THE NECROMANCER'S DILEMMA

THE BEACON HILL SORCERER
BOOK 2

SHEENA JOLIE

THE NECROMANCER'S DILEMMA

SHEENA JOLIE

The Necromancer's Dilemma
The Beacon Hill Sorcerer Book Two
Copyright © 2016 by SJ Himes
Copyright © 2024 Sheena Jolie
Sheena Jolie is the new pen name of the author formerly known as SJ Himes.
All rights reserved.
Edited by: Miranda Vescio

Cover design by Sleepy Fox Studio

CONTENT ADVISORY: Mentions of alcohol abuse. Mentions of past (not on page) sexual assault.

NO AI was used in the creation of this work of fiction or its cover. 100% human powered content.

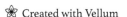 Created with Vellum

CONTENTS

DEDICATION

To everyone denied a Happy Ever After.

June 12th, 2016
49 souls.
Pulse Nightclub, Orlando, FL

1

MORNING MISHAPS

The tattoo was smooth under his tongue, Simeon's skin cool but warming the longer Angel played. Shadows and the quiet of pre-dawn covered their bed, but Angel could see the glow of emeralds from his lover's eyes, and hear Simeon growl, his chest reverberating when Angel got to one peaked nipple, laving at it before sucking the bud into his mouth. Angel bit, gentle, and Simeon bucked his hips, his thick cock slapping against his stone-hard abs. Angel grinned, and moved on to the next tattoo, a design that made no sense to Angel at all. It was haphazard, made of faded lines in a dark, mysterious blue-ish green. Made from woad, and applied to Simeon's skin over four hundred years prior.

Angel slid over Simeon, dragging his cock over the chiseled marble that passed as his lover's upper thighs, until he hovered chest to chest, groin to groin, Simeon's hands gripping his waist. Angel leaned down, Simeon lifting to meet him, and their lips barely touched, smooth and soft. Taking his time, Angel kissed Simeon with patient intent, content to explore the lips of the man he loved, his heart beating hard and fast for the both of them. Simeon caressed his back, his powerful hands bringing Angel closer, holding him safe and inciting his desire all at once.

Simeon moved, and Angel found himself on his back, Simeon between his thighs. He lifted his hips in silent invitation, grabbing his knees. A lubed finger entered him with care, opening him. Angel sighed into Simeon's mouth, their tongues entwining for a languid, delicious moment. Angel floated in a haze of pleasure and want, a pleasure that pained him as deeply as it set him free, and he keened a low whine when Simeon slid his thick cock deep inside of his ass, seating himself with a cool and smooth glide. Simeon broke their kiss, faces centimeters apart, gazes locked. Hips lifting in a controlled and devastating undulation, Simeon set the pace, each withdrawal heartbreaking, every stroke back in destructive. Angel was destroyed, mind and body broken down into tiny pieces that Simeon rearranged into a vibrating masterpiece of pleasure.

"I love you," Simeon breathed out, so quiet Angel felt more than heard the words. Angel wrapped his arms around Simeon's neck, and he clung, sobbing at each perfectly aimed stroke of hard flesh over his prostate and the sting of stretched muscles.

"I...," Angel gasped, sweat and tears running down his temples, "I love ...you too."

It was too much. The devotion and desire in those ageless eyes, the way Simeon took him apart and left him a ruin of agonized pleasure. His back arched, an orgasm slamming down his spine and erupting in his groin, cum wetting the hairsbreadth of space between their bodies. Angel yelled out his release, and Simeon gripped him tighter, hips pumping in a punishing tempo. A strong hand grabbed the back of his head, and Angel's face was pressed to Simeon's shoulder, and he bit, hard. There was no thought, no process or plan—Simeon's blood filled his mouth as Simeon's release filled his ass.

Spicy, cool, with overtones of rich chocolate, his lover's blood filled his senses and electrified his taste buds. Angel took a mouthful as another peak was reached, and he jerked and shuddered beneath Simeon. He came again, his body over-sensitized, and Simeon held him so tight that he lost what breath he had left.

He lost time. His arms and legs buzzed in the far reaches of his nervous system, his skin sizzled and the air that seeped into his shocked lungs snapped and chilled. He felt hot and cold and hovered on the edge of unconsciousness, eyes blurry. He was able to see the vague outline of Simeon moving beside him, and he twitched at the wet pass of a washcloth over his stomach and chest. He tried to move away from the damp cold between his legs and under his ass, but his body gave up.

A deep rumble that sounded like a chuckle met his ears, and Angel managed a smile at his lover's satisfaction. He was gathered close, Simeon's body still warm from their lovemaking, and Angel burrowed into his arms. A blanket was pulled over his shoulders, and Angel fell back asleep to Simeon's whispered endearments.

THE CELL ALARM shrieked at him, and Angel slapped it into silence where it skittered across his nightstand. Groaning, Angel lifted his head and came face to face with the demon warming his chest.

Eroch chirped at him, emerald green wings flapping in surprise, and Angel dropped his head back to his pillow. Eroch, the former demon that once tried to kill him, gave him a glare from daffodil-hued eyes before crawling off his chest and snuggling down onto Simeon's side of the bed. Which was empty, again.

"How hard is it for him to stay in bed until I wake up? Just once I'd like a morning snuggle," Angel grumbled, and Eroch chirruped back in a commiserating tone. The little dragon let a puff of smoke out of his nose, and smacked one of his leathery wings at Simeon's pillow. Angel chuckled, and leaned over to pet his familiar. "Aw, c'mon now. He isn't that bad. I was just complaining. He stopped stealing the blankets from you, yeah?"

Angel scratched the top of Eroch's head, enjoying the hard, pebbly sensation of the dragon's scaled hide. Eroch had a line of ridges over each eye, and he stretched out his long neck, pushing up against Angel's hand. Eroch purred, sounding much like a cat. Eroch slept with them most nights, curled up at Angel's back or warming Simeon's feet under the blankets. Simeon tended to steal the blankets, yanking it up away from the bottom of the bed, exposing Eroch to the chill during the night. Eroch hated it, and Simeon had awakened several times to a cranky dragon chewing on his toes.

Simeon was a vampire, and while his sleeping patterns varied, his lover had adapted to Angel's sleeping habits. Which meant erratic and unreliable, especially if he was working a case with BPD or a private consultation. Technically, Simeon didn't need to sleep. Angel had learned that the older a vampire got, the more resistant he became to the lethargy that came over younger, less powerful vampires during the daytime. Simeon said he still felt the urge to rest during the day, but it was no hardship for him to adapt, to be awake during daylight hours.

Angel sat up, and slid from the king-size bed, fishing around for his bathrobe. He found it hanging off the end of the bed, tangled up in one of Simeon's shirts. They hadn't taken the time to put away their clothes after they got in last night, and their bedroom activities had gone on for hours.

A crash sounded through the apartment, and Angel jumped before throwing his robe over his naked ass and running out his bedroom door. A scream destroyed the relative quiet, and Angel's heart jumped to his throat. Daniel was screaming, his cries full of pain. Bare feet slapping the hardwood floors, he ran the short distance between his bedroom and the living room, and turned to look into the kitchen through the brick arch that separated the two rooms.

Daniel was swearing and shrieking, his right hand a ruin of flesh and steam. The old kettle that used to belong to Grandma Salvatore was spilling its steaming contents across the hardwood floor, the metal container scorching the floor as it rolled and spun. Magic stunk up the room, sulfur and ozone making Angel gasp and cough. Isaac perched on the island counter, inching away from the boiling hot puddle, his bare feet inches from the disaster. Angel pushed out his will, and swept the residual magic from the room, stifling whatever caused the kettle to erupt. Isaac staggered in his attempt to escape the water, and Angel spared his brother a glance to make sure he was unharmed.

"Ahh!" Daniel screamed, falling back on the counter, holding his right wrist in his left hand. Angel's stomach roiled at the sight of his apprentice's hand. "Angel!"

"Fuck, don't move," Angel swore. The puddle was still boiling even as it spread, and steam rose to cloud the air. Isaac was in the way, and Angel couldn't get down on that side of the island without landing in the hot water that spread under the island and across the room. Isaac was going to get burned if he didn't move. "Isaac, get out of the way. Crawl over the island if you have to."

Isaac for once didn't argue, his concerned expression and the way he grimaced at Daniel's screams making it clear his brother was more worried about how badly injured Daniel was than sniping back at his big brother. Isaac slid his ass over the island, and jumped down the other side. Angel jumped over the puddle, and grabbed Daniel, dragging him to the sink and away from the danger ruining his floor.

Daniel's hand was destroyed. Daniel shrieked again when Angel took his wrist, and the agony in his apprentice's voice decided Angel's mind—he reached up and using their bond as apprentice and master, knocked Daniel unconscious.

Using the cold water was out—a burn this severe would lead to more damage if he held it under the icy water in the building pipes. Winter in Boston meant city water was artic temperatures.

Daniel slumped, and Angel pushed on him, using his weight to keep Daniel braced upright between him and the counter. "Isaac! Is Simeon here?"

"Yeah, he's..."

"I'm here, *a ghra*," Simeon said, and Angel was beyond relieved. He looked over his shoulder, and Simeon was entering the kitchen. Simeon grabbed Isaac and yanked his little brother away from the water into the living room, then Simeon leapt the ten feet over the spill to join Angel at the sink. "Let me help you. Tell me what needs doing."

"I was going to cool his hand in the water, but it's too severe," Angel said, holding the unconscious boy's hand away from his body. "We need to get him to the couch. I have to see how bad this is. We may be going to the hospital."

Simeon nodded, and with a graceful swoop, took Daniel in his arms and leapt back across the length of the kitchen to land next to Isaac in the living room. Angel grimaced, took one look at the curdling puddle that was hot enough to lift the varnish off the floor, and jumped up on the island. He walked over it, jumping down the far side, barely missing the leading edge of the mess.

"Isaac, I need you to contain that mess. Strip the causal magic from it, and cool it down."

"What?" Isaac stuttered, unable to take his eyes from Daniel's destroyed hand. Simeon set the boy gently on the couch, and Angel knelt on the floor next to him. Simeon moved away, giving him room to work.

"You're a fire mage, dammit! Absorb the heat and the magic keeping it that damn hot, and clean it up! No arguments!" Angel had no patience for Isaac's hesitancy to use magic—something careless happened in the kitchen, and Daniel paid the price.

The entire back of the boy's hand was split open by the intense heat, the skin white and thick, the flesh beneath cooked by the magic spike that turned the kettle and its contents into a kitchen supernova. The heat curled in his fingers, and the flesh was weeping fluids. Blisters distorted the edges of the worst of it, the flesh red and warped all the way up the back of his hand to his wrist. The curling of the hand was so severe he couldn't see how badly Daniel's palm was injured.

"Isaac, never mind, I need you here." A burn this bad was not life threatening—not yet—Daniel was going into shock, but he wasn't hovering on the edge of death, so Angel was unable to heal him. This injury was caused by intense and powerful heat—and so was under the purview of any practitioner with fire affinity. "You need to heal this."

"I'm not a healer!" Isaac gasped out, but he came anyway. Angel grabbed his brother and yanked him down so they were both kneeling by Daniel's hand. Angel held Daniel's arm aloft, and put his other on Isaac's shoulder.

"Isaac, all you need to do is settle into your inner sight, look at Daniel's hand, and call to the heat in the injuries. The actual temperature has nothing to do with healing—this is a mental exercise that relies on how your brain interprets and processes the injury in his hand. It was caused by heat, and you can reverse the damage," Angel instructed. He squeezed his hand on Isaac's shoulder when a wave of uncertainty crossed his features. "No room for doubt. I taught you how to heal fire and heat based injuries before you even got your driver's license, so don't lie to yourself and think you can't do this."

"How... his hand...how can I fix that?" Isaac whispered, looking sick.

"You can do it. I know you can. That power lives in you, just waiting for you to take it out and make use of it. I can block Daniel's pain as his master and supply energy for his recovery, but you'll have to do the hard work." Angel shook Isaac gently, impatient, though he made sure to hide the worst of it. Isaac had something holding him back, and his magic was sporadic, his aura flaring and dulling. Seeing Angel's impatience would get his back up and make him balk. Yet his little brother was a powerful sorcerer—all the Salvatore scions were. He could do this.

"The magnitude of the injury is irrelevant. It is fire touched, and it answers to you," Angel whispered to his little brother, and Isaac breathed out before taking a deeper, steadier breath.

"Oh...okay," Isaac gasped out, and Angel smiled. They had to hurry, or it would be harder to heal. Angel could feel the pain tearing at Daniel's mind through their link, and the boy would soon wake regardless of the knockout spell Angel used on him. Angel opened the apprenticeship link—one similar though not as intimate as the *Leannán* link he shared with Simeon. Daniel's mind was close to awakening, the pain overriding the spell, and if Isaac didn't hurry this was about to get really bad—healing an injury like this while the victim was awake would be torturous. Angel soothed Daniel as best he could, and poured energy into the boy's reserves as Isaac began to recite the spells under his breath.

Isaac always cast as if embarrassed—his Latin was spot on, and his spell work was solid. He was talented, as most fire mages were; Isaac's doubts came from that inner mental hiccup Isaac carried around and left Angel flabbergasted. One eye on Isaac's casting, another on keeping Daniel out and supplying his body with the energy to heal—the conversion of energy to matter was taxing, the drain tremendous, and there was plenty to repair and replace in his hand—Angel remained removed, watchful, but Isaac knew what he was doing once he started.

Slow motion, a horrific CGI scene in reverse, the wound and ruined flesh flowed as liquid. In the early years of his participation in the Blood Wars, Angel saw many terrific wounds, and the majority were caused by fire-based spells. Fire mages were frequent combatants in war. Burns and scorch marks, seared flesh and crispy appendages were forever etched in his memory, and yet it was still hard for him to watch as the damage done to Daniel was repaired. A decade removal from combat may not have erased his reflexes or his inability to back down from a fight, but it certainly took from him his iron stomach. He could deal with decaying zombies and corpses of deceased friends, but seeing someone under his protection so injured was too much for him. Angel swallowed back bile, since Isaac would likely vomit as well if Angel lost control of his urge to throw up. Remaining stone-faced and stoic was killing him, and he was beyond thankful when Simeon moved into his line of sight behind the couch.

His lover smiled at him, white fangs flashing in the bright morning light. Angel funneled energy into Daniel, the surge more than sufficient to fuel the healing Isaac was directing, and Angel gave Simeon a grateful smile of his own when he felt a wave of power come along the nascent mate-bond that shimmered between them. Simeon's core was a bountiful wealth of power, an expanse of primordial death magic that animated Simeon as one of the undead. Angel could tap the veil to fuel the energy he was sending his apprentice, but Daniel would feel the surge in ambient magic fields, especially this close, and it might wake him early. Simeon sending him so much power, and so selflessly, made his heart swell and tears prick at his eyes. Simeon was the better man by far—Angel wasn't worthy of his sexy vampire.

Death magic, smooth as funereal silk and cool as the taste of ice wine on a heated tongue flowed over him, through him, more than Angel was accustomed to handling outside reaching for the veil. He swayed, eyes shutting, and he breathed in and out, the magic one note of perfection, singing in his soul and making every cell in his body chime in harmony. The bond between him and Simeon was a golden cord of light, visible only to his inner sight, the once thin and fragile bond growing more solid, substantial, and the selfless gift from Simeon to Angel made it flare even brighter.

Daniel jerked, and Angel blinked his eyes open. The damage was gone. Isaac sat back, exhausted, but his work was impressive for a sorcerer who'd rather watch television than cast spells. Angel held his breath as Daniel coughed, his dark eyes opening. Sweat darkened his blond hair at his temples, and his lips were dry, but he was recovering. Angel and Isaac managed to abort the process of falling into shock, but the upheaval to his system in the last hour probably had the boy feeling wretched.

"Angel?" Daniel whispered, tears running down his temples. His poor apprentice sniffled, his arm limp in Angel's grip, and he figured the boy was terrified he was still hurt.

"Hey, kiddo," Angel smiled, and he gently took Daniel's now restored hand in his and squeezed. "Everything is fine. Your hand is all better. Can you feel my hand?"

Daniel nodded, and carefully squeezed Angel's hand back.

"Did you heal me?" Daniel asked, voice cracking.

Angel looked at Isaac and smiled. Isaac was tired and leaning back on the coffee table, and his face flushed, but he smiled back at Angel. "I didn't. Isaac fixed you right up. Good as new."

"You did?" Daniel asked Isaac, surprised. Isaac nodded, and

awkwardly patted Daniel's knee, biting his lip and not saying anything.

Daniel and Isaac may be close in age and they hung out the most, but they were still new to each other. Daniel had switched from his fear of Salvatores to needing Angel like a lifeline—the degree to which Daniel needed him was worrisome, but Angel would make sure to release Daniel from his apprenticeship as a well-trained sorcerer and balanced adult, and at this stage such dependency meant Daniel trusted him above all others. Isaac was already trained, his issues came from whatever led to his anger and magic-abhorrent behavior, and Isaac needed less from Angel as means of support. Angel had raised his little brother after their whole family died, learning how to be something other than teacher and parental unit was hard for Angel, and weird for Isaac. They were brothers, and they needed to learn to act like it. The boys were close, but the differences in how both interacted with Angel were drastic and it made things off-kilter sometimes in their own relationship.

"Thank you," Daniel whispered to the both of them. The lanky kid curled up on his side and his slow blinking and pallor told Angel that Daniel was about to fall into a natural sleep. Simeon came over, and looked down at the exhausted apprentice.

"Should I carry him to bed?" Simeon asked, and Daniel tensed. The young man was still dealing with the abuse and mistreatment he'd received at the hands of the vampire Deimos, and though he liked Simeon, the vampire made him nervous.

"No, that's ok. Isaac is gonna help Daniel to bed," Angel said, and he was grateful for his brother's short nod in agreement. "Isaac, take a nap yourself. I'm very impressed. You did a good job, little brother."

Isaac looked back at him, surprise and something like happiness in his eyes. His little brother nodded, face red and flushed, as he leaned down and carefully helped Daniel to his feet. Angel withdrew from the bond with Daniel, the boy sufficiently recharged. Sleep would help him more than anything. Isaac drew Daniel's arm over his shoulder and all but carried the blond out of the room to the hall.

They disappeared around the corner and Angel frowned, eyes to the kitchen.

Angel got up, and walked to the threshold of the kitchen, one hand on the old brick arch that marked the two rooms. He could see the whole room, and the spilled kettle had ended up on the far side of the room, blackened lines in the hardwood marking the kettle's journey from the stove. Simeon came up to his shoulder, and a cool hand gripped the back of his neck, squeezing hard enough to make Angel groan as his tense muscles relaxed. Simeon always knew what he needed, easing his tension before he even registered he was stressed.

"What happened?" Simeon asked quietly. The sounds of the boys talking down the hall filtered up to where they stood, so anything they said may be heard as well. His apartment wasn't all that big.

"I'm not sure. What did you hear?" Angel asked in turn. He looked up at Simeon, his lover towering over him. Simeon was at least a foot taller than Angel, and half again as wide. He was strength, wild yet reliable, and Angel leaned back into his hand, Simeon immovable and steady.

"I was reading the paper in the front hall," Simeon replied, "the door was open and I wasn't listening, but the boys were talking to each other as Daniel made tea. I think they may have been arguing, as their tones were sharp, but I was not paying attention on purpose."

Simeon often went to get the paper, as the windows in the hall and landing of the staircase outside his apartment were now warded in such a way that Simeon could safely step into the hall during the day and not get fried. Originally runes and wards that Angel designed to protect Simeon while letting him enjoy actual daylight didn't extend past his apartment, but Angel soon fixed that by extending that corner of his wards to include that one window. If he needed to, Simeon could now exit during daytime, heading down to the rear exit to the alley behind the building, the tall walls blocking out the sun.

Simeon could hear for a solid block in each direction, and the vampire had learned the seemingly backwards ability of turning his

super-hearing off. Angel could hardly stand humans in small quanti-
ties, so being able to hear veritable strangers talking about inane
details of their lives would drive him batshit crazy. If he were Simeon,
he'd stop listening, too.

The water was cold, though the damage done while it was hot
was pretty severe. Not even counting the damage done to Daniel's
hand, the kitchen was sorely wounded. The floors were original to
the building, and the generations of layered varnish and shellac had
turned to waxy gray and in some places peeled up in gooey strands.

"How hot did the water get?" Simeon asked, stunned as they took
in the widespread damage.

"Hot enough to destroy Daniel's hand and my security deposit,"
Angel sighed. "That old kettle should have melted, but instead it
scorched and burnt the floor and ends up against the far wall. Water
is everywhere in here, damn near, and just dropping the kettle would
have led to a smaller area of damage. This was magic, not just an
accident."

"Daniel or Isaac?" Simeon said, his big thumb rubbing along the
side of Angel's neck.

"I'm thinking both. Neither of them have the best control. Isaac
from lack of effort and practice, and Daniel from his bad education.
Kid can summon a demon and not get eaten, but some of the easiest
spells and matters of control escape him. I really want to visit
Leicester Macavoy and bitch slap him for letting Daniel out in the
world with such huge holes in his training."

"Are they a danger?" Simeon didn't look worried at all. He would
be more worried for Angel's safety, but he could handle his apprentice and little brother.

"I think this incident may be the wakeup call they both need,"
Angel said. "I'll keep an eye on them both, but they're smart. Sometimes bad things happen and it's the slap a person needs to become
better."

"You sound like you know from experience, my love," Simeon
tugged, and Angel went into his arms. He rested his cheek over the
spot where a heart should be beating. The silence there once left him

feeling odd, but now it was familiar and normal, reassuring. Simeon existed, and loved him, despite the lack of heartbeat. Even Death could love.

He smirked at himself and his romantic thoughts, and hugged Simeon tight for a moment before leaning back in his lover's arms. "Soo..." Angel started, Simeon arching a dark auburn brow at him as he waited, "Mop or bucket?"

2

NOT HIS BODIES, NOT HIS CIRCUS

Having a dragon draped all over you was a good way to get attention. Some good, some bad, most of it annoying. In this case it was annoying, as the woman in front of him in line kept turning around and outright staring at Eroch. His familiar was snuggled around Angel's neck, the collar of his heavy weather-proof sweater opened enough so the dragon could get next to his skin. Angel wore a scarf, and Eroch was tangled up in it, purring contentedly, soft puffs of smoke coming out every time the woman ogled him. Eroch was annoyed, and Angel was about to drop a hex or light the hem of her skirt up with hellfire when Simeon coughed loudly, making the woman jump and turn around. He sent a narrow eyed glare at his lover and Simeon smiled back at him, one big hand holding his elbow and reminding him he was supposed to be a grownup.

The Thinking House, a long-standing gourmet coffee house on Tremont, was overflowing with people needing their coffee hit. The line moved up, and Angel regretted his burning desire to have a peppermint latte. It was early evening, the weekend officially started, and Angel was after caffeine fortification before heading out to battle. Or shopping, really, but they felt like the same thing. He disliked people in general, and hated shopping. He got his groceries delivered, and shopping during the holidays was enough to make him exceedingly short-tempered.

This year the people he had to shop for presents for was doubled, and he still felt odd about that. Simeon was simple, all he had to do was raid the Salvatore Mansion and rescue an ancient tapestry that dated back to Ireland in the 11th century. It was small, only about the size of a movie poster, but the battle scene depicted ancient Picts and Celts, covered in woad battle markings and carrying weapons of a bygone era. It was presently wrapped up in a cotton sheath and in a pine box, the restorers able to clean the tapestry and repair a decade of dust and damp damage. The mansion may have been locked up and the furniture shrouded, but Angel hadn't been thinking clearly when he closed the old house up and he'd missed some things.

Milly was even easier to shop for. He spent all of thirty minutes searching online for a diamond necklace and a hundred-dollar gift card to The Cheesecake Factory. His teaching partner adored diamonds and cheesecake, and he had yet to vary from that very reliable and successful gift arrangement. Worked like a charm for birthdays, too. The one year he decided to change things up, she'd flat out told him to stick to what he knew, and that's what he did.

Simeon insisted it was only polite that Batiste, the Master of Boston, receive a present from them. Angel had accepted Simeon's courtship and Angel was now considered part of the bloodclan. He refused to obey Batiste or live in the Tower, and while Angel had the feeling that such a stance wouldn't be accepted from any other pair, Batiste let it go. Angel was in that gray area of being a practitioner and a vampire's bonded mate, so both sides had a claim of authority over him. Well, if he listened to any authority other than his own that is—he had trouble listening to the police, let alone the Council of High Sorcery that supposedly ruled practitioners. Though how much ruling a council of stuffy, snobbish, elitist sorcerers could do from across the ocean in Europe was beyond Angel.

Angel had no idea what to get the Master, but Simeon said he would take care of it and Angel would just have to sign the card. He'd shrugged, signed the card when Simeon brought it to him, and went back to stressing over what to get Isaac and Daniel.

He had no idea. Daniel had been in his care since autumn, two months of living under his roof and accepting Angel as his master. Daniel quickly shed any hints of his past identity, which left Angel confused and pleased, and worried on top of that. The young man was twenty years old, and had been ten years old when his whole family and two other magical clans had enslaved a vampire clan and sent them after the Salvatores. Daniel, his father Leicester, and a few retainers were all that remained of the Macavoys after the human authorities stepped in after the tragedy. Leicester avoided prison somehow, and Daniel was raised by a man who succumbed to alcoholism and agoraphobia. Daniel was no longer terrified of Angel, but he also wasn't opening up. Angel sucked at interpersonal relationships—hell, he'd never had a lover before Simeon, and he certainly didn't count a handful of hookups, and Angel was still learning as he went. Knowing how to get Daniel to open up to him and be his own man was outside his experience, especially since Angel was convinced he'd fucked up Isaac while raising him.

Isaac was the biggest mystery. He knew his brother yet didn't—he knew his brother's likes and dislikes, but the man? No idea. Isaac steadily shut down on Angel when he turned eighteen, and grew worse as the years went by, and Angel was still in the dark as to the cause.

Angel was deep in thought when he got to the counter, and the barista coughing at him brought him back. Angel glared at the rude ass but ordered his white chocolate and peppermint latte. Simeon was in line just to keep him company, but Angel ordered a small hot chocolate for Eroch, and a scone. Eroch chirped in thanks, and the barista's eyes went huge when he noticed the dragon curled under the collar of Angel's sweater. Angel swiped his card, and had to reach over and grab his receipt from the machine when the guy kept staring. Eroch ate the attention up, puffing out tiny bursts of smoke and slow-blinking his bright yellow eyes.

"Stop flirting, I want my coffee," Angel chided, and he went to wait down at the end of the counter. The barista kept on staring and Angel huffed, turning his back to the counter and crossing his arms. "My dragon. He can stare at his own. It's so rude, like no one has ever seen a dragon before."

Simeon laughed, and leaned next to him on the counter. "My love, no one has seen a dragon in this realm in hundreds of years. Would you be so sanguine if a unicorn were to be carried in someone's purse like a pet?"

"I would want one immediately," Angel said primly, arching a brow. "And I would never keep a unicorn in a purse." He was kidding. One fantastical beastie was enough—God help him if there were unicorns out there, too. Eroch gave a *meep* and poked his snout at Angel's cheek. "I'm kidding, my wee beastie. You're it for me, I promise. No sparkly horse with an antler can ever replace you."

Eroch murmured at him, and Angel smiled. He was beginning to understand the little dragon's language, and the beastie was adept with sarcasm. Eroch was as sentient as Angel or Simeon; he was just in no way human, so their behavior, while similar in many ways, was not translatable to the dragon. He was not human, and therefore would not act like one. Logic was common for all sentient species, but where people got in trouble was assuming all species had the same logic and ideas about right and wrong. Angel found following the Golden Rule was the best, boiling it down to its most basic concept: kindness.

It took some more staring from the barista and a fang-filled grin from Simeon to finally get their drinks and snack, but they eventually made their way out to the street. Angel sipped his drink while he held the scone up to Eroch, the dragon darting out from under his collar to steal nibbles. Eroch devoured the cranberry scone in about a minute, and Angel took the small hot chocolate from Simeon and held the rim up so Eroch could sip the sweet drink. Eroch was a fastidious eater, clean as can be and he left nary a crumb behind. Eroch sipped the hot chocolate, making tiny little peeps and chirps and humming happily, and the drink was gone as fast as the scone. Angel tossed the empty cup into a trash can on the street, and they walked on. Eroch went back under his collar, and hummed happily as he cleaned his snout, rubbing at his face like a cat would.

It was shopping season, with Christmas a few weeks away. Angel didn't celebrate the holiday all that much, since most supernaturals and practitioners weren't of the Christian faith. It was a human holiday more than anything, and Angel had incorporated some of the traditions into Isaac's upbringing since he sent his little brother to human public schools after they moved to Beacon Hill. That meant presents and some sort of family get together. Milly volunteered to have the dinner at her apartment this year, and since she had an actual dining room, Angel was taking her up on it.

The streets were crowded, but Simeon was obviously a vampire, and humans in this part of town weren't used to seeing a vampire walking around in public. Simeon was beyond handsome; thick, dark auburn hair, brilliant green eyes that caught the light and flashed emerald hues; and his tall, broad-shouldered frame and lethal grace set him apart from the milling throng. His pale, snow white skin and the thin cashmere sweater he wore over an equally thin tee, over a pair of dress slacks and ankle boots all broadcasted that he wasn't human. It was below freezing, snow and ice on the sidewalks and roads, and flakes were lazily falling from the dark expanse of the late evening sky. Humans were all bundled up, hats, ear muffs, and scarves everywhere. Simeon got a helluva ton of glances, half wary, half appreciative, and as they walked side by side down the sidewalk, the rush of humanity parted around them.

"What presents are left, *a ghra*?" Simeon asked, putting a hand under his elbow when Angel slid on a small puddle of slush and briny water from the street.

"Isaac and Daniel," Angel answered, tucking his collar higher when he felt Eroch chirp in complaint at the chill air. The little dragon was pouring off heat, and Angel was enjoying the fact immensely, but the wee beastie disliked the cold. He wasn't affected by it, as unaffected as Simeon, but where Simeon didn't feel the cold like a living creature would, Eroch was just highly resistant to the temperatures, and still felt them. "I have no fucking clue what to get either of them. Isaac was easy as a kid—video games. But he hasn't touched a controller since he moved back home. And I don't know Daniel well at all. He clings to me or hides in his room, and I'm afraid to push. That fucking fanghead fucked him up so badly."

That fanghead in question was Deimos, and Daniel had spent months at the undead monster's mercy, forced to work spells and do other less pleasant things for the old vampire masquerading as Elder Etienne. Angel grimaced, and sent Simeon a rueful glance of apology. Simeon shook his head once, and smiled back at him. "No need to censor yourself, my love. Deimos was indeed a fucking fanghead."

Angel snorted out a surprised laugh at Simeon's swearing, since he did it so primly. 'Fuck' sounded classy as hell when the Irish vamp used it, and it did things to his libido. "Gawd, keep swearing at me. Makes me think all sorts of things."

Simeon stopped them abruptly, people walking around them like they were a landmark, Simeon's predatory aura affecting everyone. Simeon drew him close, and leaned down until his cold lips glided over his ear as the vampire spoke. "When we get home, I'm going to fuck your tight little arse, hard and deep, in every fucking way imaginable. I will make you scream my name and beg for more. When you've cum so hard you want to pass out, I'm going to work you back up, and fuck you until your mind cannot process anything but pleasure and your body answers to me alone."

Angel shivered, his cock twitching to life in his jeans, pressing against the cold as fuck zipper. He was really glad his sweater hung so low on his hips, otherwise the entirety of the Financial District would be getting an eyeful of what Simeon's words did to his groin. "Yes, please," Angel whispered back, kissing Simeon's jaw.

Sirens wailed as a cop car drove by, distracting them both. The cruiser shut off the siren but the lights stayed on, the car easing around the corner half a block away. Angel peered down the street, and two more police cars arrived from the other direction, lights flashing. They were on Tremont walking north along a busy section of the southern side of the Financial District, on the south side of the

Common, on their way to Macy's. Angel, curious, headed in the direction of the commotion, Simeon following on his heels.

SIMEON INDULGED HIS MATE, following behind the willowy sorcerer. Angel had an unusually accurate sense for when trouble was of a supernatural bent, and whatever had happened just around the corner was agitating the humans. Simeon moved in front of Angel as the crowds surged, cries of alarm and the acrid scent of fear filling the cold air. Angel gripped the back of his sweater as Simeon cut through the crowd. Simeon was taller than most of the humans, and was able to see over their heads as they jogged and jostled each other in an attempt to get away from whatever was going on.

A warm, sweet metallic scent wafted along the lazy winter breeze, pungent and intoxicating. His fangs ached, and saliva filled his mouth. Simeon breathed in over his tongue, and the heavy scent of fresh human blood slammed into him. He growled, glad the noise from the crowd muffled the sound. He was no fledgling to be left in the throes of hunger by the spilling of blood, and he stamped down on his baser instincts.

"Someone is dead, *a ghra*," Simeon said over his shoulder. "There's too much blood spoor in the air for a human to have survived."

"Shit," Angel swore, and they jogged to reach the corner. The crowd was thinned out now, and they hit the corner and turned to look down West Street. Police cruisers cut off access on both ends of the block, and an ambulance was halfway down the street outside the entrance to a small access alley between buildings. Simeon guided Angel to the side, out of the way of a few brave pedestrians and police.

Over the next several minutes, more police arrived, and detectives arrived on scene in dark sedans. Simeon saw the rumpled suit jacket of Detective James O'Malley, Angel's liaison on the Boston Police Department. The older man exited the passenger side of the last sedan to arrive, and he was immediately surrounded by a half a dozen uniformed officers.

"Is that O'Malley?" Angel asked, and Simeon nodded. "Think I'm about to get a phone call?"

"You may well be, my love," Simeon replied, thinking the odds were good. O'Malley tended to get called on the more interesting cases, which meant the ones with suspected supernatural involvement. O'Malley then called Angel if he needed help outside department resources. "The humans are talking about the body found in the alley. Someone was stabbed, repeatedly."

"Stabbings aren't usually committed by a supernat. Most of them have claws," Angel mused, brow wrinkling. He leaned on Simeon, and the heat from his bonded lover seeped into Simeon, even with the freezing temperatures. Eroch peeked out from under Angel's chin, his yellow eyes glowing as he sniffed. The tiny dragon probably smelled the blood as well. Angel kept watching, quiet as the street was being cordoned off by yellow tape lines and uniformed cops. One was standing nearby, tying off a line of plastic crime scene tape to the stop sign on the corner, and he kept throwing Simeon nervous glances. Simeon gave the human male a thin, cold smile, and the cop swallowed nervously and hurried off, crime scene tape fluttering in the breeze behind him. Angel saw the exchange and chuckled. Simeon loved his mate's dark humor.

O'Malley and a few more detectives disappeared into the alley. Simeon leaned back, blocking off the wind and increasing snowfall, sheltering Angel behind him and the building at their back. He was reminded of another night not that long ago, when he followed his love into the chill evening and they ended up resurrecting Angel's murdered mentor.

That night was forever etched in his memory. It was the night Angel trusted him with everything. Not just letting him witness an act of proscribed magic, but it was the night Angel gave Simeon his heart and body. Angel was a frustrating mystery to most—but to Simeon he was as easy to read as a blood trail in the woods. Angel needed a foundation, trust, and honesty. He was a formidable man,

talented and powerful in his own right, and while Simeon would die
to protect his *Leannán,* his mate needed less protection than a
mundane human or even another vampire would. Forged in battle,
his mate was the scion of a powerful magical family, and while he'd
lived in relative peace the last decade, Angel's first reaction to danger
was to fight—and to fight smart. A rare combination, battle sense and
intelligence, and while Angel was occasionally foolhardy with his
own safety, his survival instinct was profound, and his desire to
protect others lent him caution.

Angel fought to win, but never at the expense of an innocent. It
was that line in the proverbial sand that let Angel claim Daniel as his
apprentice, sent him to help even people he greatly disliked, and kept
him from walking away from danger, even when his own life was at
risk.

Simeon stared down at Angel, his mate was engrossed in
watching the proceedings just down the street, and he was able to
look his fill.

Angel said once that his father was a dancer, and what lithe grace
Raine Salvatore must have had was given to his eldest son. Angel
moved with an economy of motion that most humans just didn't
have, even lifetime athletes. He wasn't one to fidget or cause issue
from boredom. He could sit in silence the whole day, just thinking,
and the quiet would be welcoming and companionable. His humor
was dark, and his sarcasm so sharp he left lesser mortals bleeding.
Snark was a relatively new term, and Simeon felt it applied best to his
Leannán. Angel was short by modern measurements for a man, only
5'7, and he was slim and lean. His *Leannán* was typical of most practitioners, his body not as sharply defined as most men his age. Angel
was far from soft, but he rarely felt the urge to exercise. Angel went to
the community center not far from his apartment and swam a couple
nights a week in the pool, a recent habit after their headlong flight
into the streets of Boston after stealing a corpse. Angel's smooth lines
and satin skin appealed to Simeon in a way that drew his focus and
desire as no other man ever had.

"You're doing it again," Angel accused with a glare and teasing pout, crossing his arms, his now empty coffee cup crushed in one of his hands.

"And that would be?" Simeon asked with a grin, turning to face Angel, leaning down to sniff at his neck and short brown hair. The blond highlights were growing out, and Simeon wanted to run his hands through the strands.

"Staring at me with that lovey-dovey expression on your face," Angel grumbled, and Simeon chuckled. He may complain, but Simeon could smell just how happy Simeon's loving regard made the necromancer.

"As I love you, and as the planes of your face are intriguing as that of an old Italian master's painting, gazing upon your visage with adoration is just something you'll need to grow accustomed to," Simeon whispered, kissing under Angel's ear. Angel sighed, his scent happy and warm with the spice of his arousal. Simeon licked the warm skin he found there, the taste of salt and the thrum of blood pulsing just under the surface making his body hum in returned desire. Though the scent of death magic his mate gave off just by existing was enough to calm his desire to bite. Angel would welcome his bite, he was sure of it, but their bond wasn't strong enough yet to grant Simeon immunity from magic poisoning.

"Only the two of you would get frisky at a crime scene," a rough whiskey-laced voice complained behind them. Simeon sighed with reluctance and pulled away from his mate, turning to nod a greeting to the gruff detective.

"Hey, O'Malley," Angel smirked, moving the bottom hem of his sweater over his groin. Angel was aroused, and Simeon growled quietly, satisfied at the reaction he got from his mate. "Do I need to answer my phone for this to be official or can we skip the call?"

"Wasn't going to call," O'Malley said, lighting a cigarette. Angel frowned, and Simeon was surprised himself.

"Why did they call you to the scene unless it's a supernat case?" Angel asked, grumpy. Angel liked to complain about how often BPD turned to him for help, but his mate went willingly almost every time, and not getting a call if O'Malley was involved was odd.

"The murderer or victim isn't a supernatural citizen?" Simeon asked, thinking that may be the only reason. O'Malley gave him a nod and took a drag off his cigarette. Simeon curled his lip at the offensive smell but refrained from commenting. He smoked cheroots so there was little room for him to complain, though the quality was far improved over the detective's cheap menthols.

"Nope," O'Malley said, looking back over his shoulder at the alley where crime scene techs were working. The coroner's van had arrived while they were distracted with each other, and the gurney creaked as it was pulled over frozen cobblestones. "Coroner and techs are saying regular old slash and stab. Victim's initial DNA test on scene came back mundane human, and the wizard on the tech crew says no magic was used. Body is a mess, though, so they called me in to make sure it wasn't a supernat kill, just in case."

"Whoa," Angel mock whispered, eyes wide. "Human on human violence? So weird."

"Yeah. Funny," O'Malley pretended to glare but his lips twitched in amusement. "Killer used a knife or two. So this one you get a pass, Salvatore."

"Dammit, I was hoping to get out of shopping," Angel grumbled. The necromancer yanked his collar higher and stuffed his hands in his pants pockets. He glowered, and sighed heavily. "Call me if something interesting happens. I'll do anything to get out of Christmas shopping."

"You've heard of the Internet, yeah?" O'Malley mused. "Wicked smart kid like yourself outta be using that instead of traipsing about in the cold."

"Shut up," Angel snarked back, cheeks red. "I tried that. I figured at this point seeing the shit in person may work better than pixels on a screen. At least I'm doing it weeks before Christmas instead of the day before."

"Inside December is still too close. Stores are gonna be crazy. Have fun," O'Malley said, grinning. "Those crowds will eat you alive, necromancer or not."

"Oh for fuck's sake, no zombie jokes! Besides, I brought him for protection," Angel said, grinning at last. He jerked his chin at Simeon, and he chuckled at the deviltry on his love's face. Eroch chirped loudly, poking his head out from under Angel's chin where he was buried in his scarf. "You, too, my wee beastie."

O'Malley stared at the dragon, surprised. Simeon found it beyond amusing how humans reacted to the familiar. Dragons were common in literature and the history of this world, yet every time a human saw Eroch, they were left flabbergasted. O'Malley quickly recovered though, having seen Eroch a few times before at Angel's apartment. Eroch eyed the detective, and Simeon laughed heartily when the little flirt winked one yellow eye at the older man before disappearing back under the scarf.

"Gets more astonishing each time I see the critter," O'Malley muttered, lighting up a new cigarette. "But yeah, you're off the hook on this one. Have fun shopping."

O'Malley threw Simeon a salute and Angel a nod, and the detective ambled back across the street to the crime scene. Simeon pulled Angel under his arm, hugging his love close. "Dammit, I guess we can either go home and you can swear at me some more," Angel whispered up at him, and Simeon tightened his arm, keeping Angel as close as possible. Angel went up on his toes and Simeon leaned down, letting Angel breathe heated words into his ear. "Or... we can go shopping. With people. Lines and stuff and more people. What was I thinking? All I'm able to think about is screaming your name as you fuck me."

Simeon looked at his watch. It was just after 7pm, the evening early yet by both vampire and mortal definitions. Angel was nipping at the underside of his chin, clever hands sneaking along the waistband of his trousers. Simeon smiled, but pulled back. His love was a temptation, and Simeon would have the sexy necromancer under him before the night was over, but they had presents to buy, and prolonging the experience would only make it worse. Simeon would know, too—he'd seen centuries of procrastination, and it never paid off.

"Shopping, my love, then we shall return to our home and our bed. I will make you scream and whimper and beg all night long after we finish our task," Simeon declared, and Angel groaned loudly, shoulders drooping. Simeon pressed a small kiss to his temple, and took his hand and tugged. Angel followed, still grumbling under his breath.

The wind picked up, and the snow began to fall with serious intent. Simeon took them back out to Tremont, and looked for a cab. The breeze was sharp and salty, the ocean in every breath over his tongue, and Simeon enjoyed the secrets the wind carried about the world. The seductive pull of blood was still there, along with a hint of something savory, earthy. Sage and lavender. Simeon sent a glance back down West Street, but he saw nothing to indicate where the new scent was coming from. The city was home to many creatures, not just humans and vampires, and he could have sworn he was scenting a fae.

No otherworldly beauty, either male or female stood out in the passing citizenry, and Simeon let it go. At least he hadn't picked up the scent of a werewolf—the wet fur smell was hard to forget.

3

WRECKING THE CURVE

"So what did you get them?" Milly asked, compact up in front of her face as she repaired her already pristine lipstick. Her makeup was impeccable, and Angel wondered if he was just missing something. He shrugged mentally, and went back to work on his laptop, checking paid invoices against outstanding bills.

"I got Daniel a sweater like mine that I'll show him how to weather-proof," Angel said, distracted by numbers and bills. He was better at math than Milly, and always ended up balancing the ledger at the end of the month. They could afford an accountant, but Milly said it was a waste as it was just the two of them in their private tutoring school, and Angel had trust issues. He wasn't comfortable with a stranger, no matter how qualified, having access to their joint funds and personal information. "It was Simeon's idea. Said the kiddo was my apprentice, and it would be a cool thing to do."

"And Isaac?" she said, snapping the compact closed and putting it into her Prada purse. Their desks faced each other across the room, a small seating area between them. The room wasn't huge, so he could see her glare quite easily from his desk.

"Ummm...." Angel slid down in his chair, trying to hide behind the screen.

"Angelus Raine Salvatore, did you flake off on Isaac's present?" Milly demanded, and he flinched as she dropped all three of his names.

"No?" Angel tried to say, then sighed, hands falling to his lap and he dropped his head back, slouching in his chair. He stared up at the ceiling and sighed even louder, frustrated. "Yeah. I have no idea what to get him. I would usually get him a video game or something, but I'm trying not to treat him like a kid. I think part of our problems now are I got so used to him being a kid I'm responsible for that I can't see the man he is now, so that's ruined all my previous experience. I literally have no idea."

Silence from his partner. Angel sat up, peeking over the top of the laptop. Milly had a perfectly manicured fingertip to her lips, her wide eyes glistening with tears. Angel blinked, and sat up some more, scooting his chair over so he could see her better. "Um...you okay?"

Milly was rarely emotional, unless she was mad. So when his partner stood, ran across the room in her extra-high heels, and fell into his lap and squeezed the ever-loving shit outta him, Angel was shocked. He hugged her back, of course, but he was clueless as to what to do when she sniffled and pressed sticky kisses to his face. "Um, Milly? What the fuck?"

"You adorable little asshole," she sniffled, peppering his hair with firm kisses while he squawked indignantly. "I have been waiting for you to have that epiphany since Isaac turned twenty-one and started going out on his own. Took you fucking long enough. I swear, I've never seen a more ingenious sorcerer, but when it comes to family and relationships you need a swift kick in the ass."

"Thanks, mum," Angel sighed, and she finally stood, ruffling his hair and making it stand straight up. The top was getting long, and he was thinking about cutting it, but Simeon liked to grab it while fucking him, so he could learn to deal with the longer length.

"So an epiphany warrants getting mauled?" Angel groused, and Milly flicked the tip of his nose with a manicured nail. "Ouch! Daggers! You have daggers, not nails!"

"The better to punish you with, my dear," Milly stated primly, and

Angel made a face in her direction as she returned to her desk. "As long as you keep in mind that Isaac is an adult and not your responsibility anymore, then you two should find your way back to each other."

"Were we that bad?" Angel asked, looking at the time on his cell. It was 5pm, and they were done for the day. On Mondays they stayed in the office of their fourth floor suite until 5pm every week so that prospective students had a reliable window for one or both of them to be present for walk ins. He shut his laptop with a soft snap and stood, grabbing his cell and keys.

Angel pocketed his stuff and opened the top left drawer of his desk, pulling out his malachite and damask steel athame and its spine scabbard. He took a spare moment to toss it on, the hilt pointing down, the blade nestled along the curve of his spine and lower back, letting him move either of his hands from hip height to withdraw the blade instead of reaching over his shoulder. It would be invisible under his coat, and his weather-proof sweater was long and thick enough to hide the scabbard and blade. Milly had long since stopped commenting on him carrying the weapon full-time now instead of saving it for high sorcery and structured casting. Angel could fight without the blade, but having it made things easier. It was sharp enough to score stone and keep its edge, and was highly reactive and sensitive to his magic, augmenting his power.

"Yes, dear, you were both that bad. Isaac resents you for some reason, and you were so focused on treating him like your ward instead of your brother you forgot how to interact. You're a smart man," Milly snarked at him, and Angel heard the old Boston accent she worked so diligently to hide creep back in as she got worked up, "but you're denser than a rock when it comes to your brother. You can get inside any of our students' heads and unravel their issues in only a few sessions, but Isaac is your blind spot."

Milly and Angel were specialist tutors—they only taught sorcerer-ranked students, and those students had to either be graduates from one of the magical schools, or students taught privately who outgrew what their families and tutors could teach or provide.

Sorcerer was the only rank out of the tiered practitioner hierarchy of power that could touch and access the veil. That was a skill not taught in most magical schools until the final year, and two semesters in tapping the veil was insufficient in making sure students had more than a grip on the basics. Angel's bloodlines and history, along with Milly's experience as former instructor at one of the premier magical schools in the country, guaranteed they had young, fresh out of school sorcerers knocking on their door every few weeks. It was mostly parents sending their children to Angel and Milly's door, and they charged accordingly. Angel knew combative magic, both defensive and offensive, and Milly was an exceptional teacher, able to provide a strong framework in the more technical side of casting and spell work.

Milly followed his lead, and Angel had an odd sense of déjà vu. It wasn't that long ago he opened the door of their office to find his murdered mentor August left in the stairwell, seconds after he was flayed open by Deimos. Angel paused, swallowing, his heart beating harder in his chest before he calmed himself. He breathed as evenly as he could, then left their inner office into the common room. Their suite had several rooms; two workrooms that were heavily warded and shielded for active magic use, their inner office that doubled as a research library, and a central common area, that had a lone small conference room with a kitchenette. They even lucked out and had a unisex bathroom, which Isaac decorated years ago in garish purples and greens. Angel joked it was the one place a frustrated student would never spend too much time in, as it was guaranteed to drive anyone out in seconds.

Isaac was in the common room, and Angel was surprised to see his brother. Isaac came with him most days, and hung out with their students between lessons, but he usually left before Angel or Milly, bored by the end of the day. He'd even taken to helping some of the more difficult cases, and it was Isaac who eventually got Samuel Serfano to ditch taking lessons with his older brother and take them one on one with Angel instead. Samuel quickly outstripped his older brother and passed the trials Angel set for him. Samuel graduated with ease, and his older brother Mark left Angel's tutelage in a huff. Angel didn't care all that much—Mark was an adult, and he was his own worst enemy, and his education and what happened with it were solely his own responsibility. Angel tried, and that's all that mattered in the end. Samuel went on to better things.

"What's up?" Angel asked his brother, stupidly nervous all of a sudden. Milly's words about treating Isaac as a brother and not a kid were echoing in his head, and Angel felt awkward. It was like they were strangers, never mind living together.

"There's nothing to eat at home," Isaac grumbled. "Daniel went to see his dad, and I'm hungry."

"Daniel went to see Leicester?" Angel asked, surprised again. Isaac nodded with a half-shrug, unconcerned.

"He got a text from his old man's servant or something. I didn't ask."

Daniel rarely talked about his father, aside from mentioning he was fine. For Daniel to go visit his father was surprising, and Angel had to make himself relax. Leicester may be a neglectful and oblivious parent, but from what he gathered from Daniel's few comments, the former head of the Macavoy clan wasn't abusive or dangerous. At least not to his son. He hoped that was the truth, he really hoped, and though he asked after Leicester to be polite, Daniel said no more than that his father was the same.

Angel wasn't stupid enough to go visit his family's once most powerful enemy. He had Daniel in his care now, and that was enough for Angel—as long as Daniel came back. If Daniel didn't come back, Angel was going to do something stupid, like getting his apprentice himself.

"There's food in the fridge. Did you just not want to cook?"

"Yeah, Blondie left an hour ago," Isaac replied, flopping down on one of the leather couches in the common area. "He said he would be back late and not to wait up for him. I'm hungry. I want pizza."

"Ooohhh, pizza sounds divine," Milly said as she left the office and shut and locked the door. Since Deimos left a body on their front step they'd taken to locking each room individually and then the outer office door. Angel backed up a step and put a hand on the wooden panel, revving up the powered-down wards that protected their office records and the books they kept inside. The wards came to life with a hum and a near audible snap, and he pulled his hand away and grinned at Milly.

"Want Luciano's or Declan pizza?" Angel asked, and Isaac jumped up with a whoop. "Isaac and I can get the pizza and meet you at your place in an hour."

"Luciano's! Luci has the best dough," Isaac opined as he grabbed his jacket and all but ran for the outer door. "I already warded the other rooms. Let's go!"

"The Bottomless Pit has given us our marching orders," Angel chuckled, pleased to see Isaac excited, even if it was about pizza. "We'll grab the pie and some soda. Pepperoni and black olives?"

"You know me so well," Milly smiled as they left the office after getting their coats, and Angel fought back the same sense of déjà vu as they went down the stairs. Milly clung to Angel's arm as they descended, her black and red heels clicking on the hardwood steps. Four flights later they were on the snowy street, and Isaac was flagging down two taxis. Milly paused on the sidewalk, her timeless face startled as she looked across the street from where Isaac was holding open a taxi's door.

"What's wrong?" Angel asked, putting a hand on her back. She jumped a bit, but gave him a brilliant smile and walked to the cab.

"Nothing, dear. I just thought I saw someone I knew. I was mistaken," she kissed Isaac on the cheek and got in the cab. "I'll see you boys soon."

Angel waved as Isaac shut the door and the cab pulled away. Isaac sprinted back to the other cab, and Angel looked up and down the street, curious as to what spooked his partner. He saw nothing out of place, cars and pedestrians braving the bad weather as the workday wound down, and headed for the second cab. Isaac was already in the back and giving the driver directions to Luciano's Pizzeria. He got in and shut the door, thankful for the heater on full blast. It was getting colder and colder, and snow was falling in increasing amounts. They might be late getting to Milly's if the weather continued to worsen.

Isaac was playing on his cell, and Angel took out his own, smiling when he saw a text from Simeon.

I am attending the Master this evening. We have several fledglings rising tonight and the presence of an Elder is needed. I love you. —S

Angel replied, smiling the whole time.

With Isaac. Getting pizza and heading to Milly's for supper. Love you too. Text me if you're staying overnight? –AS

I shall. Be safe, and my best to Milly. –S

Angel was about to put his cell away when it buzzed again.

I left the window in the bathroom cracked open for Eroch. The pigeons were back on the fire escape. –S

Angel chuckled. Eroch was in a protracted and surely futile battle with the city's pigeon population. Eroch was very territorial, and the pigeons were now his arch nemesis. Angel gave up trying to moderate the scrabble one evening when he found his wee beastie surrounded by the flamed and scorched remains of a dozen pigeons, the tiny dragon fat and happy and smug as shit after a victorious battle. Angel scolded him for leaving carcasses on the fire escape and told his familiar to make sure to wash off in the bathroom sink before coming to bed. Then he ran out into the hall and laughed his ass off. His dragon was probably going to get him in trouble with Animal Control, but it's not like the birds went to waste. Eroch regularly ate them. Apparently they were his version of a delicacy.

Angel leaned back in the seat, and sighed, tired from a long day. He was thinking about changing the studio hours, and working more evenings since he was up all night. He would be able to sleep in longer in the mornings, and have more time outside of the apartment with Simeon after the sun went down. Having a vampire for a lover was hard on his rest schedule, no matter how well Simeon adapted to a mortal's need for sleep.

Angel startled when Isaac slumped back, their shoulders touching. His not-so-little brother leaned on him, absorbed in the chirps from his cell app, seemingly oblivious to the fact he was all but snuggling with his older brother. Angel bit his lip, blinked hard a few times, and stared out the window, doing his best not to move and scare Isaac away, ignoring the way his athame dug into his back from his brother's weight.

MILLY'S TOWNHOUSE was a brick monster that sat up off the street and reminded him of an old movie set. Red brick and iron lanterns lit the front and as Angel held the entranceway door for Isaac, who was carrying the food, mindful of the slick concrete steps. A small copper plaque darkened by exposure and time was engraved with M.M. Fontaine, A.S., and Angel smiled as he always did seeing the initials after her name. The space below her name was empty, the neighboring unit in the same townhouse uninhabited for years now. Milly owned the whole building, and hated having neighbors. The uncluttered foyer was tall, and had two doors on either side, and the door on the left was Milly's multi-level part of the townhouse. Angel dug out his keys and approached her door, the metal clicks echoing around the empty space. It was barren and glaringly white from marble floors to the walls and ceilings, and it was immaculate and smelled like lemon cleanser. Old money all but screamed its presence from the paint and architecture, though Angel had nothing against wealth and living in luxury. The Salvatores and Fontaines were old magical clans, with centuries of wealth behind them and he was accustomed to Milly's home.

It was usually immaculate, at least; Angel frowned down at the melting snow and slush puddles in front of Milly's door, the welcome mat soaked. Footprints marred the pristine gloss of the stone flooring, and Angel wondered at the mess. Milly should have been home for the last hour, and the snow long melted; chunks were still intact in front of her door, and the footprints were made from a man's boot, the size triple that of Milly's dainty feet.

Angel paused, hand outstretched with his key to the door, but something warned him to wait. Whether an indistinct sound muffled through the wooden panel or some inner sense tingling away, caution had him dropping his hand and backing away.

"Angie? What's up? The pizza's gonna get cold," Isaac whined from behind him, juggling the two-liter of soda and the pizza box. "Milly knows we're coming. Door should be unlocked."

Angel blinked and looked at his partner's front door warily, his inner vision sparking to life on its own—and he swore, pushing Isaac back from the door, heedless of the soda bottle bouncing off the floor and his brother's complaints. He slid his athame free from its sheath along his spine and summoned hellfire to his hands.

"Milly isn't the only one expecting us," Angel said, anger rising to match the green flames snapping about his hands. Angel blessed Isaac's affection for Milly—his little brother didn't hesitate, his fiery red aura snapping to life around his shoulders in thin trails of flame and smoke in response to Angel's actions.

There was a stranger in Milly's townhouse, a sickly black and warped aura oozing malice and frustration. Her wards were down, most likely in preparation for their visit, and whoever had invaded her home must have forced his way in. Milly's aura, a gray and yellow flow of liquid light, glimmered softly—her light was dimming. They needed to get inside, and now. The door wasn't closed fully, and a sliver of light and movement came from under the gap. A gasp from Isaac told him his brother was using his inner sight and was seeing the same thing.

"Isaac, call for an ambulance," Angel murmured, sidling up closer to the door. Isaac nodded his head and pulled out his cell, dialing 911. Angel waited until Isaac stammered out Milly's address, and then he tensed. There was a foreign magic in Milly's home, and Angel didn't want to risk alerting the intruder to their presence by tapping the veil. Anyone ranked wizard or higher would sense him tapping the veil, and they'd lose the element of surprise. Angel focused, drawing in ambient magic, and kicked at the door, raising a kinetically-charged shield in front of him as he ran through the doorway.

Or it was meant to be a thin shield—thick enough an impediment to stop a bullet or a thrown knife, it instead became a battering ram of kinetic energy, slamming through Milly's living room, smashing the couch and splintering the coffee table. The wave of magic ripped through and devastated the room, including the man trying to hide his bulk behind one of the thick support columns that ran throughout the first level. Angel staggered, surprised, and wayward magic hissed and sparked through the air.

A gun clattered to the wood floor, and Angel ran forward, athame flaring as he tossed a restraining curse ahead of him. The tall, huge intruder took the spell and shook it off, a bull twitching to rid himself of an irritating fly. Isaac shouted, and Angel swerved out of the way, a fireball blazing past his shoulder. The ball of flame crashed into the man, and while clothing smoked and burned, the flesh beneath remained untouched.

"He's got a nullifier charm on him!" Angel shouted to Isaac, and dodged as the behemoth swung a haymaker right at his face. The man was huge, but Angel was faster. He had dropped the gun when Angel inadvertently blasted the room with a kinetic wave—the charm had weaknesses. Nullifiers were rare, and notoriously difficult to make, which meant including all types of magic in the nullifier was beyond expensive, so there were usually holes in the defenses. "Use kinetic!"

Isaac shouted something back at him, but Angel was too busy ducking and sprinting away from the man trying to crush him like a bug. Almost seven feet tall and a few hundred pounds, the huge man would have zero problems tearing Angel apart if he caught him—and with a nullifier charm on him, Angel would be dead before their magic burned through the charm's power supply.

Angel was too slow, and a fist hit him in the back of his shoulder, sending him tumbling over the remains of the couch into the kitchen. Angel slid across the floor, and slammed into the fridge. Isaac screamed, and tossed more fireballs at the bruiser, ineffective and annoying, but it distracted the big man. Isaac yelped and scrambled away as the intruder reached for him, and Angel groaned, sitting up. Isaac had never fought with magic before outside of simulated duels while Angel was training him—Isaac couldn't focus and cast and run at the same time.

Angel sat up and froze, heart in his throat. Milly was on the floor next to the stove, unconscious with a line of blood running from her mouth. She was breathing, but her face was bruised and her thick gray hair undone from its usually pristine arrangement. Angel snarled in rage, pushed off the floor, and ran at the intruder, screaming. He raised the athame at the man's back, a tidal wave of kinetic energy behind his blow—there was no honor in stabbing someone in the back, but fuck honor when the woman he loved as a mother and his baby brother were in danger—he brought the blade down as Isaac was backed into a corner between the rubble of the couch and a side table with nowhere to run.

The hellfire-infused blade bounced off the field generated by the nullifier charm, but the kinetic wave made it through. Angel landed in a tumble of limbs on top of Isaac as the wave of kinetic energy blasted the intruder out of his way, destroying a section of the doorway as the man was sent careening out into the foyer. The wave of kinetic energy had been more than Angel was expecting—the unexpected surge of tremendous power was too much for him to control, and it rebounded and revolted as he tried to pull it back before it tore the building apart.

The walls shook and the foundation groaned. The plaster walls cracked and dust rained down, and Angel mentally scrambled to control the spiraling power that was testing the limits of his control. He called the magic home, intending to spindle it inside himself until it used itself up—but that instinctive maneuver backfired.

Angel had enough time to see the intruder limp on the marble floor, seemingly unconscious, before wild magic slammed into him. Isaac's arms grabbed at his shoulders and his brother was yelling at him, but he couldn't hear anything past the ringing in his ears and the roar of limitless power reverberating through his soul.

4

A LIVING WILL

Simeon exited the limo at the Emergency entrance of Boston Metro Hospital, the automatic doors hissing as they parted for his passage. The scent of blood, sickness, and death swamped his senses, and Simeon growled with worry despite the bond with his *Leannán* telling him Angel was alive.

Startled humans cleared out of his path, and Simeon didn't have to stop and ask for directions to Angel's room—his love's scent grew stronger as he got closer. Smoke, heat, the smooth glide of peppermint and cinnamon melted over his tongue as he breathed in Angel's distinctive aroma. Simeon cleared a corner, and saw Daniel pacing in the hall outside a room, arms crossed and his head down. Worry and tension radiated off the young sorcerer, and he looked up as Simeon approached. Isaac was sitting in the hall not far from where Daniel paced, and the youngest Salvatore stood up and joined Daniel.

Daniel came forward and reached out, and to Simeon's surprise gripped his suit jacket in one hand. His wide eyes dark and afraid, Daniel clung to him, and Simeon instinctively took Daniel's hand in his, pressing the boy's palm flat to his chest. He gave a soft rumble, and Daniel relaxed, like any fledgling would when overstressed and in the presence of a master. Simeon kept his expression calm and didn't reveal his pleased surprise that Daniel reacted in such a way.

Isaac didn't reach for him, but Simeon could see his mate's little brother wanted to, and so Simeon reached up with his free hand and put it on the back of Isaac's neck, squeezing as he would with Angel. It worked on the younger Salvatore too—Isaac heaved a deep sigh, and some of the tension eased from his lanky shoulders.

"Are you both well?" Simeon asked, eyes taking in every stretch of skin and cloth. Daniel was pale but appeared fine, but Isaac worried him. His face was bruised and scraped, and he stank of fear and exhaustion. Daniel's frantic call had said that Angel and Isaac were attacked, and that Angel was unconscious. "Tell me what happened."

"We went to Milly's for pizza," Isaac stammered, and Simeon tightened his grip. Isaac took a steadying breath and continued. "Someone was in the apartment. He was...he was huge, and he had a charm, and Milly was hurt, and something happened when Angel attacked the guy, and the whole place was torn apart and...."

"Dame Fontaine was attacked?" Simeon interrupted, and Isaac nodded quickly.

"Someone broke in her place just before we got there," Isaac confirmed. "She's okay—she was just knocked out. She's down the hall in her room talking to the police about what happened. She woke up after Angel...after..."

Simeon looked at the door, and listened. Two heartbeats, one he easily recognized as Angel's, the other a stranger. He would not tolerate his mate out of his sight and alone with anyone and vulnerable. Simeon gently untangled himself from his mate's fledglings, and went to the door, opening it. A doctor stood over Angel where he lay on a bed, eyes closed and pale. He was wearing a hospital gown and the blankets were pulled up to his shoulders, with wires attached to pads running under the collar of the gown. Machines peeped and chirped in an even rhythm. There was no scent of blood or severe injury, but Simeon wouldn't be sure of Angel's health until he examined every inch of his *Leannán*. Simeon growled at the middle-aged male standing too close to his mate. The doctor gulped, the stink of fear filling the room, and he backed away from the bedside.

"Um...are you..." the doctor looked down at the chart in his hands, and then back up at Simeon. Simeon went straight to Angel's bedside, and put his hand over his mate's heart. The doctor continued to talk, but Simeon shut his voice out in favor of determining Angel's current condition himself. Isaac and Daniel came in and stood close by, the sorcerer's fledglings whispering to each other.

The bond between them was fragile, a newborn golden cord that joined their souls. Simeon's kind were not soulless monsters as Western mythology claimed—he had a soul, though his body was undead, animated by the ancient death magic that flourished inside each vampire at the moment of their turning. His soul was joined to Angel's and Simeon was able to follow the connection to Angel's body and mind. It was unheard of for such a thing to happen, but Simeon believed it was a result of their unique pairing, a sorcerer and vampire. Aided by Angel's affinity for death, they were far more intimately entwined on a level never seen before in a bond so new. Angel had a tremendous wealth of self-awareness, and through that sense of self, Simeon was able to see the paths within his mate's mind and spirit, and journey along them. He could not do this if Angel was awake—he'd only done it a few times while Angel slept, and Simeon held him through the night.

Angel was physically unhurt. There were some bruises, some minor scratches. His heart beat naturally and at a normal rate, unhurried and peaceful. Angel slept, as wonderfully handsome and beautiful to Simeon's eyes as any night he spent in his mate's arms, and Simeon withdrew carefully from his mate's spirit. Why Angel still slept was a mystery, as he was fully rested and in perfect health aside from his few bruises. Those bruises would soon be gone, as Angel had bitten Simeon the last time they had sex, and his blood would help regenerate his mate. Not as fast as a fully realized *Leannán* bond, but the blood would do until their union grew complete. *Leannán* bonds could take years to reach their full potential, and they had time on their side.

"...don't know what happened, CAT scans came back normal, may need to run further tests..." the doctor was still rambling on, "I called in for a magical examination of his aura, we should see what type of spells may have resulted in this state and what he was casting when it happened..."

Isaac whispered under his breath, "I told them no, dammit." Isaac was quiet enough that no one heard him but Simeon.

"No." Simeon said it clearly, but the doctor still blinked at him in confusion, the chart held to this chest. He knew Angel well enough after the last two years and change to know that his mate would never appreciate someone messing with his aura and examining him so deeply while he was unable to protect himself. Isaac's whisper confirmed his assumption of his mate's wishes.

"He needs a magical examination by one of our medical wizards on staff," the doctor said, and Simeon stiffened further, especially when Isaac came to his side and looked up at him, the younger Salvatore angry and tense. "This isn't an option if he is to receive the best care."

"I told them no," Isaac whispered angrily. "Angel refuses magical medical exams all the time, he flat out won't tolerate a stranger reading him that deeply. Angel changed his emergency contact and living will—he named you, Simeon. They won't listen to me, even as next of kin. Please don't let them."

His dormant heart warmed at the trust implicit in Angel's choice. Simeon hadn't even known Angel did such a thing, gave him such responsibility. Angel had such rights within the Bloodclan over Simeon and his property, but Simeon hadn't expected Angel to do the same for Simeon in the mortal world. Simeon gave Isaac a short nod in agreement, and the boy sighed in relief.

"My mate wouldn't want such a procedure done on him," Simeon told the doctor, who dared frown back at Simeon. He arched a brow, remaining still and locking his eyes on the frail human. The doctor frowned so deeply his whole face wrinkled, and he huffed out an irritated breath.

"Sir, I need to ask who you are to make such a determination. As I informed the young man, Sorcerer Salvatore has a living will, and as we cannot make him regain consciousness, we have to assume this is magical in nature. A magical examination by our practitioner on staff is standard procedure to determine a diagnosis, and only Sorcerer Salvatore's designated representative can override policy," the doctor tried to intimidate Simeon, his voice stern and his delivery pretentious.

Simeon looked back down at his mate, and gently cupped Angel's warm cheek in his hand. Angel's warmth seeped into his flesh, and Simeon closed his eyes, enjoying the heat of life that radiated out from his *Leannán*. Angel was heat and love and sex, complex and yet simple, kind and yet vicious. Death magic sang its dark song in Angel's aura, but where in another it would be a sign of supreme evil or decomposition of a mortal's spirit from a terminal illness, in Angel it was beautiful and natural. All facets of Angel were open to him, in so honest and pure of a touch, and Simeon would spend eternity loving the man sleeping in the hospital bed.

Simeon opened his eyes, and said without lifting his gaze from Angel's peaceful, handsome face, "I am Simeon, First Elder of Boston's Bloodclan, Champion of Constantine Batiste, the Master of the City. I am the bonded mate of my *Leannán,* Necromancer Angelus Salvatore, and I have the only right to determine what is best for him. You will do nothing but make him comfortable while arranging for his discharge into my care."

"I...but..." The doctor stammered, and he drew himself up to his very unimpressive height. "You can't remove him from my care in his condition. The magical examination is necessary to determine treatment."

Simeon made sure to make eye contact with the fool who dared gainsay him. He rarely gave orders—he made a request, and it was carried out. His authority was only second to Batiste's, and Simeon never had to ask twice. Human, vampire, fae, supernat—it mattered not. He spoke, and people obeyed. Only Angel dared, and with great frequency, to both disagree with him and in return order him about. And only Angel had that right.

"You will discharge him immediately. I am taking my mate home. His recovery is my responsibility," Simeon reiterated. Using his charming ability on this fool would be pointless—Simeon wanted him afraid, to feel Simeon's anger and the dangerous desire to rip apart any man foolish enough to get between him and his mate.

"I can't allow that. This is foolish. My patient needs to be in a hospital where he can get proper care, not be locked away in some dank vampire dungeon surrounded by bloodsuckers without medical training."

Isaac and Daniel gasped and swore, and Isaac got out of the way, dragging Daniel out of reach. Smart young man.

He was a predator. He may have once been human, but even then he was a warrior. He killed his first man before his ninth birthday, and drank from the throat of a mortal before he even finished rising from his earthly grave. Simeon carefully shed his veneer of civility layer by subtle layer, his eyes glowing, and his fangs dropped. He parted his lips, and the rumbling hiss of a vampire on the hunt escaped into the room. He leaned over his mate, claws extended, and growled again. The doctor gulped, sweat pouring down his temples, and fear and a hint of urine polluted the air. The doctor found his legs and ran from the room, calling for security.

"Daniel," Simeon said, easing back, soothing himself with breathing in Angel's scent so he didn't chase after the bigoted fool who paraded as a medical man.

"Yes?" Daniel asked quietly from behind Isaac, his blond head barely visible past Isaac's darker locks.

"Go see to Madame Fontaine, please. Inform her she must arrange her discharge and help her get ready to leave. I will have an escort here in twenty minutes," Simeon ordered gently, stroking Angel's soft hair. "Isaac, find your brother's belongings please. Everything, even the clothes he was wearing."

"Shit, our dad's athame is missing," Isaac swore, and he sounded exactly like his older brother. "I'll be back." Daniel and Isaac both bolted from the room.

Simeon leaned down, and kissed Angel's brow. "*Is breá liom tú,*" Simeon whispered over Angel's skin before kissing him again.

He breathed Angel in, and slowly pulled away. Part of him was hoping Angel would wake, but such things were for children's tales. Angel would wake on his own, and if he needed help, he would get it from his family and friends, not from strangers invading his most private self.

He could hear the doctor talking loudly on the other side of the ER, ordering security to evict Simeon from both Angel's room and the hospital, but the guards were wisely balking when they learned he was a vampire. His mate was famous, and Simeon's name was growing in notoriety as a result. Some of the employees surely paid attention to the papers. The ruckus was growing in volume, and Simeon pulled out his cell and sent a single text. His bloodclan would send reinforcements soon. All he had to do was keep Angel secure and safe until the cavalry arrived.

"*Is breá liom tú.*"

He barely knew a few words in Irish Gaelic, and the version Simeon spoke the most was old by a few centuries. Yet those words— he knew them by the emotion behind them. No translation needed.

I love you.

There was shouting. Some hissing. Isaac was swearing like a sailor from Gloucester and Daniel was whimpering, his grip on Angel's hand painful. More hissing. Sounded like a bunch of really pissed off vampires. Or Eroch attacking pigeons in a pitched battle for the fire escape.

Angel frowned, then yawned wide, jaw cracking. Why were people yelling and why was Daniel holding his hand? Angel had soothed his traumatized apprentice to sleep a few times since he moved in, but he didn't remember doing that recently.

Milly said something witty and scathing, but Angel's mind was fuzzy and he couldn't make it out. He hated waking up. Was he late for work? Did Milly come and wake everyone up looking for Angel? She'd never done that before. What the ever-loving fuck was going on?

Angel groaned, and opened his eyes, his vision blurry. He lifted his free hand and rubbed at them, and the red plastic band on his wrist gave him pause.

"Angel! You're awake!" Daniel cried, and hugged him. Angel patted his apprentice on the back and tried talking. He felt like he'd been asleep for days, and his mouth was dry.

"Hey, kiddo," Angel croaked out, and he coughed. "What the fuck is going on?"

"You're in the hospital," Daniel said, pulling back. Angel lifted his head and took a good look, and sure as anything he was in the hospital.

In fact, he was in bed, in a hospital room, the door to the hall opened where he could see a crowd of uniformed security and sharp suits. The suits were vampires, and Angel recognized several soldiers from the Tower. Simeon's dark auburn hair glinted with fiery highlights beneath the fluorescent lighting, and his broad shoulders and lethal grace set him apart even from his brethren.

Simeon was facing off against several men in white coats and frumpy suits, and a short cranky middle-aged man was waving a clipboard around wildly and complaining about dungeons. They were backed by armed security guards and some nervous people in more suits.

"Why is Simeon arguing about dungeons with a doctor? Am I still asleep?" Angel asked, beyond confused. Last thing he recalled was getting attacked by the angry version of a mountain troll, and... "Holy shit, what the fuck happened?"

Angel sat up fast, the shouting and a blood rush making his head spin. Daniel grabbed his shoulders and tried to push him back down, but Angel needed to sit up. He felt okay. Weird, but okay. There was an odd echo in his center, and his whole body was tingling. Toes to fingers to scalp, he felt electrified. His head was spinning and he ached in a few spots like he was bruised, but he was certain he didn't need to be in a hospital.

"I'm naked," Angel said, looking down at the gown hanging off his shoulders. "Where are my clothes?"

"Oh! Isaac went to find them," Daniel perked up and spun to the door. "I think he found them, but then everyone else showed up, and Milly and Simeon won't let them in the room."

"Yeah, um. I'm fine kiddo. Get my clothes from Isaac, please," Angel asked, needing to get some real clothing on. The chill hospital air was shrinking bits he'd rather not expose any further. He'd never been admitted before, not even when he almost died when he was twenty and several weeks ago against Deimos. The room was fucking cold and his skin felt tight and dry, and he was thirsty.

Daniel sprinted from the room and headed toward the group in the hall, that seemed to be getting larger by the moment. Angel huffed out an annoyed breath, the noise irritating the shit out of him. From what he could hear, Simeon wanted him out of the hospital and home, and the doctors were going on about Angel needed some kind of test to...he heard aura searching and magical examination, and his lip curled.

"Fuck that," Angel hissed out as he slid to the floor, flinching as his feet hit the freezing tile.

No way in hell was he allowing any stranger to examine him that deeply. He wasn't hexed—he had just needed to adjust to the extremely huge amount of power he'd absorbed and somehow managed to spindle in his core, and his mind shut down. It was an old meditation technique he'd learned from August and his father, when he was just coming into his affinity. Angel had trouble when he was a child, as his powers came on too early and his affinity not too long after that. The power surge this evening was similar to his experiences as a child. His mind went to sleep, and his spirit absorbed the power. Without his conscious mind trying to control the power, it had stopped fighting him—and it calmed. It was a last ditch, Hail Mary kind of action, and he hadn't done it since he was twelve or thirteen.

Though answering why the power was wild and immense would

have to wait, especially since a doctor in a long white coat and beady glasses snuck in around the melee in the hall and was walking over to him.

"Mr. Salvatore? I'm Dr. Ballacree. I am one of the on-staff wizards here at Boston Metro. I specialize in aural examinations and hex removal. I was sent a request to read your aura, I understand there's some concern you were hexed?" This man was tall and thin with mousey brown hair and a pinched expression, and wasn't even looking at Angel as he spoke in a distracted and vague tone of voice. Dr. Ballacree idly searched for Angel's chart, but the crazy doctor in the hall squaring off with Simeon probably had it.

"I wasn't hexed; I don't need it. I'm fine," Angel said, which he was, even with his head spinning a bit and his whole body tingling. He just felt like he spent too much time tapping the veil on full blast, instead of the steady trickle he usually used to recharge his reserves. "I don't need an examination. I'm leaving."

Angel tried standing, but the new doctor came over and put a hand on his shoulder, pushing him back down to the bed. Angel glared, and opened his mouth to tell the fucker off, but he felt a slimy sliver of magical energy glide over his outer senses, and he recoiled in shock. The asshole was trying to read him, after he said no, too!

"What the fuck! Back off!" Angel gritted out, and he slapped the other man's hand away from his shoulder. "Stop it!"

"There's no need to be agitated, Mr. Salvatore. I'm sure you think you're fine, but let a professional see first, hhmm? You've got a pretty powerful charge running through you," Dr. Ballacree said, reaching out for Angel again. "Hhhmm...what's your affinity?"

"My affinity is for kicking ass! Fuck off!" Angel pushed back at the sensation of spectral hands running over his aura, and nausea rolled through him. The doctor was taller than him by several inches, and with Angel sitting on the bed he had no leverage. The doctor pushed on Angel's shoulders, trying to force him to lay back on the bed. "Let go of me!"

Casting in a hospital was a bad idea—pure oxygen ran through pipes in the walls, and with his magic amped up, a single shove with kinetic could result in the room being reduced to splinters. That happened, and a fireball could take out the entire floor. All this held him back from casting, but that didn't stop his fist. Someone shouted his name, and Angel would have answered if he hadn't pulled back his arm and let his fist fly, cracking the creeper forcing him back on the bed across the nose. Blood sprayed and the bone snapped, and the doctor screamed, blood running down his lips and chin. Angel rolled off the bed, backing away, and the doctor was surrounded by blurs of black and brown as suited vamps materialized in the room. The doctor was restrained and yanked away from Angel, and Angel staggered back, shaking out his arms, trying to rid himself of the invasive sensation of the medical wizard's magic.

Steel bands that masqueraded as arms surrounded him, cradling him carefully to Simeon's rock hard chest. His lover turned him away from the yelling doctor and the other people piling into the room, and a cool hand lifted his chin. Simeon gazed down at him, a fond smile lifting one corner of his luscious mouth. A thumb traced his lower lip, and Angel sighed, leaning into the touch, eyes shutting. He ran his hands up Simeon's chest, caressing and touching gently as he went, and wrapped his arms around Simeon's neck. Simeon moved his hand, cupping the back of his head and urging Angel to press his face to Simeon's shoulder. He went willingly, hugging Simeon tightly to him, shivering at the rush of energy along their bond.

Their bond. It sang in his mind, in his spirit, sapphire and emerald and overtones of gold, pure and inviolate. Angel smiled, able to see the bond more clearly with his eyes shut, his inner vision open and the world shining bright. Simeon's soul shone the brightest, and beneath it, the wellspring of primordial death magic that animated the sentient undead.

Angel peered closer, ignoring the outside world, sinking below their fragile matebond, and the strength he saw left him in shock. Simeon was powerful—he was an Elder, and four hundred years old. Beneath Simeon's own personal reserves of vampiric magic, churned the ancient death magic that made him a vampire to begin with, and it was limitless. Simeon had access to his own strength, and seemed to be unaware, or perhaps indifferent to the *magica animus* that made him who he was, as Angel could see Simeon had no conscious nor direct access to the ancient death magic that dwelled within him.

And that ancient death magic was running along their mate bond, under the essence that was pure Simeon, masking it and blinding Angel to its presence. This was why his magic was amped up —this is why he almost blew up Milly's townhouse. He was a battery constantly charging, plugged in and continually being topped off. And Simeon was apparently unaware he was constantly charging Angel through their bond.

Angel stilled, even halting his breathing, as his mind tried to process what he was seeing. He wasn't tired from handling the energy that flowed unending into his core. If he were to tap the veil, he would eventually grow tired trying to wrangle the chaotic energies from the other dimension, the place where all magical energy created by living beings and active cells in all substances eventually bled through. The veil was merely a form of expression that illustrated the divide between their current reality, their universe, and the next universal layer closest to their own, and in reach of sorcerers. And it took power to use power—and Angel already had more than most of his peers.

He was adjusting, even as it overwhelmed him. He was accustomed to the veil energy, and handling the death magic he could access through his mate was more than anything he'd ever experienced before—and because it was death magic, a magic he himself produced and learned to live with and eventually ignore unless actively searching it out, he hadn't noticed. He was death magic, in a way, and he'd tuned it out. Like ignoring the sound of one's own breathing or heartbeat.

Angel sucked in a deep breath, and let out an insane giggle, trying not to panic.

"*Mo ghra?*" Simeon kissed the top of his ear, making Angel shiver. His panic receded, and Angel breathed in and out a few times, settling his nerves. As long as he didn't cast he should be fine— should be.

"Arrest him for assault!"

Angel took a hand from Simeon's neck and flipped off the crowd at his back. Strident complaints came in response, and Simeon chuckled, the sound so deep and comforting under his ear. He went back to snuggling his lover, and let Simeon take over. He was too volatile to do much of anything except to breathe in Simeon's minty chocolate scent and try not to blow up the hospital.

Simeon spoke so quickly his words were naught but a short staccato hiss, and the complaints from the medical staff faded as they were presumably herded from the room. Isaac was asking after him, and Daniel was petting his back. Angel lifted his head carefully, the room only spinning a bit, but it was enough to make him groan.

The room spun even more when Simeon swept him up in his arms, cuddling him close. Angel closed his eyes, and responded to the frantic questions from his brother and apprentice. "Guys, easy. I'm fine, just a bit dizzy. Is Milly okay?"

"I'm fine, dear. Are you sure you're well?" Milly replied instantly, and she put a slim hand on his arm. He cracked single eye open, and peered at his partner. She sported a cut along her temple at her hairline, and some bruising, but she looked a lot better than she had at her place earlier. Which wasn't hard, since she was upright and dressed and not looking like she was about to die.

"I think so."

"What happened? You just passed out!" Isaac asked, his brother's voice cracking with fear and stress.

"Isaac, I swear I'm fine. I'll be okay. Can we get out of here?" Angel asked the last bit to the room at large, and Simeon clutched him tighter.

"Of course, my love. Do you want to get dressed first?"

"Fuck yes."

Simeon sat him gently on the bed, and pointed at the door. Milly herded the boys from the room, and shut it behind them. Angel slouched, rubbing at his temples and moaning. He sat up quickly though, thinking back to the incident at Milly's home.

"Did the troll get away?" Angel asked, grabbing his pants from the stack of clothing Daniel left on the bed. He got dressed as fast as he could.

"Was it a troll? Young Isaac merely said a large man, and Milly has been unforthcoming about the identity of her assailant," Simeon handed him his boots, and Angel tugged them on. He searched for his athame, and didn't see it. Shit.

"Hybrid for sure. Did he get away? I can't see the police being able to restrain him for long. Bastard had a nullifier on him," Angel said, standing. He let Simeon hold him steady, slightly disturbed by how the power thrumming under his skin sang with overtones of joy at his lover's touch.

"The troll was not present when the police arrived," Simeon kept his hand under Angel's elbow and escorted him to the door. "My soldiers are dealing with your discharge. The hospital will be receiving a visit from the bloodclan lawyers as well for attempting to violate your living will."

"That came in handy," Angel bitched, rubbing his forehead. "What's the fucking point of having one if the damn doctors won't follow it? That creeper just went ahead and tried it anyway! I should have hexed him."

"They'll wish for a curse once my master learns of their transgressions," Simeon smiled, predatory and smug. "An insult to you is an insult to the bloodclan."

"I can handle my own insulting," Angel quipped, frowning. "Wait, that came out wrong. Fuck, I feel weird."

Simeon was there immediately, and before Angel could squawk out a protest, swung him back up in his arms and carried him to the door. Angel groaned, embarrassed, and he wrapped an arm around his lover's neck and let the stubborn vampire have his way. The door opened just as they reached it, and Simeon stepped in the hall, surrounded by a phalanx of vampiric soldiers, with Isaac, Daniel and Milly in the center with them.

Isaac walked in front of him, right behind the vampires leading the way out of the emergency room. Milly and Daniel walked on either side of Simeon as he carried Angel out of the hospital. Angel breathed a sigh of relief when he saw the hilt of his athame, once his father's blade, stuck in the back of Isaac's belt. No sign of his scabbard, but he had another at home. Angel sent Milly a look, and she pursed her lips in a tight smile, but nodded. They were going to have a serious talk about the man who broke into her place.

Angel had never seen him before that night, but he knew enough from a decade of working alongside Milly to know exactly who that motherfucker was—Milly's ex-husband and troll-hybrid, Benjamin Stone.

A fitting name for a stone-cold bastard.

5

BLOOD BONDS

"I haven't seen him in twenty years," Milly said, looking down at her cup of steaming tea.

Angel had Simeon make the tea, since his boys were too worked up to be trusted in the kitchen. The chagrin on their faces told Angel they knew exactly why they were banished from the kitchen, and they were alternating between embarrassment and sulking. Angel let them pout and focused on Milly.

It was late enough, or hell, early enough, to be breakfast, and Simeon was in the kitchen making them food. Angel spent an inordinate amount of time smiling like a loon and blushing in delight when Simeon revealed he could cook, and that he liked it. Angel asked him where he picked up the skill, and he felt like an ass when Simeon replied he hadn't always been a vampire. He learned to cook as a mortal man, and while modern conveniences were drastically different, the concept was the same.

Angel sighed in contentment and leaned back in his seat on the couch, sandwiched between Daniel and Isaac. His brother was leaning away from him, not too obvious but enough that Angel thought about getting a bigger couch. Daniel didn't care—his apprentice was snuggled up to his side, and while the boy was bigger than

Angel, he felt small and vulnerable curled up there against Angel, and the death grip he had on Angel's arm told him the night's events left Daniel severely rattled. He made a mental note to ask him about his visit with Leicester when they didn't have an audience.

"How did he find you?" Angel asked, toeing off his boots and gripping the edge of the coffee table with his toes. Milly sent him a disapproving look, but it was his house, his rules, and he smirked back at her. He gestured at her to get on with it, and she sighed loudly before taking a sip, deliberately taking her time answering. No one rushed Dame Fontaine, not even Angel.

Point made, she said, "I think it was the recent article involving the resurrected mammoth and the mention of our partnership in the Boston Globe. Your endeavors putting it back to rest after it killed those college students made national headlines."

"Were you actually hiding from him? You've been here in town your whole life," Angel asked. He ignored the comment about the resurrected mammoth. If he had a dollar for every time a bunch of idiots with some kinda talent decided to resurrect an extinct species and got eaten in the process he would be able to go on a really short but satisfying vacation to Vegas. People didn't need to have an affinity for death to be able to resurrect something—it just made things easier, and gave them the natural ability to control what they brought back. None of the college kids were necromancers and they died horribly for that lack of expertise.

Simeon came into the room carrying trays, and put them on the coffee table, two plates on each tray, laden with bacon and sausage and eggs. Simeon knocked his feet off the table, and Angel grumbled out a thanks as he took a plate.

"Hiding? No. But I thought he would be locked away for longer than he was," Milly explained, and Angel paused, a sausage link hovering midair between plate and mouth.

"He was in jail? I just thought you two split and went your separate ways," Angel exclaimed, honestly surprised. He had no clue her ex was in jail. In fact, what he didn't know outnumbered what he did.

Angel devoured a forkful of eggs and gave Milly a hard stare. "Why was he in jail? What did he do?"

Milly stared at her cup like it held the mysteries of the universe... or just some hard truths.

"He killed someone. He was in jail for second-degree murder," Milly answered him after a long moment.

"Fuck," Isaac breathed out. "Who did he kill?" Angel elbowed his brother in the ribs. Isaac winced and glared back at him.

"I divorced him while he was in prison, and I haven't seen him since he was arrested and I gave my statement. My testimony wasn't needed since he killed a man in public with multiple witnesses, so I didn't even attend his trial. I haven't seen him in twenty years, and I was hoping it would be a lifetime."

Angel opened his mouth to comment, and Milly shook her head and pointed at him. "I know what you're going to say, Angel, and don't you dare. Benjamin is not your problem to solve. I identified him to the police, and in the morning I'll apply for a restraining order. He has a warrant out for his arrest. I'll keep my wards up and watch my back. He won't surprise me again. This isn't your fight."

"He hurt you, almost killed us, and he knows where you live," Angel sat up and put his plate down with a loud smack, his fork rattling. Daniel jumped at his side and Isaac stared at him wide-eyed as he continued to eat. "You'll stay here until it's safe, dammit."

"He probably knows where you live, too," Milly replied archly. "Everyone knows where Angelus Salvatore lives in this town. In fact, I'm probably in more danger being here than I am anywhere else in the entire state, including my own apartment."

Fuck.

Milly smirked at him, and calmly sipped her tea. Daniel snickered and nibbled on some bacon, and Isaac laughed outright. He glared at his brother, and Isaac just laughed some more. "Yeah, laugh it up you two. You both live here, too."

Daniel stopped laughing and went back to eating, the remaining eggs on his plate more interesting than picking on Angel. Isaac just shrugged and kept on eating. "Been in danger our whole lives. Nothing new."

If that wasn't the truth, he didn't know what was.

Angel got up, dislodging Daniel. Isaac snagged the last bit of sausage from his plate before he grabbed it and went to the kitchen. Simeon was in there, sleeves rolled up, wrist deep in the suds as he washed dishes. Angel put his plate down next to the sink, and leaned a hip on the counter. Simeon was at times odd, even for Angel. The undead vampire lord was four-hundred-years old, a warrior and cunning predator. Yet the fact he was washing dishes from a meal he couldn't eat, and that he even cooked the meal, gave Angel a warm, almost fluid sense of sweet pain and affection.

Awe. He felt awe.

Simeon was awe-inspiring. Angel had spent his life alone, and even expected to remain that way forever, never looking for a relationship or a partner in the romantic sense...and yet Simeon filled that role so perfectly, so smoothly, that Angel had a sneaking suspicion that Simeon had been working on getting him to accept him since the moment they met, over two years ago now.

Angel slid his plate into the sink, and Simeon gave him a small smile, eyes warm with affection. Angel leaned forward and pressed his lips to his lover's shoulder, planting a firm kiss before pulling back.

"What was that for, *a ghra*?"

"Thank you for not giving up on me," Angel said, grabbing a dish towel and drying the cleaned flatware.

"I would never give up on you," Simeon vowed. Angel chuckled, and bumped his shoulder to Simeon's.

"I know that now. Still leaves me in wonder that you never thought I was too difficult. I didn't make it easy for you in the beginning," Angel admitted, playing with the towel. Simeon pulled the plug on the sink and rinsed his hands and wrists. Angel gave him the towel, and Simeon's gaze was inquiring.

"There is nothing easy about you, my love. You were a wary creature, dangerous and suspicious."

Angel huffed out a dry laugh, thinking Simeon had it dead to rights. "Am I still that way?"

"Certainly. You only trust those who have proven themselves. Such a precaution is wise, and has kept you and yours alive. You're dangerous, and that will never change. Bred for war, adapted to peace. My people call me the Celt, a throwback to ancient times when my ancestors fought with spears and bastard swords stolen from the Romans. They call me a warrior, but the term more aptly describes yourself." Simeon turned from the sink, and gently pulled Angel into his arms. Angel leaned his chin on Simeon's chest and stared up at his lover, Simeon smiling down at him. "Yet in your heart, there is an unending generosity. You believe in compassion, in second chances. You can forgive—and even better, you know when *not* to forgive."

"You make me sound like a saint," Angel whispered, their lips a couple inches apart as Simeon dipped his head.

"A warrior saint who swears with every breath he takes, and walks headlong into danger for those he loves, and never washes his own dishes," Simeon retorted with a smile, and Angel laughed.

"We have a dishwasher, ya know," Angel teased, and Simeon retaliated by picking him up, big hands cupping his ass. Angel wrapped himself around his lover, the bigger man carrying him as they strode from the kitchen. Angel tapped his shoulder, and Simeon paused in the living room.

"Milly, take the couch please. I want to go with you when you go back to your place, but we all need some sleep," Angel said, and Milly opened her mouth to complain he was sure, but he shook his head. "Sleep here for now, and let me help you. I won't hover over you like a momma hen, but please let me help keep you safe."

"Fine," she grumbled, but she gave in.

"I'll get some blankets and spare pillow," Isaac said, hopping up. Daniel took the leftover plates and trays into the kitchen and Angel heard the water turn on as Daniel began to wash up. Simeon cocked a brow at Angel and he glared back.

"No one leaves the apartment until I get back up!" Angel said loudly, and assorted muffled replies came from the depths of the apartment which he took as agreement.

Simeon carried him into their room, and the gray hue outside the windows heralded dawn's approach. They still had a while, maybe an hour. Simeon had been at the Tower, and planning on spending the night, helping with new fledglings.

"Did this whole mess fuck up your Elder duties?" Angel asked as Simeon pushed the door shut with a foot and then carried him to the bed.

"You need not worry, my love," Simeon assured him, laying Angel down on his back on the bed. Simeon stood and went about undressing Angel.

Socks, pants, underwear, shirt, everything went. Angel stroked his hardening cock while Simeon stood back and undressed himself, picking up their combined clothing and putting it all in the hamper by the bathroom door. "I'm going to worry. You spend all your time here, and not with your bloodclan. I get in trouble, and you leave. Didn't you guys have fledglings rising tonight?"

"We did, and it went very well. The younglings bonded with their masters, and only one needed to be bound to Batiste when she would not respond to her maker. Out of ten fledglings, that is a very high success rate. Daniel called me after I was no longer needed, so I was able to leave."

Simeon crawled into bed, and Angel shivered. They tugged the blankets back and settled underneath. Angel opened his arms to Simeon, spreading his legs and wrapping them around Simeon's hips, and he groaned when Simeon rested his full weight atop him.

"Don't worry about me, my love," Simeon whispered as he nibbled on Angel's jaw, licking down the side of his neck. A hard, cool but warming quickly, long cock nestled alongside his own, and Angel lifted his hips, trying to slide them together even as his head fell back and Simeon bit down on a tendon in his neck. Not enough to break the skin, but he would have a lovely collection of hickeys in the morning.

"I will always worry," Angel gasped, whimpering when Simeon

bit him again, harder. So close to danger yet not close enough. Angel cried out, hands clawing at Simeon's shoulders. Simeon biting on him, sucking up marks, leaving love bites behind got Angel revved up faster than anything, and he was begging and pleading for more before Simeon moved on to the third love bite. "Batiste has to run out of patience at some point."

"No more talking," Simeon whispered over his skin, licking at the tender flesh.

Simeon bit again, harder, and Angel yelped, his muscles melting in a rush of liquid heat and arousal. He moaned, his cock straining and aching, flesh tight and hot. Simeon eased off on his biting, and kissed Angel, firm and deep, tongue slipping into his mouth, owning every surface. Simeon always tasted of cool mint and sweet chocolate, and Angel was addicted to his taste. He dug his fingers into Simeon's scalp and yanked on the thick strands of auburn, keeping their lips together.

Simeon broke the kiss before Angel passed out from oxygen deprivation, and Angel panted fast and hard when Simeon yanked his wrists above his head with one hand, the other digging around the headboard. Angel writhed and bucked his hips when Simeon found the leather shackles, and pulled them free. "Yes, fuck yes. Please!"

Angel begged and pleaded, whispering his need as Simeon restrained each of his wrists, separately and then together above his head, tightening the leather cord until Angel's arms were immobile. Simeon ran his cool hands down Angel's arms, making him jump and wiggle. One of Simeon's hands slid to his throat, thumb under his chin, tipping his head back, while the other slid down his chest, his stomach, and took Angel's aching cock in hand.

Simeon stroked him, and Angel whined deep in his throat when Simeon added a twist to his motions, working the head, thumb spreading precum over the crown and down.

"What do you say if you want me to stop?" Simeon rumbled, and Angel had to wet his lips before he could reply. Simeon's hands both tightened, throat and cock, and he gasped.

"*Coisc*," Angel said in a whisper, harsh and ragged with lust. It didn't quite mean 'stop', but it was the easiest for Angel to say when high on pleasure. "I haven't needed to yet. Now fuck me, please."

"You frightened me, *a ghra*," Simeon declared softly. "Your fledgling calls me in a panic and tells me you and your brother were attacked. You were in the hospital, and I was afraid."

Simeon rolled his wrist, and Angel bucked up at the tight grip, nearly too painful to be enjoyable. Angel groaned happily despite the pain, and Simeon stilled his wrist. "No! Please..."

"I was scared, *Leannán*. I feared for you," Simeon rubbed a fingertip through the silky drops of precum, collecting a thick drop. Simeon put his fingertip to Angel's mouth, bathing his lips in his own fluids. Angel licked at the taste, and Simeon's finger, sucking it into his mouth. He moaned again, and Simeon squeezed his throat once before letting him go, pulling both hands away. Angel blinked up at him, dazed, aroused to the point of madness.

"Fuck me." He wasn't above begging.

"Not yet," Simeon growled, and Angel's heart tripped when Simeon's fangs dropped, eyes glowing a rich emerald flame. It happened so fast he never saw Simeon move; Angel was flipped, his wrists straining against the shackles. Simeon put him up on his knees, legs spread, cock and balls swaying heavy between his legs, his shoulders down.

"I was scared for you, my love," Simeon's voice was one long rumbling hiss, fangs making it hard for words to come out smooth. Simeon was dangerous, and Angel's whole body wanted to feel just how dangerous he was. "You need to be reminded how valued you are, how loved. How essential you are to me."

Angel bit a mouthful of bedding and sobbed with shocked pleasure when the flat of Simeon's hand slapped his ass. Fast and shocking, Angel's ass clenched, his muscles quivering. A bloom of heat came from the impact spot, and Angel sobbed into the bed when the other cheek was given a sharp slap. Vampiric reflexes meant his ass had no time to recover or his mind to separate one blow from the next. His cock jerked, precum dripping to the bed, and Angel twisted and pulled against the restraints, needing to be free, to get his hands on Simeon, to pull him close and deep, so fucking deep there would be nothing between them, not even air.

He came, shooting thick streams of cum to the bed. Angel screamed, arms shaking, fists clenched, back bowing. The blows to his ass stopped, and he was freed, even as his body convulsed and he came again, painting Simeon as his lover picked him up, turning him, and sat him in his lap.

Angel whimpered, overcome, the touch of Simeon's chiseled abs on his sensitive cock almost too much. Simeon lifted him, and a thick finger coated in lube caressed his hole before piercing the tight muscle. Angel dropped his head to Simeon's shoulder, limp and exhausted, and leaned his full weight onto Simeon, trusting him to keep him upright. His ass cheeks burned, but the stinging heat was pleasant, even as it stung from sweat running down his back and hips. More lube found its way into him, and Angel moaned loudly in approval when Simeon pulled his hand away and then gripped his hips.

Simeon impaled him slowly, carefully. Slow inch by slow inch, Angel's body opened and accepted the thick, long, rapidly warming flesh stretching him wide. The broad head nudged his prostate, and Angel jerked, moaning, before the head slid deeper into his body. Simeon touched places no one had ever reached before, and Angel delighted in the difference when Simeon bottomed out. Simeon's cock warmed, absorbing the heat of Angel's core, and reflected it back, until Angel felt like he was pierced by a wet, thick spear of molten lava. Hands cupped his stinging ass, and lifted him, encouraging him to let his knees fall wide when Simeon started to fuck Angel on his cock.

Angel's cock, softened by his own orgasm, jerked and pulsed with every stroke over his prostate, and the rhythm Simeon set let him feel every ridge and dip of the muscles across his lover's rock-hard torso. Angel managed to lift his head after trying twice, and his head lolled back on his shoulders, looking up at Simeon as his lover fucked him slow and deep. Eyes heavy and nearly closed,

Angel managed to smirk up at Simeon, whispering, "Is that all you have?"

Simeon hissed, eyes flashing a vibrant emerald, and Angel found himself on his back, legs spread wide, Simeon fucking him fast and hard. Angel grabbed his knees and pulled them up and out, and Simeon slammed his hips into Angel's, rutting like a crazed beast...or a savagely aroused vampire.

"Fuck, yes. Don't stop...come in me, please." He wasn't making any sense, but then Simeon always wrecked his brain and thought process with his cock. One strong thrust slammed into his prostate, so hard it ached, and Angel yelped as his cock unloaded again, pulsing out thick jets of cum as Simeon aimed for that spot over and over. He wasn't even fully hard, and Simeon fucked another orgasm out of him. Angel screamed, fingers digging into his legs, and his ass went on lockdown. Simeon shuddered on top of him, and Angel sobbed at the slightly cool, thick, wet jets of cum filling his ass. Simeon worked himself in as deep as he could go, grabbing Angel tight, hips jerking as he continued to come.

Angel sighed, every muscle buzzing with endorphins and pleasure. He let go of his knees, legs flopping to the bed, and he wrapped his arms around Simeon's neck, hugging his lover to him.

"I love you," Angel sighed out, kissing Simeon's neck, rubbing his nose through the soft auburn strands behind his ear. "I love you so much."

"I love you too, *Leannán*. More than I ever thought possible," Simeon rasped out, fangs finally withdrawn. His eyes glowed, softer now, not as bright. Simeon tilted his head to the side, exposing his neck better to Angel's view. Angel watched in fascinated surprise as Simeon managed to work a hand up to his own neck, a single claw sliding out an inch from a lone finger, and Simeon pierced his neck, right above the jugular.

"Shit! What are you doing?" Angel gasped out, trying to get a hand down to stem the flow.

"All is well, my *Leannán*. Drink, quickly, before the wound closes."

"What? Why? I know I've been biting you a lot, but I'm a biter, and you never complained, I thought you liked it..." Angel stammered out, watching as a thick flow of dark red blood ran down Simeon's neck to drip onto Angel's shoulder.

"It tightens our bond," Simeon whispered, and he thrust his hips, fucking his still hard cock into Angel, making him moan. "I thought you knew, my love. You have bitten me every time we made love the last several weeks."

"I like biting..." Angel trailed off, thinking about it. He'd never bitten any of his previous hookups. Never, not even the few repeat hookups he'd fucked over the years. Simeon was the only one he bit, ever.

Simeon cupped the back of his head, and Angel let him press his lips to Simeon's neck. The blood was cool, and sweet, thick like syrup. Simeon always tasted of mint and chocolate, spices reminiscent of a hot toddy or cider. Angel sucked, Simeon hissing in approval, his hips now moving again between Angel's legs. Angel drank mouthfuls, more than the brief tastes he'd taken before, eyes drifting shut.

Simeon fucked him in time to each swallow, and Angel gripped Simeon as tightly as he could, barely able to hear Simeon's murmured words of encouragement over the beating of his heart.

Angel came again, a gentle, deep orgasm, and he felt Simeon fill him up again too. Angel stopped drinking, unable to take any more, and the last thought he had was of how his blood sang in his body, and the golden cord tying them together grew stronger, more tangible.

"I'm sorry I scared you," Angel whispered, licking his lips. Simeon kissed him, lapping at the blood smeared across his lower lip and chin.

"Forgiven, my love," Simeon replied, and carefully withdrew from Angel's body. Angel went limp, his heart pounding in his ears. He felt like he was floating, the only connection to the world...Simeon's flesh on his.

Power surged through him, resonating with his soul, and Angel fell asleep, the taste of Simeon on his tongue and his lover's weight seeming to be the only things holding him down.

6

LEARNING PAINS

Angel flipped the paper, going to the section in the middle to read the rest of the front page article. They were in a café not far from the apartment, Simeon on his left and Daniel on his right. Both men were talking, and Angel peered over the top of the paper and enjoyed the sight of his lover and apprentice getting along. Daniel seemed to be getting over his hesitancy towards vampires, or maybe it was just Simeon.

It was an hour after sunset, and most humans were at home by now, so the café wasn't as busy as it would have been if they came in earlier. Eroch was curled up around his neck like a fancy necklace, though the wee beastie was a bit heavier. Angel was glad the place was nearly empty. Eroch burped, full from his cranberry scone, and Angel smiled when he felt the rumble of his wee beastie's snores.

Simeon was within reach, and Angel could almost *feel* his undead mate's presence. Simeon hummed in his space, so subtle and deep Angel could hardly distinguish the frequencies of Simeon's energies from the beat of his own heart. The *Leannán* bond between them was a translucent shimmer that coiled and spun through the air, silk spun from light and energy, and Angel could see it from the corner of his eye and sometimes when he shut them, all without summoning his inner sight. Their bond was still so new, and while a thousand times stronger than it had been the first night it was forged, Angel still feared it would shatter. Simeon said it was breakable right up until the final bond was set in place, and if it was to be broken, it could only be sundered by death or...choice. Angel's choice.

If the bond was so powerful now, and it wasn't complete, Angel was having trouble comprehending what it would be like once the final piece was in place. Not that he knew what that piece was, or what it meant exactly, but it was enough to make him leery.

Angel mentally set aside that thought, and Eroch stretched around his neck before settling back down into slumber. It was an odd sensation, but a welcome one. Eroch was his familiar, and the wee beastie served as a relief valve of sorts, siphoning off excess energy that poured into Angel from the *Leannán* bond with Simeon. It wasn't something Angel could stop, either. Eroch clung to him most of the time now, and Angel knew it was because the wee beastie was sensing the surge in Angel's personal magics from the *Leannán* bond, and was skimming from the top of the maelstrom. Angel didn't mind one bit—it was what a familiar was for, in many respects.

All Angel had to do was avoid major casting, and the endless vault of power that waited within his mate existed undisturbed. He was in trouble if he was attacked, or had to do a major working—he had yet to know how the ancient death magic would react now that he was fully aware of its presence. Angel couldn't afford to pass out again to keep himself from overloading, or destroying half the city if he sneezed.

Angel's fingers crinkled the edges of the paper. He resisted the urge to drop his pretense and tell Simeon. Tell him everything...but what if Simeon reacted badly? His mate said Angel was the only one who could break the bonds growing between them, and what if Simeon felt trapped? Felt used? If it was reversed, and Simeon was draining Angel of magical power, he didn't know at all how he would react. He was torn, so deeply he hurt from just thinking about it.

He was at a personal impasse and needed to think about his options. Protecting his lover and their bond was paramount, but it all came down to how Simeon would react if he knew. Simeon could send Angel power consciously, but seemed to be wholly unaware of the fact Angel had access to the ancient death magic that was the genesis for his existence as a vampire. Would Simeon feel used, or not care at all, generous and selfless to a fault?

Angel knew he was being stupid, and stubborn, and he had experience with putting things off, and it never ended well.

Simeon chuckled, and Angel relaxed. He went back to reading, but trying to focus on the words in front of him was difficult, despite his growing suspicions at the contents of the article.

Isaac was back at the apartment, reading Angel's Christmas present to him. Angel had gone back to Salvatore Mansion, and dug through his mother's library until he found the tome he wanted. Their great-great-grandmother had been a fire mage, a sorceress of renowned powers who led the Salvatores during some of the deadliest years of the Blood Wars. Astoria Salvatore headed the family against the Macavoys and the now extinct Melbournes, and was one of the reasons that magical clan no longer existed. Aside from her place in history, Astoria had seen heartache and loss, and Angel hoped her trials would ease whatever haunted Isaac. Her diary spanned many years of her storied life, and was a family heirloom. He gave it to Isaac for Christmas, and he supposed it was a success when Isaac spent the day reading it. His brother read it front to back several times, and Angel felt that was some progress.

In the weeks since Ben Stone attacked Milly, Christmas came and went, and now the town was decked out for Valentine's Day. The troll-hybrid never made a reappearance, though Angel had some feelers out in the community, and he'd placed tracers on Milly's apartment, geared towards those with troll blood. He would be alerted if Stone made another attempt. Milly was of the opinion that Stone was scared off, and wouldn't be back. Angel doubted it. It made more sense that Stone was biding his time, looking for a weakness to exploit.

Angel grumbled at the red hearts and ribbons and the ads geared towards sucking money from happy, and not-so-happy couples. Everyone, even vampires, seemed to celebrate the pseudo-holiday, and Angel found himself in the unenviable position of needing to get his lover something for Valentine's Day. He'd never had a lover before, so he was again stuck getting presents. Maybe sex would be enough for Simeon.

Angel went back to reading his article, one ear on the conversation at his table. Angel had begun Daniel's reeducation, and the best place to start was with the histories of the assorted beings that made up Boston's supernatural citizenry. No better way to learn something than from the source, and Daniel had asked Simeon if he could interview him about vampires. Pleased, Angel spent hours listening to Daniel open up to Simeon, and he loved his undead vampire lord all the more when Simeon patiently answered every one of Daniel's questions, no matter how awkward.

"Is it true vampires need to feed from virgins?" Daniel asked, and Angel snorted out a laugh. He kept his head down behind the paper, and bit his lip to keep from laughing out loud.

"Not true at all, Daniel. As long as our blood donor is not a practitioner, or closely related to one, we can feed from any mortal, regardless of sexual experience."

"I wonder how that rumor started then," Daniel mused, and Angel heard the scratch of pencil over paper. Daniel was taking his role as apprentice very seriously, and Angel was careful not to show how endearing it was.

"It began millennia ago, I imagine. Humans, if ill, say with any STD or other blood-borne disease, taste odd to vampires, and so we vampires as a rule tended to drink from those who were healthiest. One of the many ways to ensure our food sources weren't sick was to feed from those who hadn't yet become sexually active, and were less likely to have diseases like syphilis, for instance." Simeon's reply was matter-of-fact and even, and Angel marveled at his ability to remain nonjudgmental no matter the topic. "In this modern age, with antibiotics and the medical community's ability to treat such diseases, that precaution on our part is no longer all that necessary. The mythos still prevails though, even after all these years."

"How many donors do you have?" Daniel asked next, and Angel froze, highly interested in Simeon's answer. Simeon drank from blood bag units while at home, but Angel knew realistically that Simeon drank from donors while at the Tower. It didn't bother him, not really, since he trusted Simeon not to make it a sexual thing with his blood donors, but he still wanted to know.

"I have none in particular that are mine," Simeon answered, and Angel relaxed a fraction. "I had a dedicated few before I bonded to Angel, but I released them to another when I came to live with all of you at Angel's home. If I need to feed while at the Tower, I ask for volunteers."

"Do you need to feed more as you age, or less?" Daniel asked hesitantly, and Angel peeked up again, curious as well. At this point he was only pretending to read the paper.

"I need to feed every other day, and only a mouthful or two. If it's from a living source, like a donor, I need less, and less often. Blood units sustain me for shorter periods of time, so I need to consume more of those to get by," Simeon answered, and Angel frowned. If that was the case, then Simeon either wasn't getting enough to eat while at home, or he was eating more at the Tower. Simeon continued, "The younger a vampire is, the more they need to feed. Fledglings need to feed twice a day, and that feeding pattern continues for the first thirty years or so, then they can wean themselves down to once a day."

"So a bloodclan with a lot of fledglings needs a ton of donors, right?"

"Yes, that's true. Ten fledglings require a hundred blood donors if we wish to keep our donors from falling ill from repeat feedings. We hired an additional twenty when this brood rose," and Simeon's answer boggled Angel's mind. They paid for blood donors? He thought it was a volunteer position, and the volunteers were rewarded with a longer life span and the possibility of being turned at the end of their service.

Angel went back to reading the paper when the conversation veered toward the hierarchy in a vampire bloodclan. Finding his place in the article, Angel read the last half.

In the weeks since Angel and Simeon saw O'Malley at the site of the first murder, six bodies were found. The first three were human; the next couple were wolf-hybrid mixes, and the last was a full werewolf, a young pup of about twenty or so who hadn't been able to shift reliably yet. The previous two were considered humans, despite their publicized lineage, and the papers hadn't made the connections yet between the human victims and the supernats killed. They were all stabbed to death, and their bodies left in semi-public areas.

All murdered the same way. Mix of genders and ages, but all were under thirty. Ethnicities were varied as well, though species were cropping up in threes. Humans then weres? Angel imagined the local packs were warning their members stay out of town, and he didn't blame them one bit. Whoever was killing wasn't leaving much behind as evidence. Angel thought about it, then pulled out his cell.

He put the paper down, and sent a text.

We need to talk about these murders. It's a serial killer, isn't it? —AS

It took ten minutes for a reply, nine of those minutes spent impatiently fuming and trying to hide it. Simeon kept sneaking glances at him, and Daniel was oblivious as he diligently took notes. Finally, he got an answer.

How did you know? You been snooping about? —JO

All killed the same and left in semi-public areas. First three victims were humans, now the last three werewolves/hybrids. Not coincidence. —AS

Shit. You tell anyone? —JO

No, but I can't be the only one to have seen the possibilities. —AS

Sending a car for you. Location? —JO

Angel looked up at Daniel, thinking about it. The boy was his apprentice after all things were said and done, even if he had been skirting on the edges of treating him like a little brother instead of his student. Daniel was still wounded, pain and fear haunting the depths of his dark eyes, but there was life in him now, and he smiled more often than not.

It was time.

Angel texted back their location, and got a five-minute warning for a pickup.

"O'Malley is sending a car for me," Angel said, interrupting Daniel and Simeon. Daniel looked at him, surprised, and Simeon merely smiled, unruffled. He was probably reading over his shoulder again. "Daniel, you can go home, or you can come with me. Up to you. Simeon, you have Tower business tonight, yeah?"

"I do, my love. A meeting with Bridgerton and Batiste. I can cancel at any time, so text if you need me. Batiste understands my priorities are first to you," Simeon replied, and Daniel fidgeted. His apprentice sighed and closed his notebook, putting his stuff away in his backpack. Angel got up, Eroch chirping at his movement. Angel leaned down, kissing Simeon, slow and gentle. Daniel sighed again, even louder, and stood up as well, walking toward the door and waiting. Angel smiled, kissing Simeon one last time before pulling away.

"Love you," Angel told Simeon, who smiled at him, joy and affection plain as can be for the whole world to see. "I'll text with details. Have fun at the Tower."

Simeon took his hand, and kissed the back of his knuckles. An unmarked police sedan pulled up to the curb, and Daniel waved at the car through the window in the front of the café.

Angel grabbed his own bag, slinging it over his shoulder, adjusting his athame on his back as he met Daniel at the door. "Coming along, then?"

"Yeah. I figure I should start pulling my own weight," Daniel replied, pale cheeks flushed with embarrassment. "You've never asked me along before. What are we doing?"

"It's time, kiddo. Let's go help the cops catch a serial killer, huh?" Angel chuckled at the stunned horror on his apprentice's face, pulling Daniel along behind him to the police car waiting at the curb.

🐉

THE PRECINCT WAS LOUD, smelly, and chaotic. Angel followed behind the uniformed officer who'd picked them up, Daniel on his heels. They walked past several men in cuffs being led deeper into the building, and Daniel inched closer to Angel, nervously clutching the straps of his backpack. Angel smiled and pushed Daniel ahead of him, and they soon left the main entrance behind.

O'Malley worked in the detective's den, so called because the walls were a dark gray and the lack of windows. The large room was filled with desks, and about thirty people in rumpled suits and smelling of coffee huddled in small groups or sat at their desks, talking loudly into phones or clattering away at computer keyboards.

O'Malley was at the far wall near a door, and their escort left when O'Malley waved him off. O'Malley nodded in greeting to Angel and gave Daniel a long, considering look. Daniel flushed and fidgeted, biting his lip. O'Malley pointed at Daniel and said with a stern frown, "No puking over crime scene photos."

Daniel gaped, and Angel walked past his poor apprentice with a chuckle and a wink, following O'Malley into a conference room. A long table was covered in photos, crime scene reports, and lab print-outs. On the wall, pictures of the six victims, names underneath with each of their respective species in brackets. As Angel suspected, three humans and three werewolf/human hybrids. Only the last one was a full werewolf.

Daniel eventually came in, and O'Malley shut the door with a thud behind him. Angel walked over to the crime scene photos, recognizing the street in one set as the scene he and Simeon stumbled across while shopping. It was the first, with pictures from the subsequent five murders arranged chronologically after it. He took his time, not even seeing the rivers of blood and the terror set in the murdered victims' eyes and faces. All were stabbed, then cut open, chest cavities open to the air. Angel stopped, peered closer, and went back to the first picture, then double-checked the rest.

"He took the hearts," Angel said, and turned to send an inquiring look at O'Malley. "Same killer, same cuts, same MO in the body drops. Serial killer for certain, though I'm thinking blood magic of some kind since the hearts are missing and the bodies weren't molested. There's a macabre purpose to these killings, and it's not psychosis or an expression of sociopathic tendencies."

O'Malley snorted, taking off his jacket and slinging it over the back of a chair. Daniel glanced around, eyes darting past the grisly photos, and he hovered near the door looking lost. Angel smiled, and took pity of his apprentice. For all of two seconds.

"It took you two minutes what it took our best profilers to see in almost two months. Guess I should have called you in to begin with, huh?" O'Malley sat heavily in a chair, rubbing at his face. "It was only in the last two murders that we saw the connection. The killings were spread out across town, so different precincts caught each case."

"Which delayed the connecting of the murders," Angel said, and arched a brow at O'Malley. "Thought you all had computers and the ability to connect the dots across Town now these days?"

"Just because we can, doesn't mean we do. Too few detectives and too little talking."

Angel humphed, and crooked a finger at Daniel. "Drop your stuff and come here."

Daniel hurriedly obeyed, and came up to Angel, beyond nervous. Angel bit back a sigh and pointed at the crime scene photos. "I'll not ask you to look if it's going to make you sick. If you can't bear it, there's no shame in it. I'm used to dead bodies, and I know you aren't. Think you can do this?"

"I'll...I'll try."

"Good. Take a look, and tell me what you think," Angel nodded at the photos, and then got out of the way, walking to stand next to O'Malley.

"That wise? Kid looks like he wants to pass out," O'Malley grumbled, keeping his voice low as Daniel garnered the courage to look at each set.

"We're about to find out, but I have a feeling he'll be all right."

O'Malley grunted but said nothing, both of them watching Daniel hover over the pictures. Angel waited, patient, wondering if Daniel would see what he did. The clues were there, and if the cops had better wizards on staff, they may have caught on sooner.

After ten minutes or so, Daniel paused, finger resting on the final picture, the young wolf murdered a couple nights past. Angel waited, hoping, and he grinned when Daniel spun, eyes wide with sudden insight. "A ritual blade! Silver-edged!"

"Uh-huh. How do you know?" Angel coached, as Daniel went to the first picture, the human male whose bloody death Simeon had scented that evening weeks before.

"The cuts and the slices, even the stabs all have the same shape, and the killer made the same type of injuries, but there's a difference between the dead humans and the wolf hybrids. The wounds on the deceased wolves are seared on the edges, burnt in places where the blade lingered. Silver-edged blades would do that to the hybrids, and the burns are worse on the full-blood werewolf."

"How do you know it's a ritual blade?" Angel queried, impressed but keeping his opinion to himself until Daniel was done.

"Everyone was killed the same. Same cuts, same injuries, which I know you said already but just by looking everything really is the same. Doing the same thing over and over again means a set pattern, steps taken in order. A ritual. And the burning on the wolves killed means a silver blade of some kind, and most ritual blades are silver, or silver-edged at the least."

Angel nodded, and asked his apprentice, "What ritual requires the hearts of so many sacrifices?"

"Oh...wow. Umm there's several, across a wide spectrum of species. Most practitioners don't use blood magic, as the effects on human magic-users are very easy to see. Humans look like meth addicts, strung out and jonesing for a hit. A human would have people noticing his or her condition and most of us know the symptoms of blood magic addiction. Someone would say something. Right?" Daniel looked unsure, but his eyes were lit up and he was talking fast, excited. Angel nodded and gestured for him to keep going. "Umm...most of the fae species have old magic, earth magic that uses the hearts of sacrifices in their rituals, typically around major fae holidays and events, but such practices have gone out of use in the last hundred years or so. An expert in fae history and religion could tell us more."

Angel smiled, proud and more than pleased. "Good job, Daniel."

"I...I was right?" Daniel wrung his hands, shifting on his feet. "What part?"

"All of it, actually." Angel glanced down at the detective, who was chewing on an unlit cigarette and wearing a grumpy expression. "Don't look so sad, Jimmy. You should have called me sooner."

"Think we can keep the wunderkind? I promise to feed him, take him for walks, make sure he gets some playtime," O'Malley retorted, heavy on sarcasm and self-recrimination. Angel laughed, and gave Daniel a wink. His apprentice blushed, but smiled back at him, pleased.

"I may loan him out, but this one's mine for the next few years. Paws off."

"So we need one of them experts, huh? Would that be you?" O'Malley asked, tossing the now chewed and mangled cigarette butt at a nearby trashcan.

"That is not me, actually. If you need someone put down like a rabid dog I'm your sorcerer, but for this situation you'll actually need Dame Fontaine."

"Your teaching partner, huh? She the one with the troll for an ex?" O'Malley stood, grabbing his jacket and shrugging back into it. "Saw the restraining order come through after the break in at her place."

"Indeed she is," Angel agreed, and went to the files of each murder victim, stacking them up after collecting the loose pieces. Angel lifted the gathered files and went to Daniel, who took them with a surprised *oomph* and a frown. "I'll get your bag. You carry those."

"And where are we going?" Daniel asked, hurrying after Angel and O'Malley, Angel carrying Daniel's backpack. Eroch woke from his nap, poking his head out from under Angel's scarf with a cranky chirp when they stepped out into the larger room. Eroch stretched out, and crawled out of Angel's sweater and perched on his shoulder, flapping his leathery wings before pulling them back along his ribs. Several detectives stared, and Angel sighed in exasperation as he dodged around a few interested onlookers.

"We're going home! Hurry up," Angel called over his shoulder, Daniel all but jogging to catch up. "Everyone stop staring! Fuck! Have none of you seen a dragon before?"

7

UNANSWERED

Simeon paced away from the windows, the midnight horizon illuminated by the light of downtown and the reflection off the water in the harbor. Angel was out there, and in typical style, attracted trouble. All his love said was that he '*took the case, going back home*'.

Simeon pocketed his cell, and returned to the table where his Master and Bridgerton sat. Blood donors stood waiting along the tall windowed walls, and Simeon took his seat back, but waved off the donor that stepped forward. Their silhouettes stood out in stark relief in silent rows down the western wall, and the city glowed from between their shadows.

"You'll not partake, my child?" Batiste asked, tone casual. He heard the tension behind it, and shook his head once. This was an argument he didn't want to start.

"No need, my master."

"Have you been eating enough? The donors haven't needed to service you as often," Batiste stared hard at him, and Simeon schooled his features. Batiste's cerulean gaze was sharp as shards of ice, and he seemed to see deeper than Simeon would like. He made no response, so Batiste tried another tactic to get to what he wanted to know. Batiste smiled, a small, crooked twist of lush lips that was at odds with the chilly exterior of the city master. "How is your *Leannán*?"

"Angel is well, thank you for inquiring, Master."

"Enjoying yourself in domestic bliss, Simeon? Surrounded by all that supple flesh, and not a stretch of skin to bite. How are you handling cohabitating with living poison?" Bridgerton grinned, fangs down, and sipped from his crystal goblet. Mulled wine spiced with fresh blood, a particular favorite of the new Elder. Simeon leaned back in his chair, and tilted his head, curious.

Living poison was what vampires called humans who were magical in nature—like Angel and his family. The term was usually used as an in-species insult, and Simeon didn't appreciate the attempted slur against his love.

"So blunt. Heavy-handed. My Angelus does it far better, Bridgerton—do keep practicing." Simeon gave Bridgerton a slim smile when his jab hit its mark, the other Elder lifting a lip and snarling quietly.

Bridgerton was jealous of Simeon's *Leannán*, and Simeon was determined to keep his relationship private. It was getting harder, though—Batiste wanted Angel attached to the bloodclan, irrevocably so, and the best way to do it was through the bond. Simeon had never looked past Batiste's initial graceful endorsement of Simeon's courtship of Angel, and if he had, he would have seen what Angel saw straightaway—Batiste coveted Angel's power and his bounty of expertise and resources. Resources that now included two sorcerous fledglings—young Daniel Macavoy, and the other remaining Salvatore scion, Isaac. By asking after Angel, Batiste was really asking if Simeon had completed the bond between them, and brought Angel into the clan...and his two young charges with him.

Angel had no intention of letting Batiste or Bridgerton near Isaac or Daniel—Simeon believed his mate to be right in his assumptions that the city master and the new Elder would seek their own mates from the tempting younglings. Their kind did not make *Leannán* bonds unless love flourished at the center of the relationship, but they could create sexual relationships and foster unhealthy attachments. Even marriages—though unless love was in the center, no mate bond could grow, and a bond was ideal in romancing a mortal.

"If the nature of this meeting is to merely hound me for intimate details of my *Leannán* and his family, I will beg your leave and return home," Simeon said, and made to stand. "My mate is off limits, as any of yours would be if you are ever so lucky to be blessed with one."

"Peace, my child," Batiste replied, reaching out and resting his hand on Simeon's wrist. "I am concerned for you. I worry. Our clan, and myself, will be lessened if your union with the necromancer fails to complete. Forgive my intrusiveness, I cannot bear to see you injured."

Injured was an understatement—if Angel cast him aside, or ancient gods forbid, died—Simeon would be beyond saving. There was no healing to be done for a shattered soul. He would cease to be as he was now, and would greet the dawn to save his master the pain of killing him. Vampires that were left incomplete and destroyed by a broken bond became the *croíbhriste*.

Croíbhriste—the brokenhearted. And they were dangerous if left too long after a broken bond.

Angel would laugh and say something insulting and shocking, claiming bullshit. Simeon would too, if not for the fine tremor in the heavy weight of his master's hand. Batiste was so strong, so much bigger than the reality in which he existed. Simeon knew him better than anyone, sans Angel. And while Batiste played the coy overlord and fooled Bridgerton into thinking he was naught but a cold heart and sardonic exterior, Simeon knew intimately the passion and fire that burned in his master's heart.

It was why he believed Batiste's permission to court Angel had been naught but a gracious gift, and he was now only seeing the hidden agenda behind it. Hurt and betrayal would have been his response as a fledgling to such a cunning deception, but as he was no longer a child by any measure, he only felt caution and a vague sense of anger. Batiste meant it because he cared—but he also wanted the benefits of Simeon mated to Angel.

They may be undead, but they still lived, and Simeon had lived beside Batiste for two hundred years. Master and Elder, clanmates, and long ago, bedmates. He loved the undead lord he called master, but not like he loved Angel. And for that love, he relented. A small nod, and Simeon relaxed. Batiste's hand rested on his arm for a moment more, then slipped away.

Bridgerton glared back at Simeon, only a slim narrowing of his eyes but enough to let Simeon know that the tiny hints of byplay between Batiste and Simeon were noticed. Let Bridgerton think what he would. Simeon was secure in his position as First Elder of their bloodclan. Bridgerton could plot and plan to his heart's content— Simeon did not fear him.

"I would like to know why Simeon is allowed to live outside the clan, and still enjoy the rank and privilege of Elder. He reaps all the benefits, and does none of the duties," Bridgerton finally said, growling out each word, attacking the air with his jealousy.

Batiste leaned back in his chair, and looked every inch the feudal lord he once was. Bastard son of an ancient king, Constantine Batiste wore the impenetrable icy expression he perfected through hundreds of years' practice.

"My favored child needs not explain himself to you, Elder," Batiste reprimanded, and Simeon smiled before he could school his features. Bridgerton flinched, and dropped his eyes as Batiste continued. "And I approve heartily of his courtship of the necromancer. The why of it is not your concern."

"Forgive me, Master Batiste," Bridgerton murmured, contrite. He bowed in his seat, and Batiste let him stay that way for one long, uncomfortable moment before waving a hand. Bridgerton sat up, and sent Simeon a sharp glance, heated with anger and embarrassment.

"I called you both here for another reason," Batiste declared, and Simeon waited patiently. "There was an attempt on one of our clanmates earlier tonight, just after sunset. It was at one of the clan's clubs, and he was assaulted as he was walking to the parking structure nearby. He was able to escape, but the situation is troubling."

"Assaulted? Who was it, and did he not hear his attacker coming?"

Bridgerton was trying to hide his disdain that a vampire was almost ambushed. Their senses were exceedingly sharp, and it took a great deal of stealth or magic to sneak up on one of their kind.

"Who was it? And was he able to identify the assailant?" Simeon asked.

"One of our soldiers taking the cash deposit from the club to the treasury," Batiste dismissed, flicking his fingers. "He said he had no warning before he was struck from behind on the head. Only a passing delivery truck turning down the back alley allowed him to break away. All he could ascertain was that it was a being of immense physical strength, and his charming ability had no effect."

"Humans with anti-vampire prejudice, maybe? Or a thief after the cash?" Simeon conjectured, thinking. Depending on the club, the amount of money on the soldier could be substantial, and in the dark, a vampire could look all too human to the uneducated. "Few supernaturals in the area would dare attack our clan, and that is not hubris. We are hard to kill, and while we have our limits, they are few. Supernats know better, surely. Our alliance with Angel is also well known, and his reputation is a serious deterrent."

"Perhaps any of that. Regardless, I want the security around our properties increased. If this was an attempted robbery, I don't want it to happen again."

"As you wish, master," Simeon said. "All soldiers involved in cash drops will be doubled, and guards will be increased at all entrances. The clan's wealth is well-known; this may deter any future thievery against the clan if we appear less vulnerable."

"Agreed." Batiste stood, and Simeon and Bridgerton followed suit. "I need the room, please. Send for more donors."

Simeon nodded, and walked away, texting the communications hub in the Tower for more blood donors to be sent to the Master's penthouse. He arranged for the added security features and notified the soldier ranks of the double precautions. Their clanmates were efficient and well-trained, and would see to his orders.

Bridgerton moved with reluctance, his desire to stay with Batiste while their master fed written across his tense frame and swarthy features. Simeon paused at the doors to the suite, making it clear he was waiting on the other Elder. Batiste rarely invited other vampires to be present while he fed—it was a privilege, and one Bridgerton had yet to earn.

Bridgerton passed by him at a low simmer, and Simeon shut the door behind them. They walked to the elevator, and Simeon waited calmly for the elevator while Bridgerton worked himself up into a snit. The other Elder may be as old as Simeon, but the differences in their behavior was immense. Bridgerton was spoiled, entitled, easy to anger, and was the worst of sycophants—the kind who thought their ingratiating behavior subtle. Batiste welcomed the former unranked master from Atlanta because he had a few dozen members to his own household and numerous fledglings, and his wealth was substantial. Adding Bridgerton's resources to the clan was practical—though it seemed that welcome went to Bridgerton's head.

The elevator arrived and Simeon stepped inside, Bridgerton next to him. The guard inside backed away with a nod of respect, and Simeon placed his palm on the reader and hit the button for the garage level. Bridgerton impatiently waited his turn, and slapped his hand on the palm reader and stabbed the button for the casino level. Simeon arched a brow at the other vampire's theatrics, and pulled out his cell as the elevator descended.

Taking a car home. Meeting over. Are you home yet? –S

The speed at which Angel answered cheered him, and he read his love's text.

Just got back. Meeting with Milly tomorrow over case files. Be careful— something is happening in this city and it's not good. Love you. –AS

Love you, my Leannán. Be home soon. –S

Bridgerton snorted, and Simeon gave him a slow, cold glance. Bridgerton scowled and moved back, having been reading over Simeon's shoulder. Unashamed of his love for Angel, Simeon blacked out the smartphone screen and put it away in his suit jacket. He kept eye contact with Bridgerton the whole time, all but daring him to make a comment and voice the envious anger Simeon could see swirling in the old pirate's eyes.

The elevator came to a smooth stop at the ground level and Simeon held his place, eyes locked to Bridgerton's. The other Elder narrowed his eyes and growled, lips twitching like he wanted to flash a fang. Simeon remained still, immobile as marble. Disrespect toward his mate and their bond would not be tolerated. Bridgerton growled louder, finally lifting a lip and hissing through his dropped fangs. The elevator guard blurred as he ran from the lift, and the guards stationed outside the doors backed away as well. The elevator chimed, the doors open too long, and the sound seemed to knock some sense back into Bridgerton.

Bridgerton broke first, dropping his eyes to the side and his fingers flexing, claws having grown as tempers rose. Bridgerton snarled out a wordless burst of frustration and released a cloud of sour pheromones as he left the elevator, walking around Simeon and making an effort not to brush shoulders. Simeon watched him go, and it wasn't until Bridgerton disappeared into the casino's main doors across the lobby that the elevator guard returned. Simeon gave the guard a short, approving nod, and the guard returned to his station inside.

The doors slid shut, and the elevator went down, heading for the garage.

THE LIMO CUT through evening traffic with ease as Simeon was driven home. The late night hour meant nothing in the close streets of downtown, the heart of Boston perhaps not as densely packed as larger metropolitan centers down the East Coast, but the city was lively and the streets full of humans.

The limo pulled out of downtown and headed toward Beacon Hill, the traffic thinning as they entered the more residential area of the city. Cobblestones and red brick homes filled his view, and Simeon smiled, thinking back through the long years to when he first came to the United States. Boston was always a bustling port city, filled with a multitude of fishermen, merchants, traders, and people from all points across the world. Beacon Hill was one of the oldest neighborhoods of the city, and it showed in the remaining buildings and architecture. Some were the same, maintained through the centuries, lovingly preserved and treasured by their inhabitants. Though even a city as keen on preserving history as Boston evolved through the years, and not even the humans who studied history in great depth could even be aware of just how different their beloved city was from the day Simeon first set foot on this continent.

They were but a few spare blocks from Angel's apartment when the limo swerved, tires squealing, the driver swearing as he lost control. Simeon gripped his seat, and held himself in place as the limo slammed into the wall of a building, dust and dirt flying up and covering the windshield, the front pane of glass cracking down the center. Simeon let go of the seat and climbed forward, looking for the driver. Simeon reached the open partition, and the human man who had been driving him home groaned in pain, blood spoor filling the confines of the cab.

"Don't move, I'll call for help," Simeon said, trying to see the extent of the man's injuries through the opened privacy partition. He did not know if the human was a blood donor for his clan or one of their regular employees, and if he wasn't, then he was perhaps more injured than he appeared.

Simeon pulled out his phone and speed dialed the Tower communications hub, reaching through the opening and pressing a finger to the human male's neck, searching for his pulse. "Yes, this is Elder Simeon. Tag my limo's location and..."

The driver side door ripped outwards with a screech of metal, and the driver was yanked from his seat, the belt holding him in place snapping with tremendous force. The human was gone from his sight, and a large shadow walked down the side of the vehicle towards the backend. Simeon snarled, dropping his phone, and he spun as the rear passenger door buckled under a powerful blow.

The shadow was tall and wide, appearing bipedal and with arms as thick as tree trunks that swung at the limo door. Simeon's vision went crystalline bright and clear, fangs dropping, and battle-rage filled him. The steel door buckled, about to break, and Simeon roared in challenge. He was no creature's prey—he was the hunter.

Simeon launched himself forward, breaking through the row of windows that ran down the side of the limo, rolling as he hit the pavement, glass showering down around him. He came to a stop, crouching, spinning to face the tall creature attacking his limo.

The scent of dusty stone and fresh petrichor came to him as he pulled in the creature's defining air markers. Long years on this world told him instantly what his opponent was, and Simeon snarled in satisfaction.

Coincidences were falsehoods.

Troll.

Ben Stone, recognizable from the police report Simeon accessed on the man who attacked his mate, now stood facing him, and slapped at his chest with both fists in answering challenge and charged at Simeon. The world slowed around him, and Simeon gathered himself, sliding to the side the smallest of distances, but enough for Stone to miss him completely. Simeon raked his claws along Stone's ribs, slicing through clothing and down to skin. The man was a hybrid, and his flesh parted beneath Simeon's claws in red ribbons. If he had been full blood Simeon's claws would never have punctured his hide.

A scream of rage and pain was heavenly to his ears, and Simeon spun with Stone, leaping up and landing a foot dead center of his back, kicking hard. The hybrid outweighed him by over a hundred pounds and towered over him by several inches, but he was lumbering and slow. His great strength may be daunting for a mortal or lesser supernat, but Simeon was old and powerful in his own right. Stone flew forward from Simeon's kick, and Simeon moved at incredible speed, blurring the street around him as he ran to meet his prey as Stone face-planted the pavement.

Simeon grabbed the man's beefy arm and flipped him to his back, and slammed his foot down, the leather of his boot dark against Stone's whitening skin as he pushed so hard he cut off blood flow to the flesh and shut down his jugular arteries.

Stone gasped, dinner-plate sized hands beating at Simeon's leg, but he withstood the blows that would have broken another. His battle-rage pulled back, and the world settled. Simeon leaned over his defeated foe, Stone's efforts to free himself weakening as Simeon snuffed the life from him.

"You tried to kill my *Leannán*," Simeon whispered, enjoying the sight of Stone's eyes going wide in fear and desperation. "You harmed my friends and attacked my mate. I think Angel will forgive me for taking justice into my own hands this time."

He pushed down, the barest of efforts, and Stone gurgled, clawing at Simeon's lower leg, ripping his trousers in his frenzied and failing efforts to escape. Simeon watched, breathing in the stench of fear and sweat as death crept closer and closer to taking Stone.

Lavender and something earthy, robust like sage came in on the chill winter wind, and Simeon breathed it in, wondering for a short second where he'd smelled such a scent before—then there was warmth at his back, and a slim, leanly muscled arm wrapped around his shoulder as another snuck under his arm.

Cold and agony sliced into his abdomen, and Simeon screeched as a blade buried itself to the hilt in his flesh.

"Forgive me the dishonor, Elder, but I need my servant alive," a sweet tenor whispered in his ear, and the blade twisted in his guts.

Daniel puttered about the kitchen, and Angel paused at the threshold, wondering. The boy's smartphone was out, the screen just fading to black as he came in. He didn't hear it ring, so maybe a text from someone? Voicemail? Daniel looked lost, scared, and whatever joy and pride in himself he'd found at the police station was gone as if it never was.

"Daniel?"

His apprentice looked up from the kettle he was holding, having been staring down at the object that almost made him lose a hand. Daniel put it down on the stove, and gave him a small smile. "Yeah?"

"Is everything alright?"

"What do you mean?"

"You've been going back to Macavoy Court a lot the last few weeks. Is your father well?" Angel managed to ask without anything but honest concern showing on his face or in his voice, and was proud of himself.

Saying the Macavoy name no longer made him grimace, but he still got a twinge in his chest. He never blamed Daniel for anything in their shared past, but Leicester, Daniel's father, he blamed plenty. How the sorcerer managed to avoid prison when his wife and his brothers all ended up there was a mystery to Angel. Growing up in that place had to have been hard for Daniel, from what little he shared. Agoraphobia, depression, and what sounded like bipolar disorder was probably what afflicted the elder Macavoy, and he was convinced Leicester never accepted treatment for any of it.

"Father...Father has been ill. The last few months have taken a toll on him," Daniel admitted, hugging himself.

"Do you need anything? Can I help?" Angel ventured closer, leaning on the island.

"I may need to go see him more. Don't think he has long left," Daniel whispered. His already pale face went whiter.

"If you want, I can go with you? He may not want to see me, but I might be able to help if it's serious enough?"

"No! Please, don't," Daniel gasped out, and Angel was relieved despite his offer. He had no idea how he would handle seeing Leicester in person.

"Ok, I won't." Angel smiled, rubbing Daniel's tense shoulder. "I won't do anything unless you ask. Go see him tomorrow."

"Won't we be working on the case?"

"It'll keep until you get back. No classes tomorrow, so we can all have a lazy morning. Go see your dad, yeah?"

Daniel bit his lip, chewing on the poor bit of flesh so hard Angel winced. Daniel gave him a searching glance from under thick lashes, and he waited, patient. Waiting with Daniel always worked the best.

"Do, do I have to?" Daniel whispered.

Angel blinked, surprised. "Do you not want to see your father? Go home for a visit? You're not my slave, kiddo. You can go home anytime you want. It's just safer for you here with me."

"I hate it there," Daniel confessed, tears in his dark eyes and pain in his voice. Angel froze, again hiding his reaction. Daniel needed him to be calm.

"Is he a danger to you?" Angel asked, gently tugging at Daniel until his apprentice huddled against his side. The poor boy curled into him, and despite being taller than Angel, Daniel rested his head on Angel's shoulder and shuddered out a long, wet breath that sounded suspiciously like a sob.

"Daniel, is Leicester dangerous? Does he hurt you?" Angel asked again, firmer. Daniel shuddered again, and gave Angel a small, hesitant nod. His guts chilled with a sick fear, and he had to know. Leicester's life depended on his son's answer. "Does he hurt you like Deimos did, or does he hurt you some other way?"

Daniel sniffled, but shook his head. "Hits me, uses magic sometimes," Daniel whispered into his shoulder. Angel's anger roiled in his belly, chasing away the cold terror, and he took a deep, even breath before he lost control, got in a taxi, and went to Cambridge in the middle of the night to beat the ever-loving fuck out of Leicester Macavoy.

Angel hugged Daniel to him, and rubbed his back until he calmed. "Thank you for telling me. And no, you need never go back there if you don't want to. I'll keep you for as long as you want, probably a bit longer just in case."

Daniel gasped out a small laugh, and Angel smiled. "Go get changed and washed up, we have some case files to look over."

"Yes, Sir." Daniel pulled back, wiping his damp cheeks. There was life in his dark eyes again, and Angel inwardly cheered.

"Don't call me sir, makes me feel old."

"Sorry, sir."

"Scamp! Be gone with you!"

Daniel left the kitchen and turned for the hall to the back of the apartment. Angel gripped the edge of the island, hellfire scorching the butcher block top. He breathed, in and out, battling back the anger he thought long released. If it weren't for Daniel and what he needed right now, he would be taking years of the boy's suffering out on his father.

Such habits were what started a war that spanned generations and killed hundreds of practitioners, though, so he let go of the island and breathed out the anger, calming himself.

He left the kitchen, heading for the coffee table and the case files.

Angel staggered, falling forward, hands slapping the wall as pain ran through his abdomen.

"Fuck!" he yelled, sliding to the floor, hands going to his stomach, half-convinced he would pull them back and see blood on his palms.

"Angel!" Isaac jumped up from the couch, the old diary thumping as it landed on the floor. Isaac ran to his side, kneeling next to him as Angel shuddered, panting in fear and pain. "What's wrong, what is it?"

Angel lifted his dry and clean hands, eyes wide, heart racing. Something was wrong, but not with him. The phantom pain receded, and he felt the echo of another's agony.

Simeon.

Angel jumped up, adrenaline coursing through his veins, and he opened his senses and inner vision as wide as he could. He found the golden cord between himself and Simeon, and followed it back to his lover.

"Unholy saints, no," Angel breathed out, heart seizing in absolute terror. "Simeon!"

Angel pushed off from the wall, and ran for the front door, grabbing his athame from where it hung in its scabbard by the entrance. Angel opened the door and ran down the hall to the stairs, jumping down the steps in hazardous leaps and bounds. Isaac was yelling behind him, but Angel had only one focus, and he followed his inner vision and the compass in his soul that pointed the way to his lover.

8

LOVE'S FOLLY

Simeon thrust his head back, his skull connecting with the
face of the fae who held him. A shout and a rush of sweetly-
scented, warm blood down his neck told him he hit his target,
and Simeon slammed his elbow up and back, knocking his attacker
away from him. The blade buried in his torso slid out and sliced as it
went, opening the wound even more, until it gaped and ice cold
blood poured down his hip and groin.

Simeon kicked, knocking Stone's head to the side with a solid
thunk, and he hissed at the pain that radiated out from his center.
Simeon moved backward, keeping the prone Stone and the
newcomer in his line of sight, the wall of the building the limo
crashed into at his back.

The fae was tall as he, lean and muscled. Skin the color of dark
honey glimmered with soft hints of light, as if the frost of the winter
night clung to his skin and reflected back the meager light from the
street lamps. Long, sleek hair the shade of moss was pulled back from
a high forehead in a long queue, the end of the tail flirting with the
wind. Gray leather molded to a defined torso and lean hips show-
cased a perfection never seen in mortals. Eyes the color of mercury
framed by thick, dark green lashes twinkled, and the fae twirled the

long silver blade in his hand, Simeon's blood flying off the edges in arching patterns.

Facing Simeon, the fae smiled despite the dark crimson blood dripping from his broken nose, otherworldly features aglow with an inner light. "Best get that tended to, Elder, lest you leave your *Leannán* grieving your loss."

Simeon bared his fangs and crouched, prepared to attack. The fae twirled the blade again, side-stepping, almost dancing across the slick and icy sidewalk, balance pure and grace unhurried. Vampires moved with inhuman grace—the fae moved as if life were a dance, and only they knew the steps.

"That blade won't save you when I rip out your throat," Simeon vowed, tracking the lithe creature in front of him.

"No, Elder, I think not," the fae said, and with a flick of his wrist temperature turned from chilling to sub-zero, the wind screaming loud enough to shake windows along the street. Simeon screamed himself, hands over his ears, and he staggered, falling to a knee as the sound grew in intensity. Pressure rose in his ears, inside his head, and he yelled, trying to force out the magic threatening to crush his skull.

The male fae walked leisurely to Stone, and even through his pain Simeon was left astonished when the fae leaned down, gripped Stone by one wrist, and hoisted the unconscious troll over his shoulder. Simeon screamed again in rage, voiceless in the storm assaulting his senses. Stone was gigantic compared to Simeon, and he dwarfed the slim fae to a ridiculous degree, yet the supernat tossed him about like a toy, taking Simeon's prey from him.

The fae and his oversized burden jogged down the street, and Simeon forced himself back to his feet, swaying, but he took off after them. He tried, at least—the winds sucked at his strength, his mind confused, and he stumbled. Simeon gasped, thick blood choking him as the wound in his gut ripped even more, sending blood up his throat and out his mouth. His essence was torn open and spilling to the frozen pavement.

The wind died after an interminable passage of time, and Simeon stood, staring down the empty street. Simeon pressed a hand to his abdomen, cold thick blood oozing past his fingers. He swayed on his feet, surprised to feel weak. Centuries since an injury made him feel vulnerable, the cut from the silver blade left his innards exposed to the icy wind and the threat of second death.

He fell.

Angel ran.

He hurt, from his throat seared by the subzero air, to the soles of his feet insufficiently protected in his house shoes, each stride that hit the ice-cold pavement jarring his bones, his hands scraped and raw from slipping when he'd first made the street outside his apartment building. The fingers of his right hand were numb, the stone and damask steel of his athame freezing in the cold night air.

Simeon was somewhere ahead, so close. Another corner, another minute, a small moment of time. It felt like forever, and yet in seconds Angel rounded a corner three blocks from his apartment, and saw Simeon's limo crashed into a closed deli, the engine still running and ticking in the cold air. Angel slowed, searching for Simeon, and he panted out a denial when he saw a body flung carelessly to the sidewalk. He took a step forward before his mind caught up to his eyes—it was a human, eyes vacant and dull, neck broken from hitting the wall. He wore a style of black suit common among the Tower employees, and Angel panted in relief and ever-growing fear that it wasn't Simeon.

"Simeon!" Angel screamed, and he jogged ahead, thinking Simeon might be in the limo. The crash didn't appear severe enough to incapacitate a vampire, but Simeon might have been unlucky.

"*Mo ghra.*" The familiar Irish, whispered so quiet it might have been the wind, made him stop, sliding on the slick road.

"Where...where..." Angel increased his inner sight, and the glow of the bond led him through the long shadows between street lights. "Simeon!"

Simeon was on his back, both hands pressed to his stomach, and

Angel choked on a desperate sob when he saw the black blood that soaked Simeon's white dress shirt and his dark gray trousers. Blood puddled beneath him, and frost collected on the edges of the pool.

Angel dropped to his knees beside Simeon, and he cursed the low light. He took a quick inward breath, and in the second before his exhale, lit the dark street on fire.

Hellfire rose from the cobblestones, dancing hand-height up from the ground, swirling in the wind in joyous trails until they were in the center of a circle. Angel dropped the athame and gripped Simeon's hands and pulled them away, swallowing back bile. Green light illuminated the street, up the sides of buildings, and Angel was able to see the damage done to Simeon's abdomen.

The right side of his abdomen, from his lowest rib to the top of his right hip gaped like a red mouth, exposing dark flesh, loosened muscles, and the glistening coils of dormant organs. Angel gagged, covering his mouth with his right hand, his left shaking as he reached out and cupped Simeon's cheek for a moment. Simeon shifted, hissing through his teeth, and Angel snapped back into crisis mode at the sound of his lover's pain.

"Don't move," Angel ordered, ripping at Simeon's dress shirt, buttons flying off in all directions. "What happened? Can you tell me?"

"Fae...with a silver blade. Snuck up on me." Simeon gasped the words out, his ability to draw in enough air to speak affected by the gaping wound. Angel tugged at Simeon's waistband, checking how far down the injury went, but it appeared to stop right above his belt. Not that it helped—he was filleted open.

The incongruity of anyone sneaking up on Simeon had to wait until Angel figured out how to save him.

"What do you need to heal?" Angel asked, his inner sight in overdrive as he checked the wound for latent spells. Fae weapons were usually bespelled with secondary characteristics, like poisoning, or a spell to prevent blood clotting to ensure an injury bled out. The fae didn't fuck around.

There was residual magic in the wound tract, but nothing active, so Angel discounted worrying about spells messing with Simeon further. "Simeon! What do you need to heal? Blood?"

"Batiste...yes, blood." That made sense—Batiste could heal his clan members, that much Angel knew. Simeon couldn't feed from Angel—his blood would kill him. Angel dug out his cell, dialing a number he had never called before but Simeon insisted he have in case of emergency. It was a fucking emergency now, and Angel rocked on his knees as it rang in his ear.

"Batiste!" Angel said the second the call connected. "Simeon's been attacked. It's bad."

Batiste wasted no time in replying. "Where are you?"

"Intersection of Joy and Mt Vernon. Hurry, dammit. I don't know how to heal a vampire without blood. He can't feed from me."

Batiste made an odd sound, then replied. "Stay where you are. I'll be there soon."

Angel dropped his cell, the screen making a horrid crunching sound when it hit the pavement. Angel grabbed Simeon's hands and tugged, leaning over Simeon protectively. "I called Batiste, he's coming. I think he's going to be too late as it is, so what else can I do? There can't have been a blood source nearby for every injury you've ever had."

"Blood," Simeon breathed out. "My *Leannán.*"

"Angel!" He looked down the street, and Isaac came jogging around the corner, carrying Angel's weatherproof sweater and his boots. Isaac saw them and stumbled at the gory sight, but he gathered his resolve and sprinted down the street. Isaac jumped over the hellfire and knelt on Simeon's other side. "Shit!"

Angel wiped a hand over Simeon's cold cheek, smearing dark red blood across smooth skin. "Can you make it 'til Batiste arrives?"

Simeon opened his mouth to reply, and blood welled up over his lips, choking him. "No, no, no...don't talk. I'm sorry. I don't know how to help you except for blood. Goddammit!" Simeon blinked at him, slow, lids heavy, the brilliant green of his eyes dimming. Pain echoed down the bond between them, the vibrant gold splintering, white shards shimmering in the cord joining their souls.

"Blood," Simeon whispered, lips wet with dark, thick blood. His own blood, and leaking from him faster than he could heal. "*Leannán,* please."

"There's no one here he can drink from!" Isaac cried out, his little brother freaking out. "Maybe the dead guy? Can a vampire feed from a dead human?"

Simeon's hand, sticky and ice cold, found its way to Angel's neck, and he tugged. Gently, weak, Simeon begged him with a soft touch to lean over him, blocking the wind. The wind's needle sharp and invasive claws sliced over his back, and Angel shivered, but the press of Simeon's bloody lips to his neck stilled his reaction to the subzero caress of the salty air currents. Simeon's hand was gentle, but insistent, and Angel gasped when the sharp, smooth glide of a predatory kiss helped him understand.

What Simeon was implying terrified Angel. If this didn't work, Simeon would die. The one person in the whole world who made him feel alive, who made him feel real, would be dead, and no amount of magic would bring him back. A lifetime of promise would be cold and empty, a corpse on the frigid street, collecting snow drifts and fading from memory.

He wouldn't even be able to heal the magical blood poisoning and let Simeon keep whatever blood he took from Angel—he needed blood, and all Angel could do if this didn't work would be to watch his lover die faster. Angel cured blood poisoning by burning the offending blood out of a vampire's system with his hellfire at a microscopic level or by forcing the undead to vomit the blood, and Simeon would still die. Angel could heal mortal injuries in the *living*; if this was Isaac or Daniel, Angel could repair the wound, but as Simeon was *technically dead*, his affinity conversely failed him here.

Better to have tried than to admit he was afraid and failed. "Drink, Simeon. Take what you need. I love you."

"Angel? What the hell! No!" Isaac protested past his clattering jaws, chilled and shaking. He reached out and tried to yank him away from Simeon, but Angel put a hand up and stopped his brother.

"Drink, now!" Angel ordered his mate, and pushed his neck

against Simeon's mouth, and he winced when scalpel-sharp fangs broke the skin. Simeon growled, a feral rumble that skittered over Angel's nerves. Pain bloomed in his neck, and Angel grit his teeth and breathed through the white-hot agony of Simeon's first full draw.

He'd been bitten before. Many times. Angel bore faint scars across his body, faded by the last ten years. Taking down a vampire army that decimated his entire family hadn't been easy or immediate, and he got bit, savagely and multiple times before he managed to stop them. There were a handful of other times over the years since that night, including the fateful first meeting between himself and Simeon.

As that night went, Angel restrained his instinctive urge to pull away, and leaned into the bite. Simeon was too far gone to make it enjoyable or even employ low-level charm—Angel hissed out a breath, and steadied himself with one hand on the slick pavement as Simeon's weight pulled him down. Isaac made to come help him. "No, don't. It's all right."

Isaac sat back, eyes locked to Angel's neck where Simeon drank, deep, pulling mouthfuls that made his flesh burn. "Won't it ...kill him?"

"I don't know. I fucking hope not."

Angel went all the way down, stretched across Simeon's chest. Simeon growled again, a beast protesting the movement of its meal, and Angel stayed passive, keeping himself close to Simeon's mouth to avoid tearing. Simeon dug his teeth in deeper, and the steel bands of his arms came up, pressing them chest to chest. Each drag on the bite was hard to bear, but he took the pain, dealing as best he could. The cold stung his eyes, and he blinked away sharp frozen tears that clung to his lashes.

His hellfire died, the green illumination going dark.

A whoosh of heat surprised him, making him blink and come out of the daze into which he'd fallen. Isaac sat closer, cross-legged, knees brushing Simeon's shoulder, and his little brother held a small ball of fire in his hands. Heat poured into the small span between them, and

Angel gave Isaac a glance full of thanks. He then closed his eyes, dizzy.

He lost track of time. Usually when that happened Simeon was fucking him into oblivion, but this time his head was spinning for different reasons. He didn't know how long Simeon had been feeding from him, but if Simeon was going to get poisoned from his blood, he would be growing weaker, not stronger. Simeon held him, arms cradling him now more like a lover than a predator devouring its prey. Fingers carded through his hair, tugging on the strands. The harsh pull on his neck eased, gentled.

Fangs withdrew from his neck, and Angel went limp, collapsing totally, his limbs buzzing and his body cold. Simeon had taken too much, but Angel would have given him all if it meant saving him. Simeon shifted under him, and Angel found himself on his back in Simeon's lap, wide, strong hands brushing at his face and over his closed eyelids. A cool, soft kiss that tasted of copper and spice was pressed to his lips, and Angel opened his eyes.

A field of emerald consumed his view, and the heat and love in his mate's eyes blazed brighter than any magical fire. "It worked? It did—you're not dead. Well, super dead. Deader? Fuck, you know what I mean."

Angel's voice was raspy, and he swallowed, mouth dry. Simeon gave him a slow, sweet smile, and Angel grinned back, loopy and happy despite the spinning of his head. He looked so much better— still covered in blood and there was snow in his longish hair, but Simeon looked absolutely perfect to Angel. Simeon kissed him again, whispering over his lips, "It worked, my *Leannán*. Thank you."

"Anytime. I figured I was Julien to your Romeo there for a minute —glad I'm not right all the time," Angel whispered, grinning like an idiot. Simeon laughed and hugged him tight, rocking them both on the icy street. "You gonna tell me how that worked?"

"Certainly, but I'm sure once you've collected your considerable wits, you'll know the how and why of it faster than I can explain." Simeon sat him up more, and Angel's head spun a bit more, but his vision was clearing and limbs were regaining their strength. He was cold as hell, but Simeon for once was warmer than he was, and Angel snuggled into his embrace. He ran a hand over Simeon's abdomen through his ripped and ruined shirt, and the muscles and skin were whole and unblemished.

Miraculous.

"Fuck, I am so glad you're not dead. I just got you. And what the hell! You let some sparkly fae sneak up behind you?" Angel tried teasing, and he found himself chuckling at the bemused expression on Simeon's face. He was getting stronger, and his head felt firmly attached to his shoulders. Angel touched his neck, and winced at the ache from the wet, bloody bite wound. Simeon brushed his fingers away, and Angel frowned when Simeon put a finger in his mouth, pressed the tip to one of his fangs, and broke the skin. Simeon put his bloody finger to Angel's neck and rubbed his own blood into the bite. It tingled, and stung, but the deeper ache began to lessen.

"I think we have some talking to do," Angel murmured. Simeon nodded, agreeing. Angel licked his lips and continued, "I have something I've been afraid to tell you for a couple months."

"I've seen a shadow in your eyes for some time now, my love. I've been waiting. We shall talk, *a ghra*, but not out here in the cold. Kiss me first, then we should call the police and Batiste," Simeon said, calm and cheerful. Angel nodded, and Simeon took his mouth in a kiss that curled his toes and made his whole body feel hotter than a summer day on the dunes at the Cape.

Isaac stood nearby, hands in his pockets, doing his best to ignore his brother and his boyfriend making out on the street. Isaac was glad Simeon was okay, and he was equally confused as to how he was healed—everything Isaac knew about vampires boiled down to the fact that Simeon should be dead after feeding from Angel. Yet he was alive, and kissing Angel like a porn star.

Isaac snorted at the thought, and wandered away, steering clear of the dead man. The limo was fucked up—its front end was buried in the exterior wall of a corner deli and one side of it looked like a demi-god decided to use it as a punching bag. Something big and nasty and scary decided to attack the vampire clan's limo, and Isaac shivered, nervous at the thought of what could have done that. He might ask after Simeon and Angel were done examining each other's teeth with their tongues.

There was a boom, distant but deep, and Isaac looked up, thinking one of the military planes out of Logan was taking off, but the sky was dark and overcast, and there were no blinking lights in the clouds. A strong wind came down the street, and Isaac peered through the cold current, thinking he saw something. Air pressure grew and Isaac shook his head, and tried breathing, but it felt like he was being sat on by a forest orc. His eyes widened and he was about to call out to Angel when the air in front of him seemed to fold, to warp to his view like high heat would do on a roadway—and out stepped a blond god.

Reality swung back into *now*—and Isaac jumped, scrambling backwards as the tall, broad-shouldered Adonis sauntered towards him in a fine Italian suit and leather shoes. Gray wool clung in finely tailored lines, and a lean waist and powerful thighs made Isaac flush and his breathing hitch. An ice blue silk tie and crisp white shirt, and the darker gray on his trousers made the new vampire's white skin, blue eyes, and perfect blond hair stand out in vibrant shades. Pink, lush lips curved into a wicked, sexy smirk made him flush harder, and Isaac trembled.

He knew who this vampire was, this being of such beauty and power that his mere presence electrified the air around him and set Isaac's nerves into terrified frenzy of fascination and the urge to run.

"I was expecting to see my beloved child in need of my help. I am not complaining, not at all mind you—I was not expecting to be graced with such a delectable vision as yourself," the blond vampire said, an old, old accent lilting his words and making Isaac's belly tighten. "Angel and Simeon seem well enough. But how are you, young Isaac? Can I help you?"

The Master of Boston came closer, so much closer, and Isaac's head was screaming at him to run, to flee the predator stalking him now in long strides with a sexy smirk. Isaac tilted his head up and shuddered, mind and thoughts blinded by impossible beauty. It was as if the sun came to life in the center of a dark, cobblestoned Boston street, and it shone only for him. Beauty so perfect it hurt to look upon it, a perfection so true and pure that mortals would expire from want and desire at the merest glimpse.

Isaac breathed in, and the taste that bloomed on his tongue brought to mind icy cider and apples. An orchard slumbering in the depth of winter, fruit frozen at the peak of succulence still on the highest branches. He swallowed, copper and heat filling his senses, and he swayed on his feet.

The master stepped closer, so close Isaac trembled in fear and lust, and he froze, a mouse beguiled by a viper.

"Hello, Isaac," Batiste whispered, leaning down over him, one stone-cold hand cupping the back of his neck and holding him in a powerful grip. "I bet your kiss tastes as delicious as you look."

Soft, cool lips settled on his, and Isaac sighed into the kiss that erased every memory of any other. Heat and ice, fire and glacial cold chased sweet apples and spice across his lips and tongue, and Isaac was lost. He struggled to remember where he was, who he was, why he needed to know any of it—and suddenly it was gone.

A rush of green hellfire and an enraged scream broke the spell— and Isaac stumbled away from Batiste, terrified and shocked. He fell on his ass, hands scraped by stone and ice. Isaac was so scared he was shaking. Angel ran in front of him, spinning to face the ancient vampire he had pinned to the brick wall of the deli.

Batiste roared, struggling against the green bands of thick hellfire that held him prisoner. Angel wasn't burning the Master—he was restraining him, and considering how angry Angel looked, Isaac was surprised the master wasn't a pile of ash blowing in the breeze.

"I called you here for help with Simeon—not so you could charm Isaac and molest him! What the fuck!" Angel shouted, raising a clenched fist, and Batiste lifted into the air, his expensive suit getting ripped and stained by the old, rough brick at his back. Angel shook head to toe, and Simeon's presence at his back was probably the only reason Batiste was still alive. "Did you not learn your lesson the first time when you put your hands on me?"

Angel drew his arm back, and slammed it forward, and Batiste was tossed against the wall once, twice—again and again, head hitting with a meaty thud each time until Simeon reached out and grabbed Angel's hands, murmuring to him in words Isaac couldn't hear.

Isaac trembled, colder than ever before. Batiste charmed him? Isaac wasn't shy about kissing men he'd just met, but he had never kissed a vampire in his life, and had never planned on it either— Batiste rolled him. Swept him under with vampiric charm and stole his choice from him. Isaac wasn't like Angel—Isaac knew exactly who killed their family, and he could never forget or forgive. Simeon was nice for a vampire, and Isaac liked the Elder, but Isaac couldn't and wouldn't ever be ready for another vampire in his life, even as a hook up.

Isaac scrambled to his feet, and backed away, unsure and afraid. "He...he roofied me?"

"He charmed you," Angel gritted out, and Isaac felt sick.

"Are you...are you sure?" Isaac whispered, thinking about how wonderful that kiss had been. It felt clean, sweeping aside guilt and grief, so fresh and invigorating he had trouble letting go of the sensations still running through mind and body. "I liked it."

"He charmed you. Of course you liked it," Angel spat, and Isaac flushed, confused. "Isaac, go home. I'll deal with this."

"But, Angel," Isaac tried, but his brother glared at him, and Isaac shut up fast.

"Go home!"

Isaac backed away, not looking at the vampire held against the wall by his brother's magic. His lips tingled and the taste of apples and spice were on his tongue. He whispered as he turned, "Don't kill him, please."

Isaac ran.

He kept running until the street was a blur and he slapped open the front door of their apartment building. He took the stairs, exhausted and frantic, and fumbled for his keys with sweaty hands when he reached the door to their place. Getting inside was hard but he managed it, and he slammed the door shut behind him. Thankful he didn't set the wards when he took off after Angel, he stumbled down the hall to his room, and climbed under the covers in his bed.

Isaac huddled there, kicking off his shoes and pulling the blanket up to his chin. He shivered, mind still dazzled by the Master's kiss.

A soft chirp and the flapping of wings heralded Eroch's arrival, his brother's familiar landing beside his head. Eroch smelled of smoke and cold winter air, and the little beastie must have been hunting pigeons again on the fire escape. A small snout poked at his face, and Eroch chirred and chirped, consoling him. Isaac sniffled, and made room for Eroch to curl up under his chin. The tiny dragon purred and hummed, warming him as he hid from the world.

9

HELLFIRE AND HEXES

"*Don't kill him, please.*"

Simeon stood back, and Angel was grateful for it. If his lover tried to stop him now Angel might snap and murder someone.

Fuck, I might anyway!

"Isaac is not for you!" Angel hissed out, so mad his words came out strangled and warped.

Batiste glowered at him, still struggling against Angel's hellfire bonds. "I did nothing but kiss the youngling, necromancer. Your brother's virtue remains untouched."

Angel laughed. "Isaac hasn't been untouched since Greg Doyle got him drunk when he was sixteen. And I couldn't care less who he kisses—as long as it's his choice! I fucking felt your charm rolling over him from the other side of the street!"

"He enjoyed himself. I tasted just how much he liked it before you interrupted me."

Angel narrowed his eyes, and Simeon carefully backed away out of his line of sight.

"*Don't kill him, please.*" Isaac's whispered plea hovered on the edge of his anger. Simple, and full of emotion, it threatened to calm his ire.

Batiste bared his fangs back at him and said nothing. The fucker was pouting, which only told Angel that Batiste knew he fucked up. Anger unlike anything he'd felt in years simmered and pulsed beneath the surface, and Angel breathed in and out, doing his best not to let it overcome his control. Red hovered on the edges of his vision, and his muscles shook with adrenaline. Batiste's perfection was rumpled, and it made Angel sneer.

He had an anger problem. He knew it, hell, everyone knew it— but he wasn't a murderer. Or he wasn't trying to be one again. Angel clenched his fists harder, so hard his knuckles went white and his fingertips numb. He let go of a shaky breath, and tried to calm himself. Batiste took his chance, and fanged out, his marble perfection warping into the features of an ancient and powerful predator bred for killing.

The Master broke one bond, then another, and Angel reacted instinctively. Unless Batiste wanted to kill him and Simeon, he doubted the Master would do more than escape, but old reactions never died. Angel reached for the veil, preparing a shield, but the death magic from his mate bond answered first, a smooth current of endless magical energy filling his body and mind.

Batiste twisted, and slipped free, falling to the pavement, but Angel flicked a finger, and stopped the ancient vamp in mid-fall. Instead of green hellfire shackles, dark, shiny black smoke materialized in tentacles that wrapped and coiled around the master, stifling his screams and curses in an old dead language from across the cold sea. Angel's anger drained from him as the death magic flowed into his core, silken and seductive and gentle, the magic so receptive to his will he had no time to finish a thought before it culminated in reality.

There was no struggle. No overwhelming river of power that threatened to sweep aside his mind and shut him down. This was peace, and calm. An ouroboros that sang as it coiled within him, the song carrying hints of chocolate and mint, sapphire swirls and silver veins. It mingled with his hellfire and green death magic, and the golden cord underneath the foundation. His inner sight reverberated with the kaleidoscope of the infinity he saw within, and he swayed, at last understanding.

There was nothing of which to be afraid. Meant to be, inescapable and whole. There was only trust and love, and Simeon at the center of it all. He smiled, a tiny quirk of his lips, and he was gladdened when the last remnants of his anger faded away.

He was so tired of being angry.

"Angel?" Simeon breathed out, and he tried to give Simeon a reassuring smile.

"I won't kill him," Angel promised and he walked forward, and the smoke tentacles brought Batiste forward, forcing the old vampire to his knees in front of Angel.

"What spell is this, necromancer?" Batiste hissed past his revealed fangs, the sharp incisors long enough to drop below his bottom lip. Power, old and with overtones of crisp apple cider that made his senses sing pushed out from Batiste. Angel sighed, and pushed back with the death magic at his command. "Simeon, rein your mate in, he's gone mad!"

"I will not, my master," Simeon replied evenly, standing nearby, hands clasped calmly in front of him as he watched. "Be the man of honor I know you to be, and listen to Angelus."

Batiste growled, but his fangs retreated, his cerulean eyes glinting with anger, and to Angel's amusement, perhaps even chagrin.

"I called you here for help. Simeon was stabbed, and...I thought he was going to die. I called you for help. You said you would come, and thank you for that. I admit that by the time you got here I didn't need you anymore, but it doesn't change the fact you came. You love Simeon. I do, too. So thank you."

Batiste was listening, and Angel took a step closer, so close he had to look almost straight down to meet Batiste's eyes. Black smoke cavorted about his ankles, rubbing against him like a cat, reminding him of Eroch. "But, and this is the part you really fucked up—when you saw your chance, you charmed my brother. You're an absolute heavyweight in the charm department, asshole. You know it. You slithered your way into his mind, and while I have no issue with Isaac kissing anyone he wants—it has to be *what he wants. For real.*"

Batiste's beautiful face stilled, statuesque and perfect, even smudged by road salt and black death magic. Angel put his hands in his pockets, shivering in the cold. He hadn't the time to put on the gear Isaac brought, and his ass was cold. He wanted to go home, and take Simeon with him. Check on Isaac, cuddle with Eroch, and maybe call Milly, and tease Daniel a bit about his good showing at the police station.

"A short while ago you put your hands on me. It was a test, at least that's what you called it, to divine the truth behind my feelings for Simeon. You touched me, against my wishes and without invitation. Tonight, you had no problem charming Isaac into letting you make a move on him. He really dislikes vampires, so his reaction to you doing that uncharmed would have been scorching, and not in any way good for you. I have no doubt of Isaac's ability to fend off unwanted advances from you or anyone else—but he has to have free will."

Angel leaned down a bit, and whispered, "You've been charming your way through the centuries, haven't you? Simeon loves you, so there has to be a decent person under that arrogant facade. So instead of killing you, I'm going to let you go. I won't hurt you, but you won't be unmarked."

Horror spread across Batiste's handsome features, and Angel smirked. "I'll apologize to the fledgling. You need not worry about me charming him again," Batiste swore, and he sounded sincere. "It is habit. I always release my gift before approaching a possibly hostile situation. I knew not what caused Simeon to come to harm, and took no chances. I then saw Isaac, and Simeon unharmed, and your brother distracted me. Isaac is tempting, and I didn't think."

Batiste offered more of an explanation than Angel expected, but that didn't excuse his actions.

"You will apologize, that's true. To Isaac, in person, and only if he wants to see you. But you're a crafty old supernat, and any promise you make me regarding Isaac will have a loophole. What you seek to gain from my bond with Simeon has led you to look to Isaac. He will not be used to gain more power for yourself or your clan."

"No! Whatever you mean to do to me won't last forever! No magic lasts long on a city master!" Batiste tried to struggle, pushing his own considerable power against Angel's. He breathed out, and the black smoke stamped Batiste's efforts into nothing.

"Constantine Batiste," Angel said, voice falling into a soft cadence, his heart beating with each syllable, every dip and rise. Hexing came as easily to him as his anger, and only self-control taught to him by his mentor and father kept him from handing them out indiscriminately over the years. Yet this one time, he didn't think August or Raine Salvatore would argue his decision. Angel would hex the world to safeguard his brother. "Constantine, your charm is your weapon, your armor. Yet no purchase will it find in Isaac, no means to sway or deceive his mind or heart. He shall be forever impervious to that gift. No lies between you, be they charm or magic."

Angel lifted his hand, and a rune burned the air an inch above his palm, green and bright, and the glow reflected off the walls around them, Batiste's face, Angel's shirt and hand. Bright, searing, and full of purpose. Angel cast it off, and it shot forward, a narrow streak of green fire, and it stabbed through the black smoke, landing right over the quiet place where the undead man's heart lay.

Batiste screamed, flesh sizzling, the rune burning its presence into Batiste's chest. He would be marked, forever, until Angel saw fit to remove it. To keep Isaac safe, he might leave it there until he died of old age.

The burning stopped, and Batiste went limp. Angel let him go, the smoke receding as if it never was, and Simeon stepped around him. Simeon knelt beside his master, and gently loosened his tie and shirt, exposing the blackened skin burnt in the shape of the hex. "What does it mean, *a ghra*? And is he well, aside from a few bruises?"

"The exterior rune means 'truth', and it's woven around a design I made years ago that represents Isaac," Angel answered, walking a few steps away, kneeling down next to the dead man while Simeon tended to Batiste. "He'll heal himself just fine, and wake up his normal self. He'll just never be able to charm Isaac. Never again."

"His charm keeps our people safe, it's one of his greatest gifts. Can he still use it?" Simeon asked as he straightened out his unconscious master. Angel paused in his examination of the dead human to watch Simeon brush back Batiste's blond hair. There was affection there, and a distance Angel couldn't understand. Perhaps it was a vampire thing, to love and yet remain remote.

"His gift is intact. It just won't work on Isaac, and only Isaac. I could have done more, gone further, but leaving him handicapped to such a degree would be a death sentence. Eventually he would need it, and not have it. Though, if he tries shit with Isaac again, and Isaac rebuffs him, Batiste deserves to be lit on fire."

"Thank you for your temperance, my love," Simeon said quietly, and his battered and bloody mate sat next to Batiste's shoulder, staring down at his master. "His power has always been great, and it overshadows his good sense. He was a good man, once. Many years ago now, but I still recall his kind heart. Perhaps getting his wings clipped will teach him again that we all have limits, and none of us are gods."

ISAAC SNIFFLED, wiping at his cheeks, ashamed to be crying. He didn't even know why he was crying, not really. Hardly the first time he'd been kissed. The last time was months ago, right before an undead monster ripped Greg apart right in front of him.

Isaac sighed heavily, and sat up, dislodging Eroch. The sleepy dragon opened one yellow eye and blinked at him before wiggling down into the spot he was just in. Isaac gave a short, wet chuckle before sliding from bed, legs weak and trembling. He thought about putting his shoes back on and returning to the crash site, but the mere possibility of seeing Batiste again stopped that thought really quick.

He hoped Angel didn't kill him.

Isaac made his way haltingly out of his room, and looked into the open door across the hall. Daniel's room was dark, the bed still made. Daniel had come home with Angel, and it was late. His brother's apprentice usually went to bed early, except when Angel was still up and at home. Daniel liked being near Angel when they were home, as if the only safe place was in Angel's orbit. Isaac got it, kind of, as Angel was a badass motherfucker. He was also an asshole, but Isaac saw the merit of keeping Angel between oneself and danger. Angel laughed at danger, literally, and then owned it for breakfast.

Simeon had been attacked, his limo ambushed, and his driver murdered. Danger was coming for them again. Isaac knew the signs. He might have been very young during the last years of the Blood Wars, but he recalled enough long nights of waiting for loved ones to return from fighting their enemies to know what *impending bad shit* felt like.

Isaac made it into the kitchen, and went for the fridge, ignoring the stack of red apples on the island in a crystal bowl. The apples reminded him of the Master's kiss, fresh and clean and intoxicating. He shivered, and opened the fridge door, but a paper taped to the fridge caught his eye. It was a note. He frowned, unable to read it in the dark. He yanked it off and walked to the stove, the overhead light left on at night.

I need Angel. Hurry.

--Daniel

"Eroch!" Isaac yelled, reading the address at the bottom of the hastily scratched note. The dragon screeched and Isaac heard him flying down the hall. He flicked on the lights, and saw Daniel's smartphone left on the island next to the apples. He hadn't taken it with him. The screen was cracked and the case broken.

Isaac hadn't raised the wards when he left after Angel. Daniel had been in his room changing, and presumably Daniel didn't know Isaac and Angel left. Had someone gotten in?

He looked back down at the address, and swallowed nervously.

Macavoy Court, Cambridge. Daniel went home regularly, but this time Isaac suspected it wasn't willingly.

10

WORTH

Daniel huddled in a corner of the chaise lounge, eyes on the floor. The study smelled of damp, rotten paper, dust, and sweat. The curtains were drawn, blocking out what little light made it in from the courtyard torches. Iron shackles sat nearby on the decrepit coffee table, his wrists sore and chafed from the hard metal that had kept his magic stifled on the way back home.

Shuffling came from nearby, and he got a glimpse of a frayed hem and a scuffed slipper, the red hues faded and washed out. Pale, scrawny ankles and thin legs vanished from his view, and he hoped his father wouldn't get closer. Leicester no longer bathed, personal hygiene lost somewhere in the depths of his depression and mania. His father stank to high hell, and no amount of incense burnt by the handful of retainers remaining at Macavoy Court made a dent in the stench.

"No child of mine," Leicester whispered, and Daniel risked a quick glance up. His father paused in his rambling shuffle, twisting his fingers and talking to the air, seemingly oblivious to Daniel's presence. If he tried to leave, or move, his father would see him, fast as a snake, and he didn't know if he could survive his father's displeasure this time. Leicester tilted his head back like a bird, neck twisting as he tracked dusts motes through the air visible in the orange rays of light casting their sinister glow over the gothic furniture and dirty surfaces. He whispered, words too soft to hear reliably. "No child of mine."

Daniel gulped, and shivered, hoping to hear the sound of Angel's voice soon. He tried texting, but Brutus, his father's butler-cum-manservant had dashed his smartphone to the floor, cracking the screen. Begging for a moment to turn off the kettle in the kitchen before leaving, Daniel had scratched out the note and left it for someone, anyone to find.

I'm not coming back. Ever.

He was regretting that message he left on his father's voicemail now. Brutus wouldn't have come for him, surprising him and letting the bigger man get his hands on him. Iron shackles snuffed out his magic, and he wasn't canny enough like Angel to burn through them with pure personal power. If he just hadn't responded, kept his silence, he would be on the couch learning how to help Angel catch a serial killer. He tried to find some humor in that thought, but his father's proximity sucked all joy from the room.

Leicester went back to pacing, slapping at his head and yanking on the scraggly strands that grew haphazardly from his pale scalp. Once blond and thick as Daniel's, Leicester's poor diet and illness stripped from him his vitality and looks. His sanity eroded in the last ten years, Daniel mourned the loss of his parent, and feared the shadow of the man before him.

"No child of mine. Shame, such *shame*. Can't have it, *won't* have it. *Needs to die*."

He wanted to go home, and Macavoy Court was no longer home, not for him. Not since Deimos came and Leicester handed Daniel over without protest. He didn't know what was said between his father and the old master vamp, but Leicester had sent Daniel off with the vampire, bidding him with a scowl to obey the Elder and salvage their family name. Months of pain and humiliation followed, until a Salvatore, of all people, swept in like the angel he was named for and saved his life.

"Angel, please," Daniel prayed, whispering. "Please, hurry."

Daniel risked another glance at the ruin of his father, and the vacant eyes that stared back at him made a whimper escape despite his best efforts. Leicester shuffled over, standing too close for comfort, and leaned down, precarious and vibrating with tension. "Won't live with the shame. We won't." Rancid breath wafted over his face, and Daniel gagged, pushing back into the chaise as far as he could go.

Slap.

His cheek flamed, and he had no doubt a perfect red imprint of his father's thin hand was left behind. A thin line burned across the top of his cheek right under his eye, and Daniel wiped at it, blood on his fingertips. The Macavoy family signet ring sat heavily on his father's finger, the knob of one thin knuckle keeping it from falling off and getting lost in the debris that cluttered the floor.

"Brutus!" screamed Leicester, and Daniel jumped, shaking. This wasn't good at all, by any stretch.

"My lord?" the hulking manservant asked from the doorway, obscured by shadow. Ever-present and annoying, Brutus has seen years of Leicester's disintegration and his cruel treatment of Daniel—and done nothing.

"Did you leave the gate open? Mustn't make our guests late," Leicester shuffled closer to the doorway, words thin and reedy, almost child-like.

"The gates are unlocked, my lord," Brutus replied, monotone.

"Good, good. Hate to share our shame, but it must be done. Must be done," he finished with a whisper, scratching at his scalp again, fingers rooting through the long, thin strands that somehow managed to survive his habit.

The shadow that was Brutus gave a short bow and disappeared, and Daniel curled up into the couch, shaking.

"Fa-ather?" Daniel dared to ask, stuttering. "You...you wanted me home?"

Leicester spun, almost falling over, eyes wide, a sheen behind the dull layer for a moment. "My son...Daniel...my sweet boy..."

"Yes, Father," Daniel whispered, "I'm home. You sent Brutus for me?"

"Brutus, loyal Brutus," his father whispered, fingers randomly pointing into space, eyes tracking nothing, or perhaps more dust. "Brutus is loyal, always loyal to the Macavoys. Unlike my son. Daniel...where is Daniel?"

"You sent Brutus for me? I'm home now. Can you tell me why you sent for me?"

"Daniel!" Leicester's eyes narrowed, zeroing in on him again, his father's regard as inconstant as a compass in a shaky hand. Leicester's mouth thinned, lips tight, cheeks splotchy. "Don't interrupt me! Always interrupting me..." His voice trailed off, his father losing his train of thought before finding it again, or perhaps another altogether. "Foolish boy, useless boy. Always so useless."

Daniel huddled back into the cushions, his father hovering over him, peering down at him as if he were a bug, something foreign and unfamiliar. "Won't live with the shame. None of us will live with the shame!"

"What shame, Father?" Daniel regretted asking the instant the words left his lips, but he had to know.

Something was different, so drastically different. His father had been getting steadily worse over the last few months, and since he came home for his first visit after Angel took him in, his father's condition disintegrated rapidly. Leicester refused all doctors' treatments and resorted to tossing curses at in home nurses, and Daniel was pushed out of control by Brutus. Not that he had much control as it was, Brutus following his father's orders no matter how mad they were, and they grew madder as the seasons went on, into years, after his mother and his father's brothers went to prison for the mass killing of the Salvatores.

"Salvatore whore!" his father screamed, spittle flying from his lips. Leicester vibrated in rage, eyes wide, fingers curled to claws that hovered in front of Daniel's face. "You're his whore! You've beggared our name, our blood, our magic to a Salvatore! Filth!"

"Father!" Daniel scrambled away, trying to escape over the back of the chaise, but magic, a sickly orange and black mist rose behind where he sat, and slammed him back down. Manacles conjured from thin air grabbed his hands and legs, and he was thrown to the floor. Pain exploded through his right side, and he cried out, blood in his mouth, cheek cut from his teeth. He coughed, whimpering as broken ribs made themselves known.

"Salvatore whore..." his father was back to whispering, fingers stabbing at the air to punctuate each word. "Traitor. We kill traitors in war."

They weren't at war. The Blood Wars were over. For more than half his lifetime now, the war was ended. Yet that didn't matter to Leicester, with his fervent whispers and maniacal gleam in his eyes.

Daniel tried to break the shadow bonds, but Leicester countered him easily, as he always had. Insane his father may be, but he was still a potent sorcerer, battle-forged and skilled, and he had forced Daniel to obey him his whole life. Daniel sobbed into the dirty, thin carpet as the bonds tightened further, straining his joints and punishing his muscles. A long, horrible minute passed and the bonds relaxed. Daniel cried, tears staining his cheeks, stinging his eyes as dust kicked up from the ancient carpet got in his face.

BATISTE WAS AWAKE, and was as far from Angel as he could get without being obvious about it. Simeon kept reaching out, touching Batiste on his shoulder or forearm, small gestures the Elder appeared to make from habit. It made Angel feel odd—not jealous, not at all, just odd. There was love there, and history, and Angel wasn't a part of it. He was thankful Batiste had awoken in a subdued mood. Battling Batiste again was not on his agenda any time soon. That perfect façade was rumpled and dirty, but to look at the master he saw nothing but calm, icy control and authority.

Angel yanked his boot on, thankful Isaac brought him his weather gear when he followed after Angel's rush from the apartment. He spared Isaac a thought, hoping his little brother was all right after Batiste's charm and kiss. Now that he wasn't murderously enraged, Angel could admit the kiss was hot, but Isaac's face after realizing Batiste charmed him into it had set Angel's anger off again. He was sick of being mad, so tired of it, and yet he kept getting pissed off. He couldn't tell if he had an anger management issue for real or if he had the worst luck ever and his anger was just a byproduct of craptastic events.

"Well, the crime scene techs are gonna be pouring over the limo and the poor dead guy for hours," O'Malley said, reaching down a hand and helping Angel to his feet. Angel grabbed his athame and scabbard from the icy ground. He wrapped the leather waist straps in place and moved it around until the blade fit snugly to the center of his spine and lower back. "You going to tell me why you're covered in blood and none of it's yours?"

"Simeon was stabbed by a fae, remember? This is his blood."

"Lot of blood for the vamp to be up and walking around looking like a model from a romance book cover," O'Malley retorted, and Angel managed his first laugh of the evening since Batiste woke up, minutes before the clan soldiers and the cops arrived. "You gonna tell me how he's in one piece? Fucking cold out here, by the way. Man's got no shirt on. He might be a talking corpse, but it's still cold enough to shrivel a man's balls in this weather. You gonna tell me exactly why he's missing his shirt? Or anything other than the bare minimum you like parsing out?"

"Nope," he replied with a grin, winking at the surly detective. "And get your pervy eyes off my man, or I'm telling him you think he's hot."

O'Malley humphed and chewed on a cigarette butt, but said nothing more. He had no intention of sharing the fact that Simeon drank from him and lived. That was a secret he was keeping close to his chest. Let the world assume Batiste healed Simeon of the stabbing. It was why Angel called the master to begin with.

Angel was watching Simeon when his lover sent him a long, heated glance. Simeon did indeed look like a cover model, even covered in blood and half-naked. He'd foregone his suit jacket and shirt completely after Batiste woke up and the clan soldiers arrived. Angel smirked and enjoyed the wave of intense relief that swept through him at Simeon's answering grin. His lover was alive—as alive as a vampire could get, at least, and Angel was never more thankful for the fact he wasn't right all the time. If he'd waited for Batiste to arrive Simeon might well have given in to his second death.

The vampires were making the human police officers very nervous—the Greater Boston area boasted almost five million people, stretching from southern Maine to Fall River and southern Rhode Island, and the Boston Bloodclan was the only established vampire clan in that entire population center. Several hundred vampires out of millions of humans and other, more plentiful supernats meant humans seeing vampires in person, even the police officers, was so rare it left them wary and often afraid. The police officers gave the soldiers a wide berth, their nervousness thankfully not making them react badly to the silent and unmoving sentinels along the street.

Angel was sure he was the only human to notice a small group of soldiers that peeled off from the main group, heading in the direction Simeon indicated the fae lord and Stone went. He hoped the vampires found the bastards and ate them alive. Angel had a slim idea of what was really going on, though how Stone and this fae lord were working together left him confused. From Simeon's description, the fae who attacked him was one of the high-class lords, the near-immortal beings once worshipped as gods by human societies a few millennia ago. What a fae lord was doing with a brute like Stone left Angel worried—and he had a feeling the murders around town were connected to all of this.

What were the odds two vampires would be attacked in the same twenty-four-hour period, and Simeon would be taken down by a silver spelled blade, wielded by a member of a race famous for ritual sacrifices? He didn't like stereotyping, but he also wasn't stupid. The Universe really wasn't big on coincidences.

"You still willing to take on the serial killer case? Or things gonna change since your man got attacked?" O'Malley appeared bored, but Angel saw the tension along his broad shoulders.

"I may take a couple days to deal with this, but I'm still on it. Don't worry—takes more than an ambush attack to get us to run and hide."

O'Malley grinned, a slow spread across his jowly face that left Angel suspicious. "What's that look for?"

"You've been saying 'we' a lot lately," the detective answered, and Angel shrugged in agreement, wondering where the older man was going with his thoughts. "Used to be you did everything alone. Kept people at arm's length and never shared anything. Never talked about anything but the odd case we called you in for when we could. Never even knew you had something in you other than snark until you went and got involved with Simeon."

"Huh. Brilliant detective work." Angel winked to soften his snarky reply, and he looked away to the corpse the coroner and forensic tech were puttering over, cameras flashing. "Cops going to take this one over since the human died?"

"Mayor already called while you were using the storefront as a changing room," O'Malley pointed over to where Batiste and Simeon still stood talking quietly. "Someone from the Tower woke him and set down the rules right quick. The vamps have this one under sovereignty control as the human was one of their donors and on their payroll. We're to provide technical support and stay out of the way."

"Are you going to stay out of the way?"

"I'm not crazy enough to get involved in vampire business, no matter who was dumb enough to take them on," the detective said, and Angel huffed out a laugh. "I'll leave this one to you."

"Thanks, I think." Angel was fairly confident that the hunting party after the fae and Stone would catch up to them soon, and that there would be little for him to do after Batiste handled them. Or Simeon, for that matter.

Simeon broke away from the Master and walked across the street toward Angel. The way he strode over the icy cobblestones left Angel dry-mouthed and shivering, and not from the cold. Simeon came close, and Angel tipped his head back, eyes locked on Simeon's lush lips that were curled up in a smug, predatory smile.

"*Leannán,*" Simeon purred, pouring on the Irish so thick Angel's cock perked up and pressed against the zipper. He breathed in chocolate and cool mint, a heady spice that sung of blood and copper.

"Yeah?" Angel sighed, swaying forward.

"I'm gonna be over here, not watching you two make out," O'Malley grumbled, walking away. Angel saw him leave out of the corner of his eye. His hands found the smooth, cold expanse of chiseled pecs and defined muscles, and his hands explored, delighting in the healed and perfect flesh under his fingertips.

"Shall we go home?" Simeon whispered over his lips. Angel moaned, eyes fluttering shut, and he gave zero fucks about who may be watching as he leaned forward and sank into Simeon's kiss. Simeon's mouth was heaven, the hard press of lips and the commanding swipe of his tongue enough to shut Angel's brain down. Simeon broke the kiss after deepening it to X-rated levels, slowly pulling back, a fang catching on Angel's bottom lip. He gasped, and Simeon sucked on the sore flesh, making them both groan, a hint of blood on their lips. "Take you home, show you again how much I love you."

"Yes, please," Angel agreed, wanting nothing more than to wrap his legs around Simeon's lean hips and get that rock-hard cock he could feel against his belly in his ass. "Home, now, and sex. Lots of sex."

Simeon chuckled, and picked him up, and Angel laughed at the shocked faces of cops and vampires alike as Simeon spun on his heel and walked off down the street, heading for home. He wrapped arms and legs around his mate, and held on, and Simeon began to run so fast the streets blurred and his head spun.

Angel clung, one of Simeon's big hands cupped under his ass to hold him tight. The other roamed, teasing Angel, making him gasp and press closer. It didn't take more than a couple minutes, and they made it back to the apartment, Simeon navigating the front steps, the foyer and up the three flights to the apartment. Simeon carried him inside, mouth devouring his, and they both tore at Angel's clothing, desperate for flesh on flesh.

"Angie!"

Angel ignored the annoying intrusion, hand dropping between them to get at Simeon's waistband. "Angie! What the fuck!"

"Not now, Isaac!" Angel hissed before diving back in for another kiss. Simeon wasn't kissing him back though, and Angel groaned, dropping his head to Simeon's shoulder and groaning in frustration. Simeon gently set him down on his feet and Angel scrubbed at his face, trying to get his blood flow heading north again. "What?"

He looked up at Isaac and his brother was agitated, pale and sweaty. Eroch chirped at him from his brother's shoulder, waving his wings. Isaac swallowed and blurted out, "Someone took Daniel. He needs you."

Angel paused, shocked. "What? Who took him? When?"

"Sometime after I took off after you. His smartphone is broken and yours isn't working, I couldn't get past your voicemail. He left a note. Someone took him home, and he asked for you to come."

It took Angel a moment, and he winced as his cock finally got the message and began relaxing. His balls would never forgive him but he'd make up for it later.

"Leicester harms one hair on Daniel's head I'll kill him," Angel checked to make sure his athame hadn't fallen in their headlong dash home. "Fuck, we only have two hours 'til dawn." Angel looked up in inquiry at Simeon, and his mate nodded.

"I'll make it just fine, my love." Simeon pulled his smartphone out of his pocket, and Angel was glad it had survived the crash. Simeon sent a text, and then headed for the bedroom. "A new car will be here in ten minutes with blackout windows. I'm getting changed. Be ready."

Angel blinked at Simeon's back, then went for his bag. "Where's the note?"

Isaac held a crumpled piece of paper out, his hand shaking. Eroch cooed at his little brother, rubbing his tiny snout over Isaac's cheek.

Angel took the note, trying to smile for Isaac's sake. Angel read the few words, and swore under his breath.

"We need to go," Angel called out as he slung his green linen messenger bag over his shoulder, the contents knocking together in his haste. Simeon came out of the bedroom, shrugging into a dark Henley tee and buttoning the waistband of a black pair of jeans. Angel bit the inside of his cheek at the sexy sight but managed to get back on task.

Angel turned for the door, intending to wait for the car at the curb. It would take them twenty minutes, less than that at this hour, to get to Macavoy Court in Cambridge. Angel drew up short, almost running into Isaac who was holding open the front door. Angel opened his mouth to say something, but the set of his brother's jaw and the grim set to his mouth said he was coming, regardless of his tear-red eyes and pallor. Eroch jumped from Isaac's shoulder and landed on Angel's.

The three of them exited the apartment, and Angel let the other two go ahead while he set the wards. They sprang to life with a deep hum and Angel hurried to catch up.

11

BURNING BRIDGES

While the Salvatores and Macavoys had spent a few hundred years sharing Boston, very rarely did the twain ever meet. The Salvatores claimed Beacon Hill, Back Bay, South Boston, west to Brookline, east to the Cape, and all the way south to the Rhode Island border and the ferries to the islands. The Macavoys claimed the area north of the Charles River, all of Cambridge and Somerville, north to Medford. The river separated them, and for almost two-thirds of Angel's life, the river was the line they never crossed, unless they wanted blood spilled and spells tearing apart city streets and families.

The limo, this one with blackout windows, two vampire guards in the front and one on the rear with them, crossed the Charles and headed northwest into Cambridge. Angel instinctively tensed when he saw the signs for MIT, and the limo cruised along, the suspension taking the rough winter roads and tight corners with smooth ease. Macavoy Court was ten minutes past the campus, and Angel pressed himself back against the leather seat, vibrating. Eroch purred and chirped, winding himself around Angel's neck and nibbling on his skin, trying to calm him. Simeon was sitting to his left, and a big hand landed on his thigh, squeezing.

Angel gave Isaac a searching glance, but his little brother appeared unperturbed, his eyes curiously scanning the dark side streets and elegant old homes they passed. For Isaac, this wasn't a trip into enemy territory—this was a rescue mission, in a town he'd always had the run off once he grew up. If Angel had attempted to enter Cambridge when he was eighteen, his father would have beaten the magic out of him and grounded his ass for a decade. When Isaac was eighteen and running around town, the Wars were long over and the Town safe—well, as safe as a Salvatore could ever be in this city. It once took Angel the better part of three years to even think about crossing the territorial borders, even with the Macavoys in prison or dead, and the other allied clans decimated by police raids and exile.

If one was to be truly technical, the Salvatores won the Blood Wars, but with only a pair of free or surviving people on each side, it wasn't much to celebrate.

It was an hour and half 'til dawn, but as long as they got this handled quickly, Simeon should be fine, and if not, the limo had treated glass. Simeon and their vampire escort should be safe from the sun.

As long as they weren't ambushed by a troll hybrid and a fae lord. Angel doubted it—the fae lord and his minion had a hunting party after them, and would need to go to ground before they were caught, if they hadn't been already. Simeon took down Stone by himself, so the half-dozen vamps after the duo should have an even easier time of it. While Angel wanted to know how the fae got the drop on his lover, he would wait until he reclaimed his wayward apprentice and they were safely back home. All of them.

"How are you feeling?" Angel murmured to Simeon as the limo took one of the last turns before arriving at Macavoy Court. Less than a block now, and he tensed.

Simeon lifted his hand from Angel's leg and gripped the back of his neck, squeezing, chasing away the tension and nerves. He sighed quietly, trying to let go of his anxiety. He wasn't afraid—this was just one place he never, ever, in his whole life wanted to be, much less go there purposely. He thought he could handle it fine from the safety of his own kitchen, but now he was learning how wrong he'd been.

"I am well, *mo ghra*, healed and restored," Simeon answered, leaning down and pressing a firm kiss to his temple. Angel peered back up at Simeon, looking for signs of weariness or strain, but the strong jawline and chiseled cheekbones, combined with his devastating emerald eyes and the charming slant of his lips made Angel humph grudgingly, but he could agree Simeon looked perfectly well.

"We still need to talk about what happened," Angel stated, and Simeon gave him a small half-smile.

"We shall, I promise," Simeon agreed, and Angel had to content himself with waiting until after they dealt with Daniel and his father.

"Any plans?" Isaac grumped from the forward side seat, squinting as he tried to see past the dark window tint and the shadows outside.

"Get Daniel and go home," Angel said, and Simeon snorted softly in amusement.

"That's it? Get Daniel?" Isaac asked, incredulous. "No master plan? Just walk up and knock, then?"

"Yup," Angel replied, and despite the situation he smiled when Isaac gaped at him in dismayed shock.

"I thought Dad taught you all these combat maneuvers and battle plans and stuff," Isaac grumped, scowling.

"Combat maneuvers and battle plans?" Angel chuckled, shaking his head. "He taught me how to survive, and how to keep others alive. Nothing more fancy than that."

"Any suggestions on how not to die, then?" Isaac snarked back, and Angel got the first real glimpse of the Isaac from the last few years.

"Sure. Never make the first move unless it's to save a life. Shields up, and watch your back. Never fails."

It failed all the time, actually, but handing over fear and doubt before a conflict was the fastest way to lose. He'd never tell Isaac how many times he saw friends and family members die in conflict during the Wars. That was one part of their history he was never going to share. The Wars were over.

Isaac opened his mouth but shut it with a snap and a frown after a moment, brows making a dark slash across his brow. Angel could see his brother battling with questions he surely wanted to ask, but the limo coming to a stop on the street outside the main gates of Macavoy Court made them turn and look.

Once a grand Georgian mansion, the seat of the Macavoy clan was in disrepair and falling apart. The tall, wrought iron gates were open, and the wide stone courtyard was strewn with debris and trash. The front of the mansion was dark, though just off to the right, a dim red glow came through partially open curtains. Someone was home.

"Isaac, keep your shield ready to go, and don't hesitate to tap the veil. Don't do anything aggressive unless we're met with violence. If Leicester or his servants give us any trouble, I will handle it. You're to get Daniel out and into the limo. Our vampire friends," Angel said, nodding to the soldiers who still sat quietly in the limo with them, "won't be able to enter the premises without invitation. Simeon, too, but if anything goes to hell I will do my best to get it outside the building where you can help."

Isaac was nodding, and Simeon gave Angel a slow, single nod in agreement. "Okay, let's go knock on the door."

Simeon held him back from exiting the limo first, but he didn't mind as Simeon would be stuck out in the courtyard without an invitation while Angel and Isaac went in after Daniel. Angel wasn't taking no for an answer—his apprentice was inside, and after learning about Leicester's abuse, Angel would be damned before he let Daniel spend another hour under his father's roof. Angel was fiercely pleased he wasn't restricted to needing an invitation—as long as the mansion wasn't warded he could get in.

The wind cut through his sweater, and Eroch chirped in dismay from under his collar. Angel tugged the fabric up higher and drew in an even breath, calming himself before opening his mind and inner sight to the building in front of him.

"No wards," Angel murmured in surprise. Maybe they weren't expected? Didn't Leicester expect a visit from Angel once his apprentice was stolen? Rescuing Daniel was a certainty that Angel never disputed—but maybe not for everyone else?

"I don't see any spells or shields up, either," Isaac volunteered, and Angel agreed.

"I have no trust this is as innocent as it looks," Angel said, and Simeon nodded, his sharp senses presumably searching the wide courtyard for dangers.

"I smell Daniel, an older practitioner, and another human male, indeterminate age," Simeon supplied after a few deep inhalations. "I can smell blood, though it is faint."

"Daniel's?" Angel asked, breathing through his fear and anger.

"Perhaps, but the scent markers are dulled by distance and the wind," Simeon said, shaking his head, auburn hair catching the light from the few street lamps. "I can hear three heartbeats though, so the boy is alive."

"Perfect, let's get him back. Don't let anyone in or out except us. I don't want company at a bad time."

"I will be waiting for you here, my love," Simeon answered with a quick grin. Angel gave Simeon one last look before walking across the courtyard to the front door, Isaac at his shoulder.

DANIEL HEARD ANGEL'S VOICE, and thought he was dreaming. He'd lost track how long he'd been on the floor, struggling to breathe with what felt like some broken ribs. His grasp of his magic was sporadic, and he drifted in and out, his mind cloudy from lack of air. He wasn't too sure how he was sprawled out on the floor, but however it was, he could barely breathe. The pressure on his ribs was too much, and he wheezed and coughed every few breaths.

Trying to break his father's restraints while in one piece and cognizant was hard enough—Leicester was an adept practitioner, a sorcerer once feared across the entire Northeast for his strength and skill. It was only his mental state that left his power chaotic and unstable—and even then, Daniel was defenseless against it.

Angel's voice came again, his master's tone sharp and angry. Why was Angel angry? Daniel squirmed, trying to flip onto his side or back so he could see, but the spectral restraints holding him captive tightened and he coughed. Weakness came over him in a sick wave, and he gasped, trying to suck in enough air to hold off the darkness.

"Angel," he whispered, black swallowing his vision.

THE DOOR OPENED EASILY ENOUGH, the foyer beyond empty and shadowed. Angel took one last look over his shoulder, Simeon standing tall and strong in the courtyard, soldiers at his side. Angel turned back to the foyer, and cautiously stepped inside.

The urge to raise a shield and pull Isaac behind him was almost too much. Angel quivered with barely restrained emotions, his nerves afire, adrenaline coursing through his veins. He felt like he was back on Boylston Street when he was sixteen, fighting off a Macavoy cousin and his pals. This was horrendously surreal, and he was having trouble wrapping his brain around it.

The Blood Wars are over. Over. Just find Daniel and go home.

The door shut with a soft sigh, cutting off the cold. Isaac shifted, twitchy, and Angel gave him a small smirk. Isaac shook himself free enough from his anxiety to glare back at him. Angel slid a hand back behind his hip and gripped the hilt of his athame, and called out, "Hello? Anyone home or is this going to be the creepy intro to a horror movie?"

Isaac made a weird sound that was a cross between a gasp and a snort, and Angel grinned in the darkness. His heart was thumping, and his senses were in overdrive. *Battle-fever.*

He held still when a shadow pulled away from the deeper dark, and coalesced into a man, nondescript except for the looming shoulders and heavy, thick arms. The older man was built like a tank, his body laughably confined by a suit that screamed butler. Thinking back to some old Bond movies, this man was the stereotypical henchman, except he seemed to have natural teeth and his face was free of menacing scars or eye patch.

"Mr. Salvatore, my lord is expecting you," the bruiser rumbled out, and with the wave of one meaty paw, indicated to the right, where in any logical world a study or sitting room would be. Double doors were partially open a foot or so, the silence past them incriminating and ominous.

"How about you go first?" Angel said with a smile, showing some teeth. "I might get lost if you don't lead the way."

Isaac gave him a startled glance, but Angel held his smile and waited. The big man glowered, but slowly moved over the tiled floor of the foyer, pushing open one of the doors. Angel took a few steps forward and looked inside, his jaw clenched so hard he felt his teeth creak. Angel slid his athame free, and held it out in front of Isaac, barring his brother from stepping forward to look.

"You can either step inside the room or step out the front door," Angel gritted out, and gave the butler a stern, fierce glare. Hellfire danced in brief, firefly bursts of flame that lit the air between him and the tall, imposing man. "If you step in that room I'll take that as an admission you're partially responsible for why my apprentice is bound and bleeding on the dirty floor and that you're the one who took him from my home. If you step out the front door, I won't kill you."

The butler was a foot taller than him at least, and easily outweighed him by fifty pounds. Yet he saw something in Angel's eyes that made him blanche and carefully lower his arm from the door. The manservant backed away, and Angel kept one eye on him as he slowly walked to the front door, opening it and smoothly stepping out of the mansion.

Angel poked at the other door with the tip of the athame, and pushed it open fully. Daniel was bound in an elegantly wrought *laqueum*, a spell-trap that was used on large prey animals back when man needed to hunt their food. It later shifted into use as a booby trap, and was a favorite of feudal lords cruelly punishing those under their authority.

Like the bastard confining Daniel now. Leicester looked like hell. Wrung out, dirty, manic, and cloaked in despair and a shifty wildness that made Angel want to back away from the *not-rightness* of the man before him. Dressed in a faded robe and a bed gown that was thread-bare and ratty, the slippers on his boney feet and the thin strands of hair on his head all combined to give Angel a prime example of what happened to evil men who went insane. Leicester stared at him, eyes alight with a feral gleam and his thin, lips and sunken cheeks were twisted into a smile that chilled him to his core.

"Hello, Leicester. I've come for Daniel." Best to get things off on the right foot—his apprentice, and leaving. Fast. "Release him."

"Angelus. I haven't seen you since you were a boy," Leicester said, one hand lifting up, bony fingers waggling at his spoke. His voice was a thin hissing, the words so softly spoken Angel had a hard time hearing them over Daniel's labored breathing. "And is that Isaac? He stinks of humanity. Where is his magic? Has he none of his own? I heard he was mortal, a disgusting human spawn defiling a long revered house."

"Fuck you!" Isaac spat out, and Angel agreed.

"Foul tongue. Will you discipline him?" Leicester asked, head tilting to the side, like a bird. A crazy as hell bird.

"I'll pat him on the back later. Talk to me, and leave him out of this. I want Daniel, now."

"My son."

"My apprentice."

"He's a traitor. Whored himself to a Salvatore. I gave him to Deimos to make him worthy of our name, but he spreads his legs for a Salvatore instead. Traitorous brat, whoring magic and loyalty. Traitor to his name." Leicester said it so matter-of-factly that Angel wanted to choke him. "Traitors burn in war."

The spell erupted from Leicester so fast Angel had no time to counter. Flames screamed to life along the walls and ceiling, the dry and dusty furnishings catching faster than kindling. Angel pushed Isaac toward Daniel where he lay on the floor, and cast in the same breath. "*Solvo!*"

His spell raced ahead of Isaac, and silver and white shards of fractured light lacerated the spell holding Daniel. Isaac grabbed Daniel and pulled him into his lap, and Angel had enough time to see Isaac raise a shield around them both before Leicester attacked.

Angel ducked the foul spell flung at him, and Eroch leapt from his place around Angel's neck, screaming fiercely as he flew right at Leicester's face. The little dragon ripped into flesh and flayed open Leicester's face along his brow, wings flapping and claws digging deep. Leicester screamed and grabbed at Eroch with both hands, tearing the dragon from his head and flinging him to the floor.

Angel shouted, a wordless challenge, and flung a spell of his own at Leicester, the athame flaring to life in green hellfire as the room filled with smoke and intense heat. Angel raised his shield as the fire roared in close, unable to see if his spell connected with Leicester or not, smoke obscuring his vision. The entire room was an inferno, and Angel fell to his knees. His shield would protect him from the heat and flames, but the lack of oxygen would kill him just as fast.

Angel knelt and was able to see past the worst of the smoke. Isaac was up on his knees, dragging Daniel behind him, the apprentice trying to help. Isaac was unaffected by the heat and flames—his affinity protecting him. Isaac could tame the flames, but he had his hands full with saving Daniel. Asking Isaac to find his peace and calm and then tame the flames would be impossible—his brother was better suited to saving Daniel first.

Angel stood and dashed ahead, pushing out his shield as far as he could, keeping the flames and smoke at bay. He coughed, air thinning, and looked for Eroch. One step, then two, and he saw a crumpled tiny green form on the floor. He swooped down and reached out through the shield, thinning it enough to grip Eroch and pull his familiar back in. Eroch squirmed, but calmed once he saw it was Angel. He stuffed Eroch into his sweater and looked for an exit.

He was turned around, unable to see where the door was. He tripped, and fell to the floor, catching himself on his elbows so he didn't crush his dragon. Pain ricocheted up his arms, but nothing was broken. He looked back, and saw the foot and ankle he tripped over.

Leicester was limp and sprawled out on the floor, face bloody and Angel was unable to see if he was even alive.

"Fuck it," Angel swore, and reached back. He wrapped his fingers around a bony ankle, and yanked. Even malnourished and skeletal, Leicester was too heavy for him to drag like this.

Angel dropped his head, keeping his grip on Leicester's ankle. He sucked in air, trying to calm his racing heart and focus his thoughts. The fire was close, the carpet and furnishings falling to the flames and heat. Angel let down his guard, and the ancient death magic that now lived in his core came to his call.

Kinetic magic was usually powered by the gathering of ambient energy that was then expressed as inertia. Angel rarely needed kinetic for more than adding weight behind a blow—he used the death magic instead to give himself strength. He was smaller than most men his age, and never before had he regretted the lack of stature, and he called to his magic to make up the difference. He pulled, and Leicester was no longer a dead weight. Angel pushed himself up on his knees, cradling Eroch to him with one arm while he pulled Leicester forward another foot, out of range of the encroaching flames. He couldn't keep the shield up and get Leicester under its protection entirely—he had thinned it out so much it was nearly useless. And if Leicester wasn't dead and came to while under a shield with Angel, he would be unable to protect himself if the old man attacked. Angel called to the magic again, and dropped his shield, pulling Leicester close enough for him to switch to one of the old man's wrists instead.

Angel staggered to his feet, and guessed what direction to go. Walls of flame blocked his view in almost every direction. Leicester was easy to move but it was impossible to see, the heat so severe his lungs felt singed and his eyes dried out between every blink. He must have guessed wrong, as he fell against a wall. He coughed, even as he pulled Leicester closer. He sent his inner sight out through the wall, and laughed in relief when he learned the wall was exterior, the courtyard just a few feet out of reach. He looked down at the unconscious man next to him, and made a risky as hell decision. He raised a shield, a solid, vertical half-sphere of green energy between them and the rest of the room—the backdraft from an influx of oxygen would sear them alive if he didn't.

Angel let go of Leicester, and made a fist. He summoned more magic, and sent the wave of kinetic energy ahead of his strike, punching the wall. Plaster, wood, and stone building blocks shattered as if a giant were redecorating, and fresh air rushed over him, cold and clean. He hit again, and then again, and the hole was big enough to crawl out.

Angel tugged and shoved Leicester, pushing the man through the hole in the wall, dumping him to the stone courtyard. Angel crawled out after him, and a pair of strong hands caught him under his arms and lifted him free from the debris. He dropped his magic, and he would have fallen on his face if not for Simeon.

"*Mo ghra*! Angel!" Simeon lifted him upright, clutching him close. Eroch screeched, and Angel leaned back far enough to drag his battered familiar free from his sweater. Simeon picked them both up, swinging him into his arms, and carried him away from the building.

Angel looked back, and saw the big man he sent packing similarly lift Leicester and carry him away from the building, surrounded by Simeon's soldiers. Angel could give zero fucks about whether or not Leicester was alive—he turned back around, and was happy to see Daniel sitting in the back seat of the limo, the door open, Isaac waiting anxiously a couple feet away.

"I'm never letting either one of them out of my sight ever again," Angel said, coughing so hard he thought he might lose a lung.

"I'll help you with that, my love," Simeon said, gently cradling him all the way to the limo. Isaac ran over the last few steps, his fire-affinity bearing little brother pristine and soot-free, relief in his eyes.

"Eroch! Hey buddy, you okay?" Isaac cooed, reaching down and scooping Eroch up in his hands. Eroch gave a pathetic chirp and let Isaac snuggle him under his chin. Isaac walked back over to the limo, crawling in past Daniel.

"I get stuck in an inferno, rescue myself, my familiar, and the bad guy, and my brother worries about the dragon," Angel grumbled, and

Simeon chuckled. "You can put me down, I'm okay to stand for a minute."

Simeon thought about it, but carefully set him on his own feet, one hand on his hip as if worried Angel would keel over. He might, too, so he let the hand stay without comment.

Daniel stared up at him from where he sat on the seat, blood on his bruised cheek and lip. He had a hand holding his ribs, and tears streaked down his pale, dirty face. "You came for me."

Angel took a slow, deep breath, and smiled at his apprentice. "I'm sorry you had to go through that. And for the record, kiddo, I'll always come save you."

"You shouldn't have to save me. I'm twenty, not ten. I should be able to take care of myself," Daniel sobbed on that last part, and Angel sighed, feeling bad. The kid had no confidence in himself, his esteem as low as it could possibly get, and being abused and abducted by his own father, then held captive, wouldn't help either. Any progress he'd made in the last two months to get Daniel in a safe and happy place mentally may have just been erased.

"I'm useless," Daniel cried quietly, tears running down his cheeks unchecked. "I'm not much of a sorcerer. I'm sorry you got stuck with me."

Angel took Daniel's chin in his hand, and squeezed enough to get Daniel to look at him. "You are not useless. You are a sorcerer. You are smart, capable, sweet and a joy to be around. You're as much my family as Isaac, and I will never regret taking you into my home and care. Understand?"

Daniel gaped, mouth opening, shock in his dark, wet eyes, lashes clumped from tears. Only Daniel would look beautiful while sobbing. Angel gave him a smile, doing his best not to give into the urge to cough. He'd hack up a lung later. "Daniel, I've made a mistake the last couple of months thinking you needed time to heal from what happened, so I haven't been training you as arduously as I should have been. I'm going to rectify that. When you've been released from your apprenticeship, you'll be a sorcerer to match any the world has to offer. I am proud to be your master, and I will never regret you. I'm sorry I left you vulnerable. I didn't raise the wards when we got home earlier. I didn't make sure you were safe when I left to get to Simeon, and for that I am asking your forgiveness."

"It's okay," Daniel whispered, blushing hard. Angel let his chin go, and shuffled over to hug the boy around his shoulders. Angel could see Isaac inside the limo, his little brother's face ashen and sad, watching them from where he sat. There was something in Isaac's eyes that made Angel want to reach out and soothe him, but Isaac was not much for comfort or hugs, not like Daniel. Daniel cried into his shirt, and he rubbed his back, thinking it was a night for tears.

Or day, rather. The horizon was lightening, and it was time to go. Angel looked back to the mansion, noting the spread of the fire was being dampened by the old house wards, the ones used by the wealthy elite to prevent catastrophic damage from flood, fire, and other acts of god—or deranged sorcerers. The house was made of stone, and there were no buildings nearby for the dying fire to leap to.

"We need to go," Angel said softly, and Simeon nodded, gesturing to the vampire soldiers.

"What shall we do with Macavoy?" Simeon asked, eyes flicking down to look at Daniel before lifting back to Angel.

"Call the cops? I can wait here until O'Malley shows? You guys need to get in the limo and out of the sun. We have maybe ten minutes before things get too bright."

"I'm not leaving you alone, *mo ghra.*"

Angel looked across the courtyard. The big guy was holding Macavoy like a baby, and he shuddered. The old man was still limp and out, and Angel found no compassion in his heart. The cagey old fucker just tried to burn himself and other people to death.

He wanted to leave. Go home and take care of his family and sleep for a few days.

"I'll report this to O'Malley once we get back. Home first, then your friends can return to the Tower," Angel said, and looked away from Macavoy and his servant. "I'll keep an eye on him, and if

Macavoy survives this, I'll let the cops handle him. If he comes for us or Daniel again, I'll kill him."

Simeon gave him a slow, sweet smile, a fang visible, and Angel smiled back. Sometimes it was worth it not being the hero.

ISAAC STROKED Eroch's wings as his brother and the others piled into the limo. Dawn was really close, and Isaac was surprised they waited so long before getting into the limo and behind the protective windows. The vamps settled down around him and his family, and Isaac gave a small shiver, despite knowing they were safe, that these vamps were Simeon's soldiers and they weren't in danger.

Eroch was fine, the little dragon sore and bruised, but fine. He was grooming himself on Isaac's lap, blood covering his claws and snout. Isaac recalled the tiny beast leaping across the room, tearing into Macavoy and surely saving their collectives asses. Occasionally Eroch would pause, stare across the limo at Angel where he was holding the wounded Daniel, and then Eroch would sniff really loud, nostrils twitching, and then he'd go right back to grooming.

Isaac sighed, and while he was beyond thankful Daniel was alive and well, Angel's words to his apprentice cut deep into Isaac and his already heavy heart. Angel was fiercely loyal, but he had no room for forgiveness when it came to endangering someone. His brother hadn't blamed Isaac for leaving Daniel alone in the apartment when he chased after Angel, but he was waiting for it. Isaac was the most experienced and skilled sorcerer after Angel, and it was his job to make sure their home was secure whenever he left. Daniel has been in the bathroom, and unable to ward the apartment. Isaac blamed himself. If he'd taken merely a moment and thought before chasing after Angel, he would have been able to prevent Daniel's kidnapping.

Just another fuck-up to carry. This one was nothing compared to the guilt and grief he carried on his soul. He was doomed to repeat his past mistake, and eventually someone was going to die because of him.

Again.

12

HIS PLACE IN THE WORLD

"**Y**ou just left Leicester Macavoy there, without waiting for the police?" Milly demanded, her gray, elegantly plucked eyebrows arching high. "I'm personally surprised he's still alive. Where's the impetuous young battlemage who never left an enemy standing at his back?"

The street was packed, Valentine's Day two days away, and shoppers were crowding the ritzier section of the Market in search of gifts. Angel guided Milly around a rush of pedestrians filing out of the local jeweler, and he gave her a wink and replied, "Killing my apprentice's father in front of him wasn't an option. Daniel doesn't need grief on top of everything else. And that cranky, snotty little know-it-all battlemage you so fondly recall finally grew up. As much as I regret that, sometimes."

Milly snorted, her expression calling bullshit. Angel grinned, teasing his partner when she pursed her lips into a stern frown. "C'mon, don't look at me like that. I called O'Malley and told him what happened. He got Leicester and his burly beast of a manservant into custody. I'm charging them both with kidnapping. As Daniel's master I don't need his testimony nor does Daniel need to supply a statement unless he wants to. There's times when these archaic rules of master and apprentice come in handy."

"In this case I would agree. Daniel is too injured by recent events —his father's death might be too much. Has he spoken much beyond what you got from him the other night?"

Angel held open the glass and wood door to the apothecary shop, letting Milly enter first. Customers clogged the front of the store where the touristy items, powerless artifacts and trinkets adorned glass shelves, following Milly as she smartly walked down the narrow aisle to the rear of the store where the member's only room was located. It kept non-practicing humans from entering an area where the magical wares were stored. Anyone without magic was unable to cross the wards etched into the wooden floors. They entered the back room, the floor wards humming in approval when their magic was sensed.

"Daniel has been sleeping on and off the last few nights. Isaac has been hovering over him, and Daniel is going to end up more spoiled than Eroch at this rate. His ribs are still hurting even after a trip to the hospital and some healing spells. Times like this I wish I were an elementalist. Water affinity makes for great healers."

"If you weren't a necromancer you'd be dead, darling, and never forget that," Milly admonished, and Angel shrugged. "Will you keep working on the serial killer case?"

"I will be, and once Daniel's ribs are back in shape I'll have him helping me again. Or, you know, whenever you decide to tell me what you know, Miss Obsessed-With-Fae."

"Shush! I am not obsessed. I just love their history. The book I want to show you has pictures, unlike most books on the fae that I have, so this way we can narrow down what type of fae may have been responsible for Simeon's attack. And speaking of Simeon, have you spoken to him yet?"

Angel slid around the end of an aisle, avoiding Milly's keen obser-vational skills. She followed after him, as determined as ever, and skewered him with her gimlet gaze. "No, I haven't. The last few days have been hectic. He's been dealing with Batiste, and the aftermath of the missing hunting party he sent after Stone and the fae lord. Six vampires just don't come back after going after two targets? Someone out of the six should have come back, or hell, some undead bodies should have been found at least."

"You can't put it off for much longer," Milly hissed, grabbing his elbow and halting his meandering through the merchandise. She glared up at him, and Angel met her stare, knowing she was right. "Angel, the power humming under your skin is palpable. You've always been strong, but the sheer amount of magical energy I can sense coming from you is astronomical. It's as if you're mainlined into the veil, but I can't sense a spike in the ambient magic fields, and you're not exhausted from trying to keep the connection open full bore while charging yourself up. I know it's not the veil. Simeon managed to drink your blood and thrive on it. In the history of practitioners, there has never been a case of a vampire taking that much magic-laced blood and surviving. I know, I checked."

Angel looked around the store, but no one was within hearing distance. They were the only two in the restricted area aside from a tall, thin man who came in after them, heading for the far corner. He had his back to them, perusing the shelves.

"Do you think anyone can tell?" he asked quietly, and she frowned, thinking, still holding his arm in her small, strong hand.

"I can because I know your magic, I know you. We've been partners for so long I know your magic as well as my own. The boys may be able to pick up on it, but Isaac and Daniel already see you as a very powerful sorcerer, so they may not know that you're not your usual self. Strangers? I'm not sure. Maybe if they got really close, or put their hands on you. If they were unusually sensitive, they might pick up on it."

"This can't get out, Milly," Angel murmured, patting her hand. "The furor that would arise from vampires and practitioners alike would be madness, and I don't want to spend my days fighting off people who either want to study me and Simeon as some weird experiment, or people trying to use us to their advantage. I have no issue killing to protect me and mine—I'd just rather not have to look at that many corpses again."

"Talk to him," Milly said, firm. Angel sighed, but nodded in agreement. "Good," she said, smiling and chipper. She spoke at a more normal volume, and took off down the aisle towards the books. "That book I wanted is back here, by the way."

"This book is important, why?" Angel asked, grumpy. He wanted to go home. Too many people out and about, even if there weren't that many back in the restricted room with them. Just that tall guy in the corner. Angel still couldn't see the front of him, but he dismissed the stranger fast enough when Milly reached up, standing on her toes in her high heels, and snagged a book from the top shelf.

He peered over her shoulder, the glossy pages full of pictures and drawings. "Is that a fae fetish book?"

"Shush!" she snapped, and Angel chuckled. "It's a historical encyclopedia of different fae races, with corresponding pictures."

"And this encyclopedia has a ton of naked fae in it for what reason?" Angel said as he appreciated a slim, muscular male fae, naked except for some leaves tattooed across his fair skin. The picture was black and white, and about a century old.

"The fae societies didn't come out of seclusion until the late 1800's, and many of them refused to dress according to human standards at first, so there's going to be some nudity, okay?" Milly said, flipping through the pages. "The fae, like most supernats, are not body shy like humans, and have no need to dress to protect themselves from the elements."

"Well, slow down so I can look, too," Angel complained, and she slapped his hand away when he reached for the book.

"I am not looking at naked fae pictures with you, young man, so don't even start," Milly was adamant, and Angel gave an exaggerated sigh, holding back his smile. He had a powerful suspicion that Milly had this book at home, and hadn't shared that tidbit for a reason. Her cheeks were flushed, and Angel chuckled to himself. Milly was hard to fluster—but apparently she had a fondness for supernatural men.

Milly stopped near the end of the book, and turned it around, holding it up so he could see. One side was a full-page picture, showing a male and female fae. Long dark green hair, pale skin, and perfect features. Angel blinked, and took another look. "They look like the fae lord that ambushed Simeon."

"I thought they might," Milly said, frowning.

He pulled out his smartphone and took a picture, sending it to Simeon.

"Is that a new phone?" Milly asked him with a smirk.

"Yes, you know it is," Angel said with a drawn out exhale. "Who are they?"

Milly flipped the book back around, and ran her hand down the page with the description. "High court Sidhe, descendants of the fae ruling classes from the British Isles and Northern Europe around three thousand years ago to early medieval times. They were hunted to near extinction about five hundred years ago. There's estimated to be less than a hundred high court Sidhe left in the world as of the 2000 census. About fifty percent of them fled to the New World when the Colonies were established."

Angel got a text back from Simeon, and he held it up to show Milly.

They appear to be the same species of fae that attacked me. –S

"We have a winner," Angel said, and plucked the book from Milly's hand. She smacked his shoulder, and he ducked, teasing, "I'll take this. Save you from yourself. Can't have you daydreaming over fae porn while at work."

"You are an asshole." She crossed her arms and sniffed, narrowing her eyes. "You're going to read it at work, aren't you?"

"Yup."

Milly glared at him and stomped off, heading for the spell ingredients shelved along the far wall.

Angel put the book under his arm, and went toward the front of the store to pay for it. He got halfway up the aisle when someone stepped in front of him, almost knocking into his shoulder. He swerved, and he bumped into a display of attuned crystals. The stones lit up, a cascading shower of hellfire green and emerald, and

Angel carefully backed away, the lights fading. Attunement stones were used for divining affinity in youngsters who hadn't yet presented definitive signs, and they were notoriously fragile.

"What the hell," Angel growled, glaring up at the tall man in front of him. "I know I'm short but I'm the only person in the damn aisle. Watch yourself."

He went to go around the asshole, but a long arm came up in front of him, blocking his way. Angel stopped, and bit the inside of his cheek. Losing his temper in a public apothecary surrounded by magical devices was such a bad idea. "Excuse me."

"Mr. Salvatore. A pleasure to see you again," the asshole said, giving him a slimy, over-friendly smile, and that's what clued Angel in.

"Hey, Doc. What can I do for you?" Angel gritted out, resisting the urge to punch Ballacree in the face again. He must have been healed at the hospital because there was no sign of the broken nose Angel gave him when the doctor refused to stop examining his aura. "Need me to break another bone?"

"I was wondering if I might take you to dinner, perhaps a coffee? I understand you enjoy coffee quite a bit," Ballacree said with another odd, thin smile that made Angel want a hot shower and lye soap. Angel was left confused and shocked by the out of the blue offer, and his spine tingled with the urge to retreat. Every instinct Angel had screamed stalker-alert. Ballacree took a long step toward him, peering down at Angel like he was a snack. "You go to that café next to the Common several times a week, so you must like it. I wanted to discuss my examination of you at Metro. Your aura was intriguing, so enticing. We never had a chance to finish. And call me Alfred, please."

Alfred? Why would he call anyone stalking him anything other than creeper?

"Okay, several things inappropriate just happened," Angel said, backing up a step so he could keep Creepy Stalker Doctor's hands in view. "One, you violated me and my rights when you examined my aura. Discussing it publicly and without my permission is also a big

Fuck You. I broke your nose, remember that? I can do it again. And I should, since you've been stalking me if you know my coffee buying habits. Two, I'm so unavailable that the Devil has to make a reservation a lifetime in advance just to claim my soul. Three, I am going to set your ass on fire if you take another step toward me."

Ballacree was advancing, one step at a time, as if approaching a skittish animal. Angel wouldn't bite, but he would attack.

"Mr. Salvatore, there's no need to be hostile. I am sure we'd get along beautifully if you only gave us a chance. Come have some coffee with me."

Gave us a chance? Us? Creeper alert!

Ballacree was trying to get in his personal space, the taller man seeming to hover over him. Angel swallowed his irrational fear of the medical wizard and stopped backing away. He put the fae book on a nearby shelf, and stood his ground. He lifted his chin, and met the clearly crazy eyes of the sociopath in front of him.

"I am going to fuck you up if you take one more step, Doc," Angel warned. "Pretty smart predator, aren't you? Stalking potential victims at work where they're presumably helpless or warned against using magic in the hospital. Seeing me here, surrounded by very reactionary artifacts and magic supplies that could light up if the wrong spell hits them; must have been a perfect opportunity. But let me make one thing very clear. It's *Necromancer* Salvatore, you crazy fuck, and I don't need my magic to kick your ass."

Something must have clicked in the doctor's lizard brain that his prey wasn't all that vulnerable. He blinked, and took a long, slow step away from Angel after a tense moment. Angel didn't advance in return—there was no need. He kept his face emotionless, impassive, and hardened. He was not vulnerable, nor defenseless, and never anyone's prey. "Try this on me again, or anyone else, I will know. And I won't let you escape. Run, now, while you still can."

Ballacree gave him a shifty, yet thorough glance that made Angel want another shower, and then backed up again. Angel said nothing —this was all on Ballacree now. Angel had his athame, and while the blade was meant for casting, the edge was dragon-tooth sharp and long enough to stab clean through a man. He had no problem using it in self-defense.

Ballacree must have seen enough to convince himself Angel was not worth it, and the medical wizard turned away, and left the backroom. Angel watched, able to see the doctor vacate the store and walk down the street through the windowed front, then out of view.

Milly all but ran to his side, vibrating with rage. "Was that creepy guy the doctor from the hospital?"

"Yes, he was," Angel said quietly, grabbing the fae book from the shelf and putting it under his arm. His heart was racing and he felt dirty. He wanted nothing more than to curl up in Simeon's lap and let his lover soothe away the nasty feeling of Ballacree's eyes running over his body.

"Are you okay?"

"I'm fine, Milly. Not my first stalker, unfortunately."

Angel took out his cell, and typed up a short email, sending it to O'Malley. Angel had stalkers before, years ago, not long after the end of the Blood Wars. Necromancer groupies and humans obsessed with practitioners latched on to Angel as either a hero or a murderer—and fanatics came in all shapes and sizes. He got rid of them, eventually, either through the passing of time, or throwing them in jail. One or two met less than pretty ends—it wasn't murder if it was self-defense. He learnt that lesson early and often as a teenager.

Detailing the encounter, Angel sent the email, then put his smartphone away. He would tell Simeon in person. "I need to pay for your fae porn, then we have to get to the office. We have students coming in soon."

"It's not porn."

"Whatever lie you have to tell yourself."

Angel took a breath, and let it out, glad he could smile and mean it. He was still mad, but it was dissipating faster than usual. Holding on to anger was exhausting. Milly was standing next to the attunement crystals, the gems glowing a silvery gray and white. Milly's affinity was for air, the wind, and weather-magic, and the crystals reflected her affinity back out to the world. It was beautiful.

Angel grabbed one of the larger crystals, which flared with hell-fire green in his hand, and cringed at the outlandish price. Daniel's affinity had yet to make itself known—but that was fine. Daniel was only twenty, and at an age when a sorcerer's powers hit their normal range and settled, and affinities were made known. Angel and Isaac, like many Salvatores before them, had their affinities come on them early in their teen years. The crystal may provide Daniel with some insight and a welcome distraction.

Milly gave him a searching glance, as if to make sure he really was doing all right. He gave her a short smile, wrapped his free arm around her shoulder, and walked them to the counter to pay.

Simeon narrowed his eyes, while Angel gave him a sweet, slow smile that made parts of his anatomy very happy. Sweet was rarely a word applied to his *Leannán,* but in this case, with that devilish glint in his green-brown eyes and the wicked slant to his lush lips, Simeon knew it was the right word.

His blood tastes of spice and fire, peppermint and cinnamon. Heat and sweetness. Strength and vulnerability.

"Flirtation and tempting me will not distract me from the topic, *a ghra,*" Simeon drawled, and he chuckled with satisfaction at the way his words made his mate shiver. "That foolish mortal has been stalking you. He must be stopped, whether by mortal law enforcement or by my hands. This behavior cannot be allowed to flourish—it only gets worse."

Angel gave him a half-shrug, and Simeon was alternately proud of his mate's unconcern and left frightened by it. Angel was formidable—but he could be hurt. His body was still mortal, easily damaged and broken. Not even a full-fledge *Leannán* bond was bullet-proof.

"I told O'Malley and he pushed a restraining order through," Angel said, stepping right up to him, his shorter mate tipping his head back to make eye contact. "Not that it's going to do any good but then I'm not worried. I've got a mate who's sexy as fuck and deadly, who loves me. And a dragon who likes tearing the faces off crazy assholes. I'm good."

Warm breath over his face, sweetened by tea and Angel's scent made him moan softly, and he leaned down, sniffing along Angel's neck, nuzzling the smooth, heated flesh. Angel's bravado and nonchalance was as endearing as it was frustrating. Though the way his mate all but melted against him when he nipped on the silky skin just behind his ear made Simeon think less about potential dangers and more about how it felt to pin Angel down and fuck his sweet, tight arse. Too long since he had the pleasure, Simeon laved at the spot, nipping it again, making Angel moan and shiver. The scent of arousal filled the air, heavy in sex pheromones and Angel's specific scent, spice and sweetness.

A vibration and tiny pinpricks with a solid weight crawled onto his shoulder, and Simeon sighed, pulling back from Angel. Eroch settled on Simeon's shoulder, staring intently at them, the little dragon's whole body vibrating from the force of his chirring purr. A small puff of smoke came from twitching nostrils, and yellow eyes glowed while Eroch sniffed and investigated Simeon's face. A couple pokes at Simeon's cheek, and Eroch pulled back, settling his leathery wings along his back and grooming his neck ridges, content now to ignore them both.

Angel laughed under his breath, and gently nudged Eroch off Simeon's wide shoulder, the tiny dragon hissing a complaint as he took to the air. The underground garage of the Tower was a cavernous space filled with less than a third of the vehicles it could potentially hold, and the dragon's chirps echoed off the concrete columns and ceiling. Eroch landed with a distant thump on top of the Master's personal car, a blood red Porsche with black matte accents, and the alarm sounded. Eroch screeched, and blew a long lick of flame at the car's hood, before taking off again in a frenzy of disgruntled squeaks and flapping wings. Smoke rose from the blistered paint on the once pristine car, and Angel choked on a laugh as Simeon sighed quietly.

"I won't say a word," Angel laughed, hugging him.

"We won't need to," Simeon said, pointing up at the cameras placed along the ceiling at regular intervals. "The clip will have already been seen by the communications hub up in security, and Batiste will be getting a text any moment."

"Oops?" Angel shrugged, smiling.

"We should get home, before my master decides to call me back upstairs to discuss the habits of your familiar." Simeon took Angel's hand and tugged him toward his private car, the low black Jaguar waiting with seemingly restrained lethality. Angel went around to the passenger's side and got in, holding the door open for Eroch, the little dragon zipping in from wherever he had been causing mischief. Simeon got in the driver's seat, and turned the ignition.

"I love your car," Angel said, clicking in his seat belt and holding Eroch in his lap. "Why don't we use it more often?"

"Because I cannot have my wicked way with you while driving, so we use the clan drivers and the limo?"

Angel smiled at him, and sank happily into the soft leather seat, sighing in contentment.

"We could get you one of your own, *a ghra*, so you need not rely on taxis anymore." Simeon broached the subject carefully, wondering how Angel would take the suggestion. It was not a matter of money—Angel was wealthy. Substantially so, in fact, to the point he had more than he or his brother could spend in a lifetime. The fact that Angel rarely used his family money and used his teaching income for expenses said a lot about the man his mate was, and Angel never really spent the money on anything big. Angel paid for his household expenses, and the needs of his brother and apprentice, and that was it.

It was only the property taxes on Salvatore Mansion that Angel used his trust fund money to pay for, and the rest lay languishing, accruing interest and dust.

Simeon took them from under the Tower, heading back through downtown toward Beacon Hill. It was a twenty-minute drive, though faster when they made the trip, most residents at home in bed while they were both still out and active.

"I think my license is expired, honestly. I haven't driven a car since I was twenty." Angel shifted, hugging Eroch to his chest, the little dragon sniffing at his face with soft, happy chirps. "It's a nice thought. I have two designated spots in the back alley I never use, aside from when you bring your car home, like now."

"What kind do you want?"

"Can I have this one?" Angel asked, yawning. His mate was tired, and the soft seat and warmth pouring from the dash were relaxing him, his heart rate slowing. "It smells like you."

"Certainly, my love." Simeon would give Angel anything, anything he wanted, regardless of what it was. Even the world. He knew Angel enjoyed his scent, as the man stole his pillow every morning when Simeon got out of bed. Giving Angel his car wouldn't be a hardship— as his *Leannán*, Angel co-owned everything Simeon possessed. He was certain Angel had no idea, and that was one more thing they needed to discuss.

The drive through the city was relaxing, Boston lit up despite the late hour, the streets empty, a fine coating of fresh snow covering everything, and the Jag left tracks in the virgin snow. Eroch was sleeping, a hint of sulfur and blood hovering about Angel's familiar, and Angel's own scent and the beat of his heart told Simeon that Angel wasn't that far off from sleep himself. Simeon made sure the heat was up, and navigated the tight streets of Beacon Hill, passing the statehouse, and turning a block from the apartment townhouse, twisting the sleek car through the confines of the rear alley to pull into one of Angel's unused parking spots next to the rear entrance.

Simeon turned the vehicle off, and gently rubbed Angel's shoulder. His mate blinked and yawned, noticing they were home. They unbuckled, and Simeon made it around to Angel's side of the car after the doors were shut and he locked it, roping an arm around Angel's shoulders to guide his sleepy mate and his slumbering burden inside.

Angel unlocked the rear door, and they stepped into the narrow back foyer and faced the even narrower staircase that went up four flights. Angel was on the third floor, in the largest of the apartments. The stairs were too narrow for more than one person to go up at a time, so Simeon swept Angel up into his arms and took the stairs as fast as he could. Angel was tired—he voiced no complaint at being tended to in such a way, and it gave Simeon a warm, satisfied feeling to care for his mate.

Angel was by now used to his speed, and his heart rate stayed even and steady. Simeon got them to their door in moments, and he tilted his head, hearing two sets of heartbeats within. His mate's fledglings were home, and Simeon tapped the door with his shoe, hoping whichever one of them was closest would hear. He could put Angel down and use his own keys, but Angel was moments from sleep, and his mate needed a quiet and peaceful night.

The wards hummed, at such a pitch even Simeon could hear, and Angel mumbled and shifted in his arms. The door opened a few inches, and the wards made a soft hissing noise. Isaac peered cautiously out the door, and he opened it fully when he saw it was them. Long accustomed to Angel's wards, Simeon carried his mate over the threshold, feeling the wards welcome them home.

"Is he okay?" Isaac whispered, the young man's expression of worry and a twinge of fear making Simeon pause and give him a short nod in assurance.

"Your brother is just tired," Simeon replied, and Isaac's shoulders slumped in relief. He got out of the way, and the fledgling shut the door. He felt again that odd sound-sensation, and looked back, to see Isaac checking the wards. Usually Isaac raised the wards and that was it—he was giving them more attention, and Simeon was interested in why. "Has there been trouble?"

Isaac jumped, and gave him a guilty look. "Um, no. Not really. Uh, Angel told me about the stalker guy. I don't want some sexual predator breaking in while we're sleeping."

Simeon gave Isaac soft smile, and the lad relaxed. "Thank you, Isaac. Get some sleep, yes? I will be on guard tonight. Take yourself off to bed. You too, Daniel." Simeon gave the apprentice a stern look where he sat on the couch, and Daniel stood immediately, then headed for his room with a wave.

Leaving the fledglings to put themselves down for the night, Simeon carried Angel and Eroch to their room. He shut the door behind them with his foot, and Eroch leapt from Angel's arms, diving into the bed and wiggling under the covers out of sight. He took a chance on squishing the tiny beast, and lay Angel down on the bed, his mate limp in slumber, his handsome and almost pretty features relaxed and smooth.

Simeon moved gently but quickly, removing Angel's clothing and then sliding his mate under the covers. Angel barely reacted, aside from grabbing Simeon's pillow and dragging it close, burying his face in the downy white pillow and giving a happy sigh. Simeon stripped, leaving on a pair of silk sleep pants, and then left their room. He prowled through the apartment, taking his time to scent the air, the drafts in the hall and living room, clearing each area as he went. All the windows were locked, runes appearing in brief flashes on the glass at certain angles. The streets outside were empty, due to the late hour and the increasing snowfall. Simeon padded soundlessly down the narrow hall, pausing outside both boys' rooms, hearing them breathe slow and deep, both fledglings asleep. No scents but their own on the air currents under the doors, and no foreign heartbeats.

Satisfied their home was secure for the moment, Simeon returned to Angel, shutting and locking the bedroom door, before heading to the en suite bathroom and making sure the window to the fire escape was latched. It was, and Simeon checked the snow on the iron and steel landing, looking for disturbances. There were none, and Simeon peered down at the side street below, listening. He could hear, if he wished, the heartbeats of the other mortals in the building, but he reined in his senses, focusing them outward, looking for anyone who may be outside in the cold, far too interested in Angel's apartment.

Nothing, but that may change. Stalkers rarely concerned themselves with practicalities when they grew increasingly focused on their targets, and the skewed romanticism of mooning over an unrequited love in the winter night might appeal to some. Not to mention the fae lord and his troll, who for unknown reasons decided to attack Simeon and try to kill him. There were six vampires missing, and not even Batiste could find them. The threats posed by both a mentally disturbed mortal and powerful supernats were enough to warrant extra caution on his part.

Simeon returned to bed, and slid under the covers. Angel mumbled in his sleep, crawling until he lay draped over Simeon. He smiled, hugging Angel to him, and enjoyed the warm, limp weight and the thrumming of blood through Angel's body. It was a symphony of sensory delight, and Simeon relaxed, floating in the edge of slumber and wakefulness. He didn't need to sleep, but he could relax.

MORNING CAME TOO EARLY, though from the angle of the sun it was closer to noon than dawn. Angel yawned, his jaw cracking, and he sat up, pushing back the covers. The curtains were pulled back, the room bright and sunny. Blinking sleep from his eyes, Angel wasn't surprised to find himself alone in bed. Simeon was always up before him—there were rarely any mornings in which he woke in Simeon's arms.

"I need to chain him to the bed," Angel said under his breath, and a chuckle at the door made him look up. Simeon was coming in the room, carrying a tray. He shut the door with his shoulder and brought the tray to the bed, setting it on the nightstand before leaning down and kissing Angel on the forehead.

"Breakfast in bed?" Angel asked, puzzled. "Did I give you a blowjob in my sleep?"

Simeon chuckled, standing back up and pulling the blankets back. "You did not, though I would never say no to such an honor. Milly called, said she wasn't feeling well and that she wouldn't be in. Before you ask, I believe she has a small cold, and is not being held hostage in her apartment. Now run to the bathroom, *a ghra*, while I fix your tea."

"Yes, sir," Angel saluted, and stumbled from bed, heading for the bathroom. Eroch was in the sink, lounging. "I don't need a cat—I have a dragon."

Eroch flapped his wings, giving him the stink eye while Angel used the toilet. Angel chased him from the sink by opening the bathroom window enough for the dragon to slip outside to the fire escape, and the squawk of pigeons and the *voosh* from a flaming torrent told him the Pigeon Wars were back on. Eroch fed himself adequately while decimating the flying rat population. Angel washed up, then made his way back into the bedroom.

Simeon was waiting in bed, the covers pulled back, holding the tray. Angel climbed back in bed, and snuggled up against Simeon's side. Tea, croissants, and some fresh fruit with vanilla yogurt made his breakfast, and Angel kissed Simeon's bare shoulder in thanks. Accepting a cup, Angel moaned in delight at the robust Earl Gray, and drank most of it down before coming up for air. Simeon chuckled indulgently, and broke off a piece of croissant, the pastry so fresh it steamed as it was pulled apart. Angel nibbled as Simeon fed him piece by piece, their eyes catching each other's gazes, heated looks and slow sexy smiles passing between them. Simeon fed him by hand, and Angel couldn't find the impetus to complain, enjoying every moment.

Eventually he ate as much as he could, and he licked fruit juices from Simeon's fingers, sucking them clean. His cock throbbed between his legs, heavy and full and aching. He was naked, and his whole body felt flushed and overheated, Simeon's cool skin a welcome reprieve from the heat coursing through him. Simeon set the tray on the nightstand, and gathered Angel to him, rolling Angel to his back and settling between his thighs.

Simeon rested his whole body on him, and Angel moaned breathlessly, spreading his legs wider, wrapping them around Simeon's firm ass and crossing his ankles. Simeon nipped at his lips, before taking his mouth in a devouring kiss, full of fangs and tongue and wet heat. Angel lifted his head and ran his fingers through thick auburn hair, holding Simeon to him as they ate at each other's mouths, breathy moans and gasps the only sounds between them.

"Please," Angel breathed out, lifting his hips, begging. Simeon knew what he wanted, what he needed. Emerald eyes burned, the vibrant depths seeing every secret and desire he held unvoiced, devouring whatever walls remained between them. "Please."

Simeon was gone but for a second, but it was too long, his return above Angel with the tube of slick enough to make him cry out with needy relief. He found himself manhandled, hips lifted onto a pillow, ankles on Simeon's shoulders as lubed fingers worked themselves into his ass. The barest amount of prep, and then Simeon slid home, the burn exquisite and necessary, the pain soothing the sharpest edge of Angel's need.

Angel clung, bent in half and keening when it wasn't enough. Closer, deeper, harder. Simeon heard his pleas, half-formed and nearly indistinct from his gasps and whimpers. Simeon lifted him with one arm around his waist, and plowed his thick length hard and fast, pistoning at a rhythm that drove wails from Angel's chest, desperate cries for release. Hips rammed against his ass and thighs, rocking him on the bed, but Simeon held him fast, held him in place, not allowing him an inch to move away. He had no option but to take it, and he took it all, his body opened and accepting of the silken steel length working inside of him.

He hit his peak fast and hard, crying out a choked exclamation of startled relief. Simeon growled, right behind him, and flooded his ass with rapidly warming seed. Teeth lanced his neck, and Angel arched into the bite, mouth open and gasping for breath. Long draws on his flesh made his orgasm roll on forever, his release spilling and spreading between them, wet and slick and messy.

Colors and light blurred, streaks of movement in his vision. He closed his eyes, shuddering. His perception narrowed to the teeth imbedded in his flesh, the thick cock in his ass, and the powerful suction on his neck. There was a deep and yet delicious ache beneath the bite. His eyes shut, and he lay limp beneath Simeon.

Reality fell away. His consciousness floated, and golden cords slithered and hugged about him, cradling his spirit. Cold, sweet fluid filled his mouth, dripping past his tongue, and he swallowed reflexively, the golden cords singing and shivering in response.

Simeon.

My love. My Leannán.

Whispers in the turbulent dark. Were they from within, the endless depths that filled his very core, or did they come from the undead man whose breath drifted over his face and neck?

WAKING up this time was a clean break between unconsciousness and mindful awareness. Infinity swelled and sang beneath him, within him, and it was the arms about his torso that anchored him to this world, this reality. Angel breathed, slow and even, and pushed the universe away, until he was just in bed, wrapped in the arms of the man he loved, watching the sunlight reflect off the armoire and the few pieces of artwork on his walls.

Eroch was sleeping at his side, head tucked under his wing, tail twitching as the little dragon dreamed. Simeon stroked his arm, big hand warm from Angel's own heat, the touch soothing and full of love.

"Are you back?" Simeon whispered, words stirring his hair. Angel squirmed until he could look at Simeon face to face.

"I am," Angel replied, quiet. "Where did I go?"

"The place where the bond between us lives," Simeon answered, his green eyes crystal clear and honest. Angel lifted a hand, and brushed back Simeon's bangs, the deep auburn strands glowing bright red in the midday light. Never more glad he'd warded the windows to protect Simeon from the harmful radiant sunlight magic that killed his kind, the sight of Simeon in sunlight was unforgettable.

"I heard you, in that place," Angel told him, questioning.

"As I heard you," Simeon confirmed.

"What does that mean?"

"The last of the mate bonds is nearly complete," Simeon explained. "Once it is in place, our bond can never be severed, but for death."

Angel brushed a thumb over Simeon's sharp, high cheekbone, and breathed out the words he should have said weeks ago. "The death magic, the ancient power that animates you...I can access it. It eclipses even the veil, and I cannot stop it. It pours into me, a river of death magic, and the mate bond between us makes this so."

Simeon gazed back at him, impassive, eyes searching over Angel's anxious expression. Angel waited, breathless, and then Simeon spoke.

"A matter of time and love, *a ghra*. I wasn't expecting it to happen so soon, but it's not a horrible thing that's come to pass, my love."

Angel blinked. Thumb paused in its sweep over flawless skin and sharply defined features.

"Wait. You knew this would happen?"

13

THINGS FATE FORGOT TO MENTION

Angel sat up, Simeon's arms falling from around his waist. He scooted back, until he sat against the headboard. Simeon leaned on his side, head propped up on one arm, gazing up at him with an amused expression, eyes twinkling, mouth quirked up in a wry grin.

"You knew this would happen?" Angel demanded, and Simeon's smile grew teasing, indulgent.

"T'was but a matter of time, as I said. The *Leannán* bond is soul deep, *mo ghra*. All that I am, all that you are, all that we are together, as one."

Angel opened his mouth, but shut it with a snap, finding that for once in a very long time he had nothing to say. Simeon waited, infinitely patient, love and amusement plain to see in his smile.

Long minutes went past, and Simeon's open gaze and smile never wavered. His equilibrium and patient demeanor irked Angel, but more from an odd sense of being denied the confrontational explosion he'd actually been dreading for weeks. "This is anticlimactic and it's making me grumpy."

Angel's words and his subsequent frown made Simeon chuckle,

and Angel resisted the childish urge to pout. Simeon's chuckles went on long enough to make Angel crack a smile, and he relaxed.

"Alright, all on the table, or bed, rather. Tell me everything about the bond. Has this happened before? A necromancer and vampire binding?"

"Yes, and no. The exchange of energies between a vampire and his or her bonded lover is typically one-sided, if the vampire bonds to a human mortal. This is the most common pairing—the mortal gains advanced healing, resiliency, increased senses and longevity. There have been a few rare occurrences of a vampire and a practitioner bonding, but none above the rank of witch, and never a necromancer. The exchange of energies is dependent upon the pair. Some things translated over, but it was never the same, and unpredictable. Similar to what happens to werewolves when they form a mate bond, though more specific and the results are random."

"So what's different about us?" Angel asked, thoughts racing ahead.

"I think you know, from the look on your face."

Angel mused over a single thought, his mind latching onto the implications. The healing bite on his neck was proof enough. "The death magic that animates you is accessible to me because I am a necromancer. No other practitioner would be able to access it at all, let alone be able to sense it, even if they were bonded like we are. My death affinity is the deciding factor here. Death magic cycles into me, and parts of me cycle into you. That transfer of power is why my blood isn't lethal to you—the magical energies in practitioner blood is carried out of you and back into me along the bond."

Simeon gave him a short nod, and said, "I'm not too cognizant of the fine particulars, but all vampires bonded to practitioners in the past have developed immunity to magical blood poisoning."

"I seem to be getting a lot from you, and aside from magical blood poisoning immunity, what do you get from me?" Angel asked, curious. Simeon sat up and leaned on the headboard beside him, one arm pulling Angel alongside him.

"I am not sure, my love. Whatever I may gain from you through our bond has yet to present itself. I do know that your blood is as potent as the Master's, maybe more so, and the healing properties are amazing. I haven't needed to feed since you healed me. The blood I took this morning should see me through the next week or more."

Angel touched the bite on his neck, the pain a pleasant burn. It was dry, no longer bleeding, and the previous bite hadn't scarred. He was certain this one wouldn't either.

DANIEL WAS IN HIS ROOM, sleeping off a pain draught Milly had fixed him, Eroch curled on his pillow beside his head. Angel gently closed the bedroom door, and tiptoed back to the living room. Simeon helped him back onto the couch, and Angel moved around stacks of photos and papers.

The case files made an inelegant sprawl across the coffee table, gruesome pictures of slain humans and wolf-hybrids flowering like crimson blooms amongst the white sheets of paper and forensic printouts.

Angel reclined on the couch, head in Simeon's lap, reading the fae encyclopedia he'd bought at the apothecary shop.

"Is that porn?" Isaac asked, leaning over the back of the couch and peering at the glossy pictures.

"Yeah, from Milly's stash," Angel said, absentminded.

"Milly has porn? Wicked cool!"

"It's not porn!" Milly groused from the kitchen where she was fixing tea.

"Then why are they all naked?" Isaac called over his shoulder, tilting his head as he took in one especially fine specimen of supernatural manhood. Angel grinned, and put a hand on Isaac's face, pushing his brother away. Isaac grumbled and smacked Angel's hand, but he walked off anyway.

"Stop leering at something I'm reading. All kinds of wrong. You can borrow it after I'm done."

"Pages clean, please."

Simeon was laughing, silent chuckles under Angel's head.

"Men are gross," Milly complained with a sniffle. She shuffled into the living room, reclaiming her chair, wrapping the afghan back around her shoulders. She held a cup of steaming tea under her nose, closing her eyes as she breathed in the warm vapor. "Oh, this is good."

"We could have gone to your place, instead of you traipsing across town with a cold in the middle of winter," Angel said, sending her a concerned glance. "It would have been easier on you."

"I chose to look at it this way—if we get attacked again, I won't be stuck cleaning up my place," Milly said, between long sips of tea. "My insurance company was very upset this last time."

"Why were they upset? It's not your fault your crazy ex came calling."

"I think it was the fractured foundation and demolished living room that was the biggest concern, my dear."

"Oh," Angel mouthed. "Oops.'"

Milly gave him an indulgent smile and went back to drinking her tea.

"So you two had your talk, then?" Milly said abruptly.

Angel gave Milly a warning glance, his eyes going to Isaac and back. She frowned, and sat back. He glared, but her gaze remained unwavering. Acquiescing, he sighed loudly and closed the book with a thud. "Yes, we talked. We're on the same page. Apparently Simeon being able to drink from me is a side effect of the mate bond and perfectly normal."

"And the rest of it?"

"Same thing—normal, for us at least."

Isaac wasn't listening, his brother occupying one of the arm chairs, his nose buried in their ancestress's diary. Angel shrugged, and went back to reading his book.

Angel gave up reading after a long minute. "Milly, why would Stone be working with the fae lord?"

Milly put down her empty cup, and snuggled back into her chair, drawing the afghan tighter around her shoulders. "Benjamin was always an aggressive man. He was a frequent participant in bar fights and scuffles. That's why he was in prison—he killed a man in a bar fight. If the fae was after someone willing to throw a punch and never ask why, Ben would be perfect."

"So...coincidence that a fae lord, someone who already has a huge amount of power in his own right, just happens to hire your troll-hybrid ex-husband as his bruiser? One who comes to Town, and decides to break into your place with a nullifier charm? C'mon."

"I don't think it's a coincidence at all."

"I don't either." Angel sat up, throwing the book on the coffee table. "Look, this is what I think is going on."

Simeon, Milly and Isaac all gave him their undivided attention. Angel rubbed his face hard, then ran his fingers through his hair, not caring if the too long strands stood upright.

"People, human and supernat, are being murdered. Evidence points to certain rituals favored by specific races of fae. Obscure religious rites that would only be known by those particular types of fae. There's a small handful of rites across the globe that require living hearts removed by silver blade, and we can discount human blood magic since there is no signs of mental instability in the killer. The kills are sterile, clean, and identical with each subsequent murder. Blood magic drives the wielder insane, so that's not what we're seeing."

Angel got nods and murmured agreements from his audience.

"Milly gets attacked at her place. Her ex, with no spellcasting magic of his own, is wearing a nullifier charm. Those are rare as fuck, incredibly hard to make, and it was tailored to rebuff her type of magic and mine. That means whoever made the charm knows us, our magic, and planned for the chance Stone would come up against us. My use of kinetic magic is not well known. Choosing between nullifying death magic and kinetic, it's easy to see which one the charm's creator would pick."

More nods. Good, they were following along.

"Okay...Milly."

"Yes?"

"I know you taught at some of the best schools in the country. Aside from technical skills, what else did you teach?"

"History of Fae Societies in Northern Europe and the Great Purge."

Milly's face, already naturally pale, went whiter. Angel sighed, and gave her a nod. "I think the fae lord Simeon encountered is the one who found Stone. Neither of us are hard to find. I think this time, Milly, you were targeted to keep your expertise from coming out. Eventually, the murders would come to me, and the killer couldn't take the chance that I would involve you. Sacrificial hearts mean black magic, death magic—and I'm the only necromancer on the East Coast. Keeping me out of the way has to have been his plan the whole time. Stone had reasons of his own going after you—the fae gave Stone the means. They made the error of assuming you were vulnerable. With you out of play, I'm handicapped or too distraught to function."

"He was right. If you and Isaac hadn't come when you did, I would be dead or kidnapped."

"But we did make it, and you're safer now. You've got precautions in place. I think the fae lord sees there's no point in taking you out now. He lost his chance, so killing you now is pointless. Keeping Stone under wraps now, since there's an APB out on him, is probably why we haven't seen him again."

"So why the hearts? Why did he attack Simeon?" Isaac asked, face scrunched up in confusion.

"I'm not sure about the hearts. But I think why Simeon has to do with the fact he's a vampire, and not just my vampire." Angel leaned back, and took Simeon's hand in his. "When your limo was attacked, was it just Stone?"

Simeon nodded, green eyes bright in his face. "Yes. The fae lord appeared just as I was about to kill Stone. He was not present that I was aware of when the limo crashed."

"And that hunting party you and Batiste sent after them? Still missing?"

"Yes."

Angel pointed with his free hand at the pictures of the slain victims. "Most rituals are effective with one or two sacrificial hearts. Having six is overkill, no pun intended. There's no need for six hearts, when one or two suffice. So, to me, that says the killer isn't getting the results he needs. So he goes out, gets another heart. He's progressing through different species, and each species has intrinsic qualities to them that would augment or change a sacrificial working. A werewolf hybrid has more power than a mundane human—a full-blood wolf has more than a hybrid." Angel pointed out each of the different species as he explained.

"The fae lord, from the circumstances Simeon described during the attack, has the ability to hide, and disguise his escape. The vampire hunters would never have found him if the fae went to ground and stayed there...unless he wanted them to find him—I think they are dead, otherwise they would have returned by now." Angel squeezed Simeon's hand in sympathy. His lover wore a tired and saddened expression, and it made his heart ache just thinking about how Simeon must be feeling. "Simeon?"

"My love?"

"I know a vampire turns to ash in sun and fire. But if a vampire was to be killed by removing the heart, would the heart and body remain intact?"

"Yes. A vampire might be healed if the heart is returned in time, but the body decays swiftly after a short time. Magic and some modern chemicals can sustain the heart intact. We as a people have had human scientists try such a technique before. They met unpleasant ends."

"Disgusting and I'm glad you took them out." Angel rubbed Simeon's hand, and looked at Milly and Isaac in turn. "If we follow the common and publicly perceived hierarchy in the supernatural species' power scales, vampires are at the top, with some species of fae equivalent or even higher. Agree?"

Milly and Isaac both nodded in agreement. "Right. So Simeon's limo is attacked by Stone because the fae lord sent him out after vampires. They are proving too hard for Stone to handle on his own, so I think the fae lord began to tail Stone to make sure he was able to pull it off. The clan had some attacks on vampires before you were hit, right?" Angel asked, and Simeon gave him a short affirmation. "So, Ben Stone goes after Simeon because the limo obviously belongs to the clan, so there's bound to be vampires in there. Stone doesn't strike me as the smartest tool in the kit. Simeon defeats Stone. The fae lord comes in, stops Simeon, but doesn't kill him. What was it he said to you?"

"The first thing he said to me was, 'Best get that tended to, Elder, lest you leave your *Leannán* grieving your loss.'" Simeon frowned, remembering. "He knew I was bonded."

"How do the fae perceive mate bonds?" Angel asked.

"To the fae, there is no more sacred bond than that of soulmates." Milly fussed with her empty cup, looking between Angel and Simeon. "He probably realized who you were. Your mate bond with Angel is common knowledge in the supernatural community. That's probably why he left you alive. To kill someone bonded would have been dishonorable."

"But killing a dozen people is acceptable." Angel grumbled, but he got her point. Sometimes necessity won out over honor. She shrugged helplessly.

"Maybe the vampire hearts he has now will be enough. Maybe he's got what he needed, and he's done killing. I still don't know what ritual the fae lord is planning, but whatever it is, it's fueled by unwilling sacrifice. That says 'evil' to me. Agreed?" Angel looked around the room, and was satisfied at the resolve and stern expressions on his family's faces.

"He needs to be stopped. So this is my plan. Stone is the weak link. The fae lord, if he is High Court Sidhe like the book suggests, is an unknown player. I've never fought against a fae before. Too damn rare. Tracking him is pointless. That's why I'm going after Stone. I either track him to the fae lord, or make him talk. Stone needs to be stopped, and so does his boss. Find Stone, we find them both."

"This doesn't sound good," Milly said, frowning at him. "What are you planning?"

"Troll hunting, of course."

"RUN THIS BY ME AGAIN," O'Malley said, spitting out the words and actually getting in Angel's face.

"I'm going hunting, and I want the police to stay out of my way." Angel stood resolute, the older and taller man trying to stare him down.

"And when you say hunting, are we talking tracking and then you'll call the cops and let us take the bad guys down, or are you going in for the kill?"

"The fae lord has presumably killed six vampires," Angel stated, chin up, eyes level. "Please tell me what super-secret weapon the police have that can handle a High Court Sidhe and a troll-hybrid that took out six vampires."

"You don't know the vampires are dead," O'Malley challenged. His tone was getting rougher, louder, and the precinct around them in the detectives' den grew quiet. Angel kept his eyes on O'Malley, indifferent to the audience watching and listening.

Angel arched a brow, letting his thoughts express themselves clearly on his face. His disbelief at that possibility was strong. Simeon's soldiers were loyal and obedient to him and the Master—they would have returned if they could. And no vampire would let himself be taken hostage. It wasn't in their nature.

O'Malley exhaled loudly and threw his hands up in defeat. "This serial killer has been terrorizing the town for weeks, and the mayor and the chief have both been breathing down our necks to get this solved, and you want the police to stay out of your way? I brought you in to help, not take over! So what, I go home and wait by the phone?"

"Not so bluntly, but yes," Angel replied. "I should have been involved from the start. We both had the chance at the first murder, weeks ago. People are dead because we failed to see the truth. I will rectify this as best I can, but it will be done my way, and I will not have anyone else killed going after the fae lord and Stone. They are beyond the current resources of the BPD."

"But not beyond you?"

"I am the only one capable of taking them out," Angel said, his words carrying over the silence in the large room. Papers rustled, the vents overhead wheezed out in complaint against the cold, and Angel could almost feel the weighty regard of the varied law enforcement officers in the room. O'Malley glowered at him, and Angel tried again. "This is my city. I will stop them."

"I could just ignore you," O'Malley ventured, and Angel gave him a small, tight smile. "In fact, I think I should go straight to my captain and tell him we need to reevaluate our consultation contract with you."

"You can ignore me, but I thought ahead. I'm sorry, James, I really am. If I didn't care, I wouldn't be here warning you off," Angel said, regret coloring his words. There was a commotion at his back, and the ripple effect of having The Master appear in the middle of the precinct, with no warning or sign he was present swept across the room, humans gasping and swearing in alarm.

Batiste sauntered into the room to stand next to Angel, and O'Malley and several detectives nearby took a step or two back, instinctively responding to the threat emanating from the supreme predator in the room. Angel gave O'Malley an apologetic glance, and walked back to the door.

He tried the nice way. Time for the hammer.

"Detective O'Malley, I am here as sovereign leader of the Boston Blood Clan to assert my clan's right to vengeance and justice, for the assault on several of my children, and the kidnapping and presumed murder of six of my soldiers. As such, with my authority, I am ordering the BPD to stand down. The fae lord and the serial killer are more than likely one and the same, and due to the corroborating evidence supporting this theory, the investigation into the serial killings is closed. Boston Police will not hinder or restrict Necromancer Salvatore's actions or obstruct justice mete out at his discretion. Your cooperation and assistance into this matter is duly appreciated, and I must offer my sincere gratitude for the BPD's efforts."

O'Malley said nothing in reply, his swarthy face reddened by anger and likely embarrassment. Angel suffered a twinge of guilt, and then banished it. He waited, and O'Malley eventually gave the Master a slow, short nod in agreement.

Angel left the room. The Master could find his own way home, as he found his way there to begin with. Angel was just thankful Batiste answered Simeon's call and took their side.

Angel walked down the hallway, hands in his pockets, certain he may have just damaged his relationship with the BPD, erasing the last few months of improvement since Grant Collins left on his forced sabbatical.

The door swung shut behind him, the hallway long and empty to the front. Angel steeled his spine, and walked on, determined to begin the hunt. The city was his for the night, and if his plans came off correctly, the dawn would see the threat posed by Stone and the mysterious fae lord laid to rest.

14

BEFORE THE HUNT

The sun set, obscured by a heavy cloud cover and the buildings to the west across the river. Angel palmed his athame, and checked he had his linen bag strap tight across his chest so it wouldn't slam about if he had to run. He slid the blade into the scabbard at his back, and tugged his sweater back into place. He touched a finger to the window facing the street, feeling the zing from his wards responding to his touch.

"Angie?"

"Isaac, I swear to god if you call me that one more time..." he complained, shaking his head. Angel turned from the window, and he glared at his brother standing a few feet away.

"Yeah, still gonna do it," Isaac retorted, waving off any threat Angel was about to make. "Are you sure you don't want me to come along?"

"Simeon and I will be fine," Angel assured his brother. "I swear, we will be fine, and we will come back."

"Yeah, but..."

"No buts," Angel teased, and Isaac grumbled at him under his breath about annoying older brothers. "Daniel is still injured. Milly is sick with the flu and can't help. And you're a capable sorcerer, little brother, but you have no combat experience. You'll get there, one day, but jumping in right now at this point will mean I'll have to protect you while hunting."

Isaac bit his lip, thinking about it. Angel could almost see the thoughts spinning in his brother's mind. Isaac was stubborn—the last few months of brotherly peace felt artificial, and Angel kept waiting for Isaac to snap, to reveal the surly and argumentative young man he knew was buried under the facade Isaac was carrying since Greg Doyle's murder. Even before, when Isaac lived with Angel the first time, Isaac never thought things through, always arguing and defying Angel for the sake of it. Perhaps he was wrong, and Isaac was different, a new man after the recent traumas, but old habits die hard. Wondering if this time Isaac would revert back to his previous behavior, Angel waited.

"I remember those nights when I was a kid," Isaac blurted, eyes wide, dark and troubled. Angel frowned, but let Isaac continue. "I know you think otherwise, but I remember the first night Dad took you out, the first time you fought the Macavoys. I was ten? You were seventeen? Maybe? It was a short trip into disputed territory, and Dad wasn't expecting trouble, but it turned into a nightmare. That's what Dad called it. He said it was hell, but he smiled the next morning at breakfast, prouder than shit, that his son fought back without flinching. He called you fearless."

"Isaac..."

Isaac shook his head, and pointed at Angel, stopping him from moving forward. "I remember it very clearly, because that's when things started getting crazy. The War turned, and we were winning. I heard everyone. Mom, Grandpa, August, everyone. 'The Salvatores have a necromancer. We're going to win.' I remember them all, saying it with smiles on their faces. 'The only necromancer on the entire East Coast,' and 'no one can match him, he's one of kind.'"

Angel breathed in, battling back the memories. Isaac was right. Their family had lauded the rise of his powers, his affinity's growth in his later teen years. Angel had pushed himself, becoming one of the youngest sorcerers and battlemages in the Blood Wars. He learned to fight without mercy, and enjoyed the favor and praise of his family for it. Even when he killed.

Isaac sat on the couch, picking at his nails, looking at the floor. He risked a few steps closer, and Isaac looked up at him and the raw pain on his brother's face made him pause. "Isaac?"

"You were special to everyone because you were a necromancer. They were right—one of kind. But those nights and days during the War...every time you left, I prayed to whatever deity who would listen, 'Let him come back. Let him come home. He's the only brother I have, he's one of kind.'"

"Isaac." Angel was gutted, heart sundered. He choked, covering his mouth to stifle a sudden sob.

"I wanted to go with you, near the end. I wasn't more than a kid, and my powers were just starting to come in, but I wanted to follow you. Stand next to my brother and fight our enemies—not because you were already famous, but because you were my big brother, and I loved you." Isaac went back to looking at the floor, and Angel was helpless to stop the pair of tears that scalded his cheeks as they escaped his eyes. "I used to watch you leave, and every time that door closed I was afraid you'd never walk back in again."

Angel gave up restraint. He pulled Isaac to his feet and hugged his little brother, so tight he made him cough. "I am coming back. I swear," he whispered, voice rough from tears and a pressure in his chest that felt like, if it broke, he'd cry forever. Isaac's hands clutched at his back, fisting in his sweater, grasping, as if searching for a grip strong enough to keep him from walking out the door. Isaac's tears wet his neck, his shirt collar, his little brother sobbing quietly. Angel bit his lip, shutting his eyes as tightly as he could, forcing his own tears back.

He had to leave, and Isaac had to stay. There was no choice in any of this, but for them all staying safe inside, and chancing that someone else may die because they did nothing.

Angel pulled back, and gently grabbed Isaac's face in his hands, wiping away tears, his brother's eyes wet, cheeks flushed, misery on his expressive features. "I'm sorry."

"Don't be sorry for caring about me, about anyone. Never apologize for loving someone. There is nothing you have done that I can't forgive. You're my little brother, and I love you, too."

Isaac gasped, choking on his tears, and he backed away a step, stumbling a bit. He wiped angrily at his face, embarrassed and awkward, a teenager all over again. Angel's heart ached, and he was at a loss. Something was wrong, beyond Isaac's worry that Angel may not come home again once he stepped out that door. Isaac wiped his sleeve over his eyes, and he backed away again.

"Isaac? What is it?"

"Do you mean it?"

"That I love you? Of course."

"No!" Isaac's voice rose sharply, then fell to a whisper. "That you'd forgive me anything?"

"Isaac, I know you. The worst you've ever done was leave your wallet at home and then get picked up for public intoxication, then calling me for bail money and a ride home. I've forgiven you each time for that, no matter how pissed off and annoyed I was at the time." Angel smiled, trying to calm Isaac, to tease him back down from the emotional edge he was on.

"I'm not...I've done...I'm not a good person." Isaac's protests were weak, his eyes so full of misery that Angel's instincts rose to the fore. There was something more, hints of an old behavior. "You don't know. You're wrong."

"What do you mean?" Angel asked quietly, intent on watching Isaac's reactions. "What's wrong?"

"*A ghra*, the sun has set, are you ready..." Simeon came out of the bedroom, Eroch fussing on his shoulder, the little dragon flapping his wings and making a ruckus.

Simeon took one look at them both, and then stepped back in the bedroom, shutting the door. Isaac was a statue, expression tormented, eyes down and refusing to look at Angel.

"We can talk when you get back, yeah. I'm gonna go check on Daniel." Isaac took off down the hall, and Angel tried to stop him, but

Isaac's longer legs took him out of reach. Isaac disappeared into Daniel's room, the door closing with a click behind him.

Angel grumbled under his breath, frustrated.

"My love?" Simeon called to him softly, concern in the sexy lilt of his voice.

Angel shook it off. He wiped his own eyes, confused, saddened, and more than willing to knock down that door and demand answers, but they had more pressing matters.

"I'm fine," Angel said, backing away from the hall and walking to the front door. Simeon's expression kindly called him on his bullshit, but his lover said nothing to contradict him. Eroch jumped from Simeon's shoulder to Angel's, and Angel opened his sweater enough for the dragon to crawl inside and curl around his neck.

"Let's go hunting."

"The weather hasn't been favorable for hunting by scent," Simeon mused, sucking in a lungful of cold air. "There is no spoor left to follow, *a ghra*."

Angel stepped up beside him, boots crunching in the fresh snow on the sidewalk. They were standing where the limo had nosedived into the deli front, the brick wall a jumbled mess. Angel reached into his pocket, and pulled out a sandwich bag. Angel opened it, the smell of blood and troll coming off the battered piece of fabric he withdrew. "What is that?"

"A piece of your suit jacket. It's the one you were wearing when you fought Stone. It has some of his blood on it." Angel shook out the fabric, and Simeon shook his head.

"The scent may live on in his blood, but if the trail itself is abolished, I cannot track him from here."

"I figured. I have a backup plan, actually." Angel gave him smile, a mysterious gleam in his eyes that made him want to drag Angel in and ravage his mouth. Angel continued speaking, pulling his bag around and opening the flap. "No point in scrying for him, not if he's carrying a nullifier charm on him. That would be useless."

Angel rooted inside his bag, and came out with a small metal object. Light glittered off the tiny artifact, and Simeon was surprised to see it was a dog whistle, at least a couple hundred years old from the style. Noblemen in the Old World would buy such things for their huntmasters, handing them out as gifts or symbols of favor.

Carved and intricate, the silver whistle had hunting hounds running after a small fox, the designs so small and minute that from a distance they blended together. About four inches long, the thin pipe dangled from a necklace, which Angel wrapped around his bare hand, the ends of the whistle sticking out on either side of his fist.

"Don't interrupt me," Angel said softly, eyes falling shut. Simeon knew by now not to do so, but it was habit for Angel to say such, part of his ritual.

Simeon made sure he was just behind Angel and to the left, able to guard his front and back. Angel was vulnerable when he performed structured casting—his attention focused fully in the working, and he tended to be oblivious to what was going on around him.

The early evening was quiet, so still a tableau that the snow covered cobblestoned street could have been a painting. Simeon could hear the hiss of snowflakes falling and the hum of cars a few blocks away. The sky overhead was brighter than a clear sky would be —the low-hanging cloud cover reflected the ambient light from the city below. He was suited to hunting at night, and so the street, the alleys, even the shadows in storefronts were all penetrable to his gaze, though to Angel it would be dark and shadowed.

Angel's hand, the one holding the whistle, rose higher, chain swaying. He held it just over his head, and Simeon watched, curious. Vampires and practitioners rarely mixed, and the majority of spells Simeon had seen over the centuries were usually cast in battle, or at him and his clanmates.

"*Canes infernales,*" Angel whispered in Latin, eyes still shut, lips barely moving. *"Exaudivit vocem meam. Audite sermonem meum. Ut praeda offeratur, et sanguine."*

Hounds of hell, hear my voice, heed my command. I offer you blood, and prey.

The sidewalk beneath their feet vibrated. The fresh snow hissed, and a thick cloud of steam escaped as the snow melted so swiftly Simeon had trouble seeing it happen. Cobblestones in the street shook, stones cracking, the sounds sharp as gunfire in the quiet.

A shape rose from the street a few feet in front of them. Simeon held his ground, trusting in his mate to have whatever entity he summoned under control, though every instinct he had said *danger*. Green flames, indistinct and flowing as water, snapped and hissed, the hellfire solidifying as the figure grew higher, wider. A long, wide muzzle cracked open by white fangs was the first to appear from the twisting flame and shadows, followed by a large head, thick neck, powerful, high shoulders and a sloping, long back that ended at powerful haunches. A long, scraggly tail with mane-like feathers of fur completed the image, and Simeon was rocked to his core, equilibrium lost for a short moment.

"Cú Faoil," Simeon whispered, and the hellhound shook out its fur before taking a step toward him, nose twitching as it scented him. He risked extending his hand, and the beast licked his fingers, grumbling, pleased with him. The hellhound stood waist-high on all four large feet, and if it were to stand on its hind legs, Simeon had no doubt the beast would be taller than him.

It was bigger, slightly bulkier than its modern descendants, the Irish wolfhound—the beast looked as it would have two thousand years earlier. The hellhound shook itself out again, fur settling, green hellfire sparking amidst the longer strands of dark gray fur. Its eyes were depthless voids of embers and flame, green to match Angel's magic and the hellfire that danced in the air as it moved across the stones.

"Do you like him?" Angel asked, and Simeon gave Angel an awed nod.

"He is a *Cú Faoil*, my love. Such a sight, I thought never to see.

They are the forebears of the wolfhounds of today, last seen centuries before even I was born," Simeon placed a hand over his heart, and gifted Angel a short bow, his mate flushing a lovely red across his cheeks at the gesture. "Thank you for the chance to see such a marvelous beast."

"I used the death magic I get from our bond," Angel said, and held out his hand holding the whistle. Simeon took it after a short glance, and Angel nodded. "The magic came from within you, and shaped the hellhound that answered my call. He's yours."

"Mine?" Simeon asked, fingers tracing the designs etched into the metal. "Will he not disappear once the spell is done?"

"Well..." Angel smiled at the hellhound sniffing at his sweater. Eroch poked his head out, took one look, and ducked back inside Angel's sweater. "Usually with an artifact like this, the hellhound will answer to whoever holds the whistle and can maintain the manifestation of the hound's form on this plane. Usually they are used for hunting prey that can't be found by mortal means—like a fae lord, for instance. Then the spell is released and the hellhound returned from whence it came. But this time, I tied the beast's form and the whistle to the death magic that cycles through our bond, and once you use the whistle, the artifact and the beast it summons will be bound to you specifically. He's yours, if you want him."

"Your incantation, it offered blood and prey?" Simeon said, brows furrowed. The hellhound padded across the street, sniffing curiously at the ground. Simeon was surprised to see snow melt under its paws, large, clear imprints left behind. Steam rose under its paws as it strode over snow, and Simeon tightened his hand on the whistle.

The beast was powerful, dangerous. The magic his mate could wield again left Simeon in awe.

"Once it finds the fae lord and Stone, either one of us can cut our palms and let it drink, or..." his voice trailed off, Angel watching him, as if for his reaction.

"Or?"

"You can set it to the prey, and let the hound attack. He will attack until you call him away or the prey dies."

"If I summon it again?"

"If you want to summon him again, only if you set him a task will he need to be paid in blood or prey, or both. If you summon him to hang out and watch TV, then you can dismiss him again without paying a price."

Simeon eyed the beast, its fiery eyes staring back at him. It was waiting. Its purpose was to hunt, and to kill. Simeon stroked the whistle with his thumb, almost able to feel the hum of magic in the artifact.

"Thank you for the gift, *a ghra*. I will wield it wisely."

"You're welcome," Angel said, and blushed as he said it. "It's just a spectral beast long extinct on this plane, bound to serve you and destroy things. And hey, he looks badass."

Simeon laughed outright and pulled Angel into a hug, kissing his lips. Angel chuckled before melting into their kiss, moaning quietly as Simeon thanked him with lips and tongue. He gently eased back, Angel blinking at him, lust having blown his thoughts askew.

Angel coughed, and then put his hands in his pockets. "Um, right. Let's go make puppy-chow out of bad guys."

SIMEON'S REACTION to the hellhound was making Angel's year. The hound came to heel prettily, Simeon murmuring to it in Irish Gaelic, a dialect older than the one spoken in modern times. Seeing the beast cavort on dancing paws and whine eagerly when Simeon petted its head made Angel snort out a laugh, grinning so wide his face hurt.

"Blow the whistle already," Angel said after a minute or two of hellos. It was cute and all, but the big, slobbery demon-dog had a troll to find. Simeon sighed in a forlorn manner, but winking at him, put the whistle to his lips and blew. No sound emerged that Angel could hear, but he felt the magic stirring.

The reaction was instant. The beast's behavior went from joyous companion to bringer of death. It went stiff, head held high, tail straight, eyes focused ahead. Angel held out the scrap of cloth with Stone's blood on it, and the beast snuffled at it, nostrils flaring as it dragged in breath after breath from the cloth. Eventually it shook its head, body quivering. Angel put the scrap back in the bag and tucked it away safely.

"He's ready," Simeon said, putting the whistle on its chain around his neck and tucking it out of sight.

"This outta be fun," Angel quipped, and his jaw dropped when Simeon said a short, sharp word in Gaelic—and the hellhound leapt forward, a streak of light and flame. "Shit!"

Simeon's arms came around him, and he found himself being carried, Simeon chasing the hellhound as it tore through the streets, braying. The sound was deep and sonorous, echoing off brick walls and shaking windows. It was a haunting wail, eerie and disturbing. He wanted to hide from such a sound, more than grateful for the safety of Simeon's arms.

SIMEON PUT him down in a narrow alley, just off the street. The walls were high and narrow, and the hellhound snuffled at the dirty ground. Rats squeaked, tumbling over themselves in abject terror as the beast ambled deeper into the alley. Light glowed at the far end, and Angel could make out the silhouette of bare tree branches and iron fences.

"Where are we?" Angel whispered, their journey too swift for him to keep track of every turn.

"The end of Court Square," Simeon said softly, his whisper loud in the heavy silence.

"Then that's King Chapel ahead of us at the end?"

Simeon nodded, and Angel frowned. They were out of Beacon Hill, by about a block, and a thirty-minute walk from the apartment. A handful of moments via vampire-piggy back, but still disturbingly close to where he lived.

The hellhound woofed, a gentle booming noise that drew their attention. Angel hurried forward. The hellhound wagged its tail and jumped in place, about halfway down the alley, and it went back to snuffling when Angel drew near. The beast was pawing at the ground, slush and mud going everywhere. Simeon said something in that melodic language of his, a short chiding word, and the hellhound whined, but backed away. Angel knelt, and with a regretful sigh, ran his hands through the muck.

"There's something here," Angel murmured, fingers running over a metal seam in the stones and cracked concrete. "Wicked! I think it's a door."

"Let me, my love," Simeon bade, and Angel scrambled over a couple feet. Simeon ran his fingers through the mud, and stopped at one spot. He paused, then curled his long fingers down deeper. "Get ready. I cannot hear below us. There may be dangers I can't sense."

"Dangerous things in a dark hole under a back alley in one of the most supernatural cities on the planet? Nah, I think we're totally safe," Angel quipped, crouching on his feet, Eroch chirring around his neck. Simeon shot him a look, and Angel shrugged, grinning. "I'm ready."

He tugged on the death magic singing through his soul, and the pure tone that echoed make made his heart race. Shield or fireball, depending on what may be waiting on them in the dark.

Simeon pulled. At first, nothing happened, and Angel's breath caught in his throat. A long moment passed, then there was a rumble, a sigh of sound. An air pocket pushed through the mud and erupted, splattering them with gunk. Then a wet rushing noise came from the hole that opened up as Simeon lifted what must have been several hundred pounds of stone and concrete. The slab was thick, over a foot, and about five feet across. The hellhound whimpered happily, and leapt into the void, green hellfire lighting up the darkness below them. Simeon pushed, and the slab crashed to the alley, shaking the ground. Angel gaped, and had to adjust himself, his cock stiffening behind his zipper. Simeon didn't even break the vampiric equivalent of a sweat. "Holy shit."

Simeon gave him a slow grin, and Angel found himself wishing they weren't hunting bad guys. Eroch chirped, and Angel jumped, startled.

Simeon took out his cell, and tapped the screen a few times. "I've told the Master about this entrance. I think we may be in danger of losing cell service."

"Good idea." Angel took out his cell, tagged his location, and sent it to Milly, with instructions not to tell Isaac unless they weren't in contact by dawn. He had no idea how deep the hole went, or where, but the city wasn't that big. They were either going to end up in farmland or the cape.

The hellhound barked impatiently, and Simeon gave him a sly wink before leaping into the dark. "Are you coming?" Simeon's voice called up from the black after a long moment, and Angel chuckled.

He jumped.

15

UNINTENDED EVIL

olid, thick arms stopped his descent, and Angel pressed a kiss
to the corner of Simeon's mouth in thanks as he was lowered
to his feet. He looked up at a rectangle of light, blinking. It
was a drop of about twenty feet, and he gulped. "Really glad you went
first."

Simeon chuckled, and helped him straighten out his gear.

The tunnel was made of cut stone, dripping with moisture and
moss. The floor was curved, the tunnel circular and looked to be a
few centuries old. Angel looked back up, then ahead, and guessed the
tunnel went straight, matching up with the alley. Eventually,
depending on how long it was and if there were no turns, they would
end up at King's Chapel. He looked behind them, and saw nothing
but utter black.

Angel held up his hand, and snapped his fingers. A green ball of
hellfire appeared, and he tossed it into the air. About the size of a
grapefruit, it hovered a foot or so above their heads. A miniature
green sun, it illuminated the tunnel, casting their shadows on the
walls.

"Dead end that way," Angel said quietly, pointing behind them at
the solid rock wall. He turned back around, the tunnel stretching out

ahead of them into the darkness. The hellhound paced a few yards away down the tunnel, easy to see now in the deeper dark that it glowed with an inner fire of its own. Its eyes were brilliant in the shadows, and Angel grinned, still pleased he was able to use the huntmaster's whistle after all these years. "Can you see?"

"I can. I don't need the light, *a ghra*, but it doesn't hinder me. Be ready to put it out if I say so, though. We may need to remain hidden so as not to give away our position."

"Say the word, and it's out," Angel said and gestured ahead, letting Simeon take the lead.

Simeon took his hand, and led the way into the tunnel.

The stone underfoot was wet, but not frozen, and the temperature was still cold, though warmer by a few degrees. The hound's snuffling and the scratch of claws on stone was as loud as his breathing. Simeon made no noise, and if it weren't for the larger hand holding his, it would be impossible for Angel to know he was there if the light went out.

Eroch stirred and climbed out of Angel's sweater, perching on his shoulder, one front hand-like paw clutching at his ear to steady himself. "A necromancer, a vampire, a hellhound and a dragon all walk into bar..."

Simeon made an inelegant noise, and squeezed his hand. "Are you nervous, my love?"

"Walking in the total darkness in some subterranean tunnels beneath the city? I'm fine," Angel said with a smile, though his heart was beating a bit faster than normal. Simeon didn't call him out on it though, just held his hand and kept walking forward.

Eventually Angel detected a slope, the tunnel angling down, and the rocks under his feet grew slick. Simeon held out his arm, and Angel had no trouble swallowing his pride and borrowing some of Simeon's balance. The hellhound had no need to worry about such things as slipping, its wide paws and huge claws giving it traction no boots could match. It thankfully wasn't tracking at a headlong pace this time, its nose to the ground and its long tail out. Occasionally it would lift its head, sniff the air, and then continue onwards. There was never a light ahead—it remained dark.

They walked. For what felt like ages. Angel knew from checking his watch that it was less than an hour, but the intensely close surroundings of the tunnel and the deprivation of light made it seem longer. The angle became even more extreme, and Angel gave a serious amount of thought to just sitting on his ass and sliding down the tunnel. At this degree of descent, they were going deeper more than they were going forward, and Angel had a feeling they were somewhere beneath King's Chapel.

Ankles aching and his legs burning from the angle, Angel moaned in gratitude when the tunnel leveled out, and the walls on either side opened up. They paused, and the hellhound whined, tail wagging.

He sent the light in front of them, and breathed out in amazement. "Fuck me."

Columns rose from the ground, carved stone that depicted odd creatures and foliage. Angel counted, and from what he could see, the thirty-foot ceiling was supported by a dozen columns, two neat rows of six marching down evenly the length of the room. The walls, just out of view until he increased the light, were smooth, flat, and appeared to be made of unbroken stone.

"Are we alone?" Angel asked as quietly as he could, his whisper echoing in the cavernous space.

Simeon tilted his head, listening, and grimaced. "I cannot tell. I hear no heartbeats, but that doesn't mean much. The subway runs nearby," Simeon said, pointing to the left wall. "It's the Park Street entrance, and there's still trains running."

"Ask Fido," Angel whispered, and Eroch chittered in amusement. Simeon called to the hellhound, and it wagged its tail before loping ahead down the length of the room. "What does that mean?"

"It's your spell, *a ghra*," Simeon replied. "But I'm certain there must be someone or something here."

Angel sent the green light ahead, feeding it energy, making it grow in size. His eyes ached at the increase of light but he was able to see the vast room more clearly. The dull gray stone now shone a vibrant shade of green, and the columns were even more disturbing. Simeon took the lead again, and Angel followed behind.

He approached one of the columns, and the artistry was astounding. Fae females and males lay entwined in beds of flowers, with forest creatures frolicking amidst trees and bushes. Words in languages he'd never seen before were chiseled into the roots of trees, along the petals of flowers, amid blades of grass. He walked around the column, the scene unending, with other scenes he could not make out stretching above his head toward the ceiling.

Angel walked to the next column, his footsteps echoing, and found himself looking at a new scene, the relief carved in stone of two fae males, features identical, standing on the prow of a ship. They were dressed in armor and leather, swords on their backs, both of the men staring straight ahead. The waves of the sea, the sweep of a gull's wings, even the long braids in their hair were carved so delicately, so perfectly, that Angel was left awed. It was art, at a level he'd never seen before. Such work must have taken several lifetimes.

This column too had words carved into the details. He tried deciphering them, but the alphabet was wholly foreign to his experience and he couldn't figure it out. "Fae language, maybe?"

Eroch chirped at him, the little dragon confused as well. Eroch made no move to leave his shoulder and explore, and Angel couldn't blame him. The columns were beautiful, but the room was cool, the atmosphere chilling and somehow sterile.

It felt lifeless.

"Angel." Simeon's voice echoed off the walls, his lover sounding far more distant than he was. Angel jogged towards the call, and he passed nearly all of the columns before he came to the end of the room—

It wasn't the end.

A long, low dais about twelve feet long and three feet high was near the far end of the room. The wall, about twenty feet beyond the dais, was crumbling in, large stone blocks tumbled about like children's toys. Roots grew through the broken wall, a whole mass of them, as thick about as Angel's waist and dark brown in color. Thousands of offshoots and minor roots sprawled across the wall, ceiling, floor, the longest of which touched the dais, and the object on top.

Simeon came out from the shadows, startling Angel. Simeon put a hand on his shoulder, and pointed to the dais. "What magic is this?"

"Dear Hecate, fuck me," Angel breathed, eyes wide, heart pounding. "Is that a coffin?"

Shaped like a coffin, the glass box was longer than it was tall, the planes grimy, shadowed, but clear enough Angel could see that it was occupied. Angel summoned the hellfire sun, and set it to glow above the box. "It's a coffin."

"I can't smell death. Maybe a very old body?" Simeon asked, stepping forward. Angel grabbed his elbow and tugged, shaking his head.

"Don't step any closer." Angel pointed to the floor, and the runes etched into the stones made his pulse race. "I may not be able to read the language on the columns but those runes are clear enough. Anyone who steps in there is at risk of being affected by the stasis spell."

"Stasis?" Simeon backed away, and gave Angel an incredulous look. "What's a stasis spell and who's in the box?"

Angel looked down at the runes, noting the age and the style of the carved symbols. They were old, older than anything he'd seen still in use, except for the runes maintaining the wards at the Tower. Those were two centuries old, at the minimum, placing them around the era of the Revolution. These runes appeared similar in presentation.

"Angel?"

"Give me a few minutes," he replied, distracted. "Make sure we aren't ambushed."

Simeon grumbled at him, but walked away, calling to his hellhound. Eroch sat on his shoulder, tiny head tilting and twisting as he peered at the glass coffin on the dais. He made no move to leave his shoulder, which Angel was thankful for. Whoever cast the stasis spell knew dark magic, ancient spells of which their only purpose was torture and misery.

Angel walked around the dais, careful with each placement of his feet, not wanting to step on a rune hidden by root or dirt from the collapsed wall. Some of the roots were as large as tree themselves, and the smallest made nets of pale cream tendrils across the stone dais. The thinnest of the roots just touched the glass of the coffin, as if it had taken them centuries to grow that far and only just made it.

The top of the coffin, covered by dust set to grime, clouded the planes of glass and rendered the occupant impossible to discern. The coffin appeared to be sealed, unopened since it was placed. There was a dark smear across the top, and the closer Angel got, the more his stomach wanted to turn over.

"Fuck."

"My love?" Simeon appeared out of the shadows, concern on his handsome features.

"There's burnt and rotting bits of flesh on the top of the coffin," Angel said, wanting to spit as the odor that arose from the mess filled his sinuses. "I think we found where the hearts were going."

"So the fae lord and Stone are the serial killers?"

"I'm pretty damn sure at this point," Angel confirmed, kicking aside some roots to look at the runes beneath. "I have a theory, and it's crazy, but so is finding a creepy Snow White under the city in a fae temple."

"We're alone for now, my love. The hellhound hasn't picked up a new trail yet. He keeps coming back to the roots and the coffin when I ask him to track."

"Hmmm. Maybe he needs another hit off the scent scrap."

"Perhaps. What was your theory?"

Angel pulled his bag off, mindful of Eroch on his shoulder, and put it down next to a big root. Angel jumped over a mess of roots, getting closer to the outer band of runes. "These runes are for a stasis spell. Stasis spells are proscribed, forbidden, just like the resurrection spell I used on August. It's dark magic, death magic, but this spell wasn't cast by a necromancer. This sorcerer was talented, knew the runes and incantations, but not a necromancer."

"How can you tell?"

"Because I can access it," Angel said, and let his own death magic loose.

The runes lit up, golden symbols that blazed like bonfires, before cooling to subtle embers of light. "If a necromancer cast this, it would be locked to him or her, and I wouldn't be able to take it over so easily."

"Is that wise?"

"Not really, but if I want to know what's in the coffin, I need to," Angel replied, and with a shrug, stepped inside the stasis field.

"Angel!"

Angel held up a hand, stopping Simeon from crossing the runes. He waited, and the spell remained stable, the runes waiting. "I'm fine, I promise."

"Your recklessness will drive me to an early grave, *a ghra*," Simeon muttered, glaring at him, arms crossed.

"Pfft," Angel smiled back. "You'll outlive me."

"I'd rather not, thank you," Simeon retorted, still scowling. "What are you doing now?"

"Getting a closer look at our mystery host."

Simeon muttered something in Irish that sounded like swearing, and Angel winked at his mate.

The spell still stable, Angel strode to the dais, climbing up on it next to the coffin. Nose wrinkling in distaste at the decaying mess, Angel leaned over, and wiped the glass above where the head should be. Blinking in surprise, Angel sat back, took a moment, then looked again, longer this time.

"My god, he's gorgeous," Angel murmured, shocked and pleased.

"He?"

"Simeon, there's another fae in here." Angel sent a flash of fire over the rotting organic crap on top of the coffin, burning it to ash instantly. He wiped it away, and eventually the glass was clean enough to see the fae, from head to waist.

So perfectly preserved he may have been sleeping, dressed in garments that reminded Angel of paintings from the Revolution. The light cream shirt he wore was open at the throat, pulled back to expose a muscled chest and a lean build. And the gaping wound over his heart.

"That's why he's in stasis," Angel murmured, looking up at the roots spilling from the wall, to the tiny tendrils just touching the coffin. "They were trying to save you."

Angel looked up at Simeon, and explained. "He suffered a mortal blow. There's what appears to be a sword wound to his chest, and it damaged his heart. I know some fae are so hard to kill they may be considered immortal, but I think a blow like this to the heart would be enough to stop one. The stasis spell was primarily used as imprisonment, for captives and hostages, rendering the person inside perpetually frozen in all ways. But they aren't meant to be permanent —the spirit of the person in stasis is left in limbo, hovering between this world and the next, deprived of sensation, emotions, thoughts. It was once used as a means of torture—anyone woken from a stasis spell would find themselves very willing to cooperate with their captors."

Angel stood, and jumped from the dais, crossing the runes again with a flash of golden light. He picked up his bag, and carried it over to Simeon.

Angel put down his bag, and faced the whole dais, the collapsed wall behind it in perfect view. He pointed to the roots, following them down to the dais. "A stasis spell lasts until the sorcerer who cast it releases it, or it runs out of power on its own. Usually that's after a few weeks. Never have I heard of a stasis spell that lasted longer than that without it being shut down, and recast."

Simeon smiled at him, tugging him close and pressing a kiss to his temple. "You're so happy discussing horrible things, my love."

"Funny." Angel poked Simeon in the side, and continued explaining. "The roots served as a time fuse of sorts. The stasis spell was set, and the roots were drawn to the coffin. When the roots reached the coffin, that was a signal that the spell was failing. In this case, once the spell fails, the fae inside will die, unless he was healed in time."

"How did the sorcerer who cast it make the spell last so long? Those roots have been growing for hundreds of years," Simeon mused. "And you said he wasn't a necromancer? How then has it lasted this long?"

Angel was about to answer, but another beat him to it.

"I slit his throat, and his sacrifice powered the spell, vampire," a beautiful, accented voice said, and the roots within the wall writhed and split, cracking like kindling.

A door, shadowed and dark, opened inside the roots. A pale hand appeared, wrist covered in gray leather.

Simeon crouched in front of him, a shriek of bloodcurdling decibels coming from his fanged mouth. The hellhound barked, appearing from the shadows, sliding to a halt in front of Angel and Simeon, its hackles raised and head down, teeth bared.

The fae stepped out from the hole in the roots, green hair slipping in a long braid from his shoulders. His other hand held a mass of flesh, dark blood dripping from the sundered heart.

16

BROTHERLY LOVE

Angel raised a shield, surrounding him and Simeon, the hellhound just outside the barrier. The beast would be fine —it couldn't be hurt. The shield burned hellfire green, clear as lightly colored glass and impenetrable. The fae lord gave him a lovely smile and a nod, as if greeting him on the street, calm and collected, an immune to the discordant image he presented—beautiful and bloodied.

Simeon stayed crouched, and Angel cautiously put a hand on his mate's shoulder. He rubbed, hoping to soothe Simeon back from the edge of his hunting rage. He needed a thinking, wise Elder in this moment—the time for the apex predator might be needed, but not yet.

"Greetings, Elder Simeon. I am Cian Brennan," the fae offered with a sweet, short bow, an elegant motion that brought to mind dancing. The words, polite and endearing, cut through Simeon's rage and made him shudder under Angel's hand. Simeon stood, but kept an arm in front of Angel, despite them being safe behind his shield. "It is a pleasure to see you again, and whole."

"No thanks to you," Angel shot back, pissed off. "You gutted him like a deer and left him to die."

The fae, Cian, jumped gracefully from the roots, walking across the expanse of floor and net of roots, stopping on the other side of the dais directly across from them. He placed the bloody heart on the coffin, amusement crossing his features as he took in the cleaned glass. He smiled down at the figure in the coffin, and Angel sucked in a breath.

Twins. Cian and the fae in the coffin were twins.

"Elder Simeon appears whole and unharmed." The fae replied, his smile sweet, beautiful. Angel's heart tripped at the perfection, his breath stuttering. "Did Constantine get to him in time, or perhaps you healed him? I heard such things were possible, when a vampire bonded with a practitioner."

"My mate restored me to health," Simeon said, his words carrying a hissing undertone.

"Congratulations," Cian said in turn. "Your bonds are complete, then. A blessing upon you both."

"This is creepy as fuck," Angel interrupted. "Can we get back to the fact you've been killing people for the last few months so you can resurrect your almost-dead brother?"

Cian's face went blank. His eyes, a mercurial mix of gray and blue, pulsed with an inner light. Magic moved in the temple, and Eroch hissed quietly in Angel's ear. Cian's eyes flicked to the tiny dragon, widening a fraction, the only response Angel could see in the fae.

"How do you know what I intend?" Cian asked, words flat, sharp. He looked down at the runes, which still glowed, and he made a soft sigh, as if he'd just received good news after waiting far too long. His gaze narrowed to Angel, and then his eyes pulsed again, the colors swirling. "You are indeed a necromancer, then. I was not sure. I've been...away."

"Don't know how you missed that," Angel grumbled, and Simeon gave a reluctant snort of amusement. "That's what you're doing with the hearts—trying to repair your brother's heart, so he'll survive once the stasis spell collapses."

"Ruairí is my brother," Cian said quietly. "For him, I would do anything. I would kill a hundred pure souls if it meant his survival."

"Is that what you've done?" Angel asked, pointing at the heart dripping on top of the coffin. "Is that a pure soul, sacrificed for your brother? It's going to fail, you know."

"A vampire's heart. Immortal, and so perhaps worthy of restoring Ruairí."

Simeon growled, tense as piano wire and just as ready to snap. Angel's own heart ached for his lover's loss, and he wanted nothing more than to smack the superior and patronizing smile off the fae lord's face. "You killed one of the vampires Batiste sent after you and Stone."

"Regrettably, yes." Cian pulled a silver dagger from a hidden sheath on his thigh, and held the blade above the intact organ. "I will kill them all to restore my brother."

Recalling what Simeon said about returning a removed heart to a fallen vampire, Angel acted without thought.

"*Solvo*," Angel whispered, and loosed the spell. It arrowed across the room, and tore through the runes of the stasis spell. The runes burned and smoke rose, and the root system groaned and creaked.

The whole temple shook, and Cian was knocked back from the coffin, falling amidst the roots. "No!" His scream was tormented and furious, and foreign magic, unlike anything Angel had felt before, rose in the temple.

"Go now!" Angel shouted, and dropped the shield in time for Simeon to blur towards Cian.

Eroch screeched, and leapt into the air, circling above Angel's head. The hellhound chased after Simeon, and shouts and vampiric screeches came from the other side of the dais. Angel sprinted for the coffin, intending to stop this once and for all, the heart still resting on top.

A blow landed on his side, and Angel tumbled head over heels, crashing into a column. He coughed, blood flying from his lips, and gasped, trying to draw air into his abused chest. He looked up, eyes streaming tears, and fear slithered over him as he watched Ben Stone emerge fully from the opposing column, the mountain troll-hybrid stepping from the stone as if it were living. The huge man grinned down at Angel, cracking his knuckles and laughing.

Stone had been here the whole time. The hellhound brought them to Stone—he'd been a part of the temple, in the stones around them. A trait that usually only came with full-blood status, Angel realized he'd made a terrible error in calculating their prey's capabilities and he was about to pay the price.

"C'mere, little man," Stone said, his voice deep and reminiscent of gravel crunching underfoot. "Smash you to bits of blood and bone, then I'll go for my bitch of a wife."

"Fuck you," Angel said, spitting blood at Stone. He pushed up the column, regaining his feet. A fist the size of a melon came swinging at his face, and Angel ducked. The column behind his head shattered, and Angel ran, ducking a follow-up swing.

Stone was slow, but he had one goal—to crush Angel.

Eroch dived, latching onto the back of the troll's head, and flame erupted from his jaws. Stone bellowed, shaking his head, trying to dislodge Eroch. Angel took the distraction, and summoned as much kinetic energy as he could, pooling it between his hands. "Eroch!"

The dragon leapt away, flaming as he went, leaving behind scorched flesh. Angel released the kinetic energy, and air warped as it barreled ahead.

Stone took the blow, and nothing happened. "Fuck!"

Angel scrambled away, running behind another column. Stone was laughing, obviously enjoying himself. He must have had kinetic energy added to the nullifier charm. A complete charm would be impossible to deplete without sufficient time—Stone would crush him before he could.

Stone lumbered around the column, looming over Angel. Eroch was flying above them, shooting flames at Stone. His skin burned, clothing failing under the intense dragon fire. His coat and shirt fell to scraps hanging from his waistband, and Angel used the distraction to get further away. Eroch was too fast for Stone to hit, his flames traveling farther than Stone could reach. Eroch forced Stone back, away from Angel, his little dragon enraged and letting the troll know it with prejudice.

Angel ran for the center of the temple. Stone shouted and came after him, one arm up to block the flames coming from the furious beastie above him. "Simeon!"

A streak of green and shadows raced past Angel, the hellhound colliding with Stone. The ground shook, Angel falling to his knees. Pain raced up his legs, jeans torn, but he climbed back to his feet and turned.

The hellhound ripped into Stone's leg, the troll bashing at the hound, blows landing on its head and shoulders. The hound growled, impervious, chomping through Stone's clothing and hide like a hot knife through butter. The hound may be born of death magic, but it had a physical form—and teeth that was as real as any canine's. The flames that burned over its fur and haloed about its head and eyes made no mark on the troll, the charm deflecting the death magic of the hound, but not its bite.

Eroch flamed over and over, and the hound bit through the troll's left knee, bone cracking. Stone screamed, and fell to his knees. Eroch screamed in triumph while the hound leapt for Stone's throat.

It was over so fast Angel had trouble believing it.

The hound bit deep, its jaws eclipsing the troll's thick neck, and he shook his head, worrying at the flesh. Stone tried to force the hound off, but with a solid, fast jerk of its jaws, Stone's head left his body. The headless body fell forward, blood spraying over the floor. Angel dodged a thick spurt, the rich metallic scent of warm blood heavy in the cool air. Eroch landed on the corpse, flaming it while screeching in victory.

The hound dropped the head with a thick splat and a happy wag of a long bushy tail. Its eyes glowed, flames brighter, the spell resolving itself as the hound's physical form released. A howl echoed through the temple, the price for the hunt paid, until Simeon summoned him anew.

Angel exhaled a shaky breath, adrenaline making him dizzy. He spat on the floor, leaning over, hands on his knees. "Oh, that was so gross. And cool. But gross."

Eroch was chittering to himself and cleaning his face, wings out and fanning. Steam rose from the little dragon's body, his emerald scales glowing around his snout and on his chest. "You are so badass."

Eroch chirped, happy, then went back to cleaning himself. Angel stood upright, and stumbled on shaky legs for the end of the temple. He hadn't heard anything from that part of the room. Weird magic rose and fell in waves, Angel's own magic sparking and flaring in response. The ambient magic fields were chaotic, as if someone was tapping the veil and then releasing it, over and over.

He cleared the dais, and stopped. Simeon and the fae lord Cian were locked in a horrific tableau. Simeon was standing over the fae lord, who was on his knees, covered in slashes from claws and teeth. Simeon had his claws buried in the side of Cian's neck, frozen in what must be millimeters from ripping out his arteries. What made Angel's heart stutter and skip a beat was the root that was buried in Simeon's back—too close to his heart. So close, that one twitch of the root would put wood through his heart, killing him.

Simeon's pain-filled eyes met his own, and he tried to smile. "*A ghra*, walk away. Don't look."

"No...look, necromancer." Cian coughed, blood running over his lips. "Look at what you've done."

Cian raised a bloody hand, fingers shaking as he pointed to the dais. Angel ripped his gaze from the tangled duo and looked at the coffin. The stasis spell was falling apart, the runes dying one by one. The body within would be freed in moments, and then the grievously wounded fae would die.

"My brother will die, murdered by your hand," Cian gasped out, tears running down his blooded cheeks. "My life is nothing compared to his. Therein lies a pure soul, a hero, a noble man untouched by the world's evil. I am nothing without Ruairí. And so shall your mate be nothing if my brother dies."

"Tell me what you want," Angel demanded, but he knew. If there was one thing Angel knew without a doubt, it was what Cian was going to ask of him.

"Angel, no. There is no need, *a ghra.* If this one here can kill without remorse for his brother, then imagine what that one must be like. Walk away, my love, and let me finish him." Simeon jerked as the root twitched, and Angel wanted to throw up, his terror so acute at the thought of Simeon dying right before him. He shook his head, tears running from his eyes, hot and scalding.

"I won't watch you die. I love you, dammit. I'm too selfish to be noble." Angel wiped at his face, spreading dirt and blood, begging for Simeon to understand. "You wouldn't let me die, so I won't see you go before me!"

"Hurry, necromancer, or we all die," Cian whispered, eyes locked on his brother's form. The last runes were flaring, the spell coming to an end.

"If his soul passes before I can restore him, I will not resurrect him. He'll be a revenant, not alive, not as he was, not if I pull him back across the void."

"I care not. Do it!"

Angel jumped to the dais, knocking the vampire heart from the top of the coffin. He gripped the lid, and pushed, the heavy glass lid refusing to budge for a frustrating moment. It released with a snap, and Angel pushed it away. It fell to the ground, shattering, the sound deafening. The last of the runes flared, and then died, and Angel slammed his hand down, covering the wound.

Eyes the shade of clear amber opened, startled. A shade so pure and lovely Angel fought not to be distracted. Angel reached out, blood flowing from the ruptured heart beneath his fingers, and he summoned all his magic, the death magic coming to his call. Desperation made him pull on the mate bond, and the primordial magic within Simeon answered.

As he had once with Daniel, Angel used the death magic huddled within the dying fae lord to reach out and tried to grab the soul hovering on the precipice. Angel closed his eyes, falling into the cavernous void between life and death, chasing after the fae's soul as it hurtled towards the Other Side.

In his short life, Angel had only ever healed mortals, human practitioners that took life-ending injuries and spells. He could not heal the undead, not with death magic—he could only ever heal the living. How to heal a fae was unknown to him, but the fae were living creatures, so he might be able to do it.

Once the soul, the spirit, fell from the precipice and entered the Other Side, Angel could not heal the injured. He could resurrect, bring the soul back to a dead body, but it was beyond even his affinity to truly bring someone back to life, a living soul in a living body, restored and pristine. Such an ability was in the purview of the gods, and only them. He had the narrowest of windows in which to succeed, and time was running away from him.

Angel chased after the soul, Ruairí's death imminent. Desperate, Angel poured all of himself into the fae, his own spirit loosening from within his mortal coil. He reached, further and further, Death so close Angel sensed a Presence, the Void looking back. His mind and spirit made one last attempt—and he leapt after the departing soul, falling from the precipice. Angel cried out, despairing at his failure even as he caught the fae's soul before it was swallowed by the blackness. He fell, spirit loosening from his body.

Angel!

The golden cord of his soul bond went taut, jerking his descent to a rough halt. A horrible tension grew, the weight of the fae's soul pulling his own apart, the bond with Simeon unrelenting.

Simeon, help me!

The golden cord sang, the death magic it carried joining in harmony. Strength filled him, sewing him back together, pulling him and the fae's soul back from the Void. Angel used the bond to find his way back to his own body, all but dragging the fae's soul behind him.

He came back to himself, slumped over the fae, Simeon's worried calls in his ears, the fae lord screaming. Angel gasped, lungs burning, eyes watering. He clenched his hand in the ruined, warm flesh of the injured fae's chest, and returned the soul to the body. Flesh knit, blood ceased to flow from the deep wound, muscles and tendons and nerves stitching themselves back together. Angel poured all the power he could into the healing form under his hand.

Angel panted at the effort, terrified by how close it had been, heart racing in an attempt to prove he was alive too. Beautiful amber eyes blinked up at him and there was a confused, kind smile gracing perfect lips. Ruairí breathed, chest rising, a wide, red scar in place where a gaping wound had been. Angel smiled in return, a reflexive response to such beauty as that smile.

"Ruairí!" Cian cried out, heartbreaking and yet joyous. Angel looked over his shoulder, to where Simeon and Cian were locked together in their deathly stalemate.

He made a choice, hoping love would win out over violence.

17

PAYING THE PRICE

"Let each other go," Angel gasped out. "He's alive. Let Simeon go. Simeon, it's alright. Just stop, both of you."

"My love..."

"It'll be fine."

Simeon withdrew his claws, and the root fell from his back. Cian dashed towards the dais, and Angel fell to the ground out of the way. He crawled to Simeon's side, where his lover fell when the root pulled away.

Simeon reached out for him, and Angel pulled his head and shoulders into his lap. He wrapped his arms around Simeon, and held his wrist to Simeon's mouth. "Drink, baby. Please."

Simeon gripped his wrist, and fangs bit into his flesh. Angel shuddered, but held fast. Simeon drank, and Angel buried his face in Simeon's hair, so thankful to have his mate in his arms. "You pulled me back," Angel whispered in Simeon's hair, dropping kisses amongst the strands. "You pulled us both back. Thank you. I love you so much."

Simeon rubbed his forearms, soothing, loving touches that calmed his racing heart and settled his frayed nerves. Simeon drank great mouthfuls that made his arm pinch and pull, but he accepted the pain with a grateful heart.

Sobs and laughter reached them, and Angel looked to the dais. Cian had Ruairí in his arms, the brothers weeping and laughing in happiness. Joy glimmered in the air and on their skin, hair lifting gently in a nonexistent wind. They spoke to each other in a language Angel didn't recognize, the words lyrical and sweet, almost intoxicating to hear. Their reunion made his heart hurt, the love coming from both men almost too much to witness.

A chirring cry echoed through the room, and Eroch flew over the pair on the dais, and he landed on the ground next to Angel. "Hey, wee beastie. So proud of you."

Eroch puffed up, flapping his wings. Angel cast a glance at the fae lords, who were in their own world, paying them no mind at all. Angel shifted, and with his free hand pulled out his cell. No service, but he wasn't surprised. He opened his texting, and wrote a short message, adding the recipients before setting it to send once there was a signal.

"I need you to do me a favor, Eroch. Take my cell, and fly back the way we came. Get my cell to the tunnel entrance, and leave it there, okay? Then come right back."

Eroch tilted his head to the side, stared at the cell he held out in his palm, and Angel waited. He knew Eroch understood, but the beastie was not a pet, and could refuse. Eroch nodded, an odd gesture to see from a creature that wasn't humanoid. Angel quietly thanked the dragon when he leapt onto Angel's hand, grabbing the cell with his front legs. He chittered, wings flapping. Angel focused his will, summoning a tiny green hellfire star to stay with Eroch, lighting the dragon's way through the tunnel. He had no idea if Eroch could see or not in the darkness, but the beastie was doing him a favor, acting as a beast of burden, so it was a small kindness. Eroch took off, his usual effortless leap slightly cumbersome, but he flew fast enough. He disappeared into the shadows of the temple, the tiny hellfire light keeping pace.

Simeon pulled his fangs from his wrist, and Angel hissed at the sting. His wrist throbbed in time to his heart, and he groaned, dizzy. Angel helped him sit up, and Simeon pulled him in, taking his mouth in a savage kiss. Anger, frustration, love, all of it was in Simeon's kiss, demanding Angel respond with fervor.

Simeon pulled back, and Angel crawled into his lover's lap, hands roaming over his back, searching out the place where the root had pierced his back. Smooth skin ran unblemished under his fingers, and he embraced the intense relief he felt at the discovery Simeon would be fine. Simeon held him, the steel bands of his arms refusing to relinquish their hold on Angel, and he burrowed his face into Simeon's chest. Tears came, and he let them, enjoying the feel of Simeon holding him.

HE HAD no idea how much time passed, but he jerked awake from his doze when a hand touched his shoulder. Angel sat up, wiping at his face, and jumped when he met amber eyes and a wide smile.

Simeon growled quietly, and Ruairí held up his hands, kneeling beside them. He looked at the way Simeon held Angel in his lap, and the fae lord chuckled, murmuring something softly in his own language that spoke of amusement and sympathy.

Angel shook his head, and said, "I'm sorry, I don't know what you're saying."

Ruairí tilted his head, much like Eroch did, and the fae lord's expression turned rueful. "Forgive me, necromancer. I assumed you knew my tongue. The last necromancer I met knew it better than I do."

Ruairí's voice was astounding. Deep, smooth, accented with a lilt much like Simeon's, it made Angel shiver, his attention captured by the sound. As charming as the sound of a babbling brook or the song of a forest wren, it captivated and seduced. Simeon's arms tightened around him, and Angel breathed out, blinking as he let go of the sensations generated by the fae lord.

The red scar on his chest was smaller, less vibrant, and even as he watched the wound continued to heal. Ruairí would be perfect once again, his own natural healing ability able to restore such damage. Angel frowned, and Ruairí looked down, touching the wound and sighing.

"The blade that cut me down struck true and sure," Ruairí said softly, giving a half shrug, the motion elegant and endearing. "I could not heal, not so grievous a wound. My heart was damaged past the point I could heal. Cian told me what he did. Last I recall, I was on the battlefield, cutting through British infantry attempting to retake the city. My brother loves me, as I love him, but that does not excuse nor allow the evil he committed in my name."

"He murdered innocents. Humans, werewolves, vampires. All to save you," Simeon growled. "Cian must pay."

"And so he shall, without complaint," Ruairí promised, gesturing behind him. Cian knelt beside the dais, his mercurial eyes locked on his brother, as if afraid to take his gaze from his twin, lest he disappear. "We owe you a debt, necromancer. A debt that may never be repaid. Cian will accept whatever punishment comes his way from the human authorities."

"From the bloodclan, you mean," Batiste said, making them all jump but for Ruairí. Batiste appeared behind Cian, standing over the kneeling fae.

Vampires emerged from the shadows, over a dozen of them. Bridgerton appeared beside Batiste, carrying Stone's head by the hair. He threw it to the ground, and it rolled until it smacked into Cian's knee. The fae lord bowed his head, as if waiting for a blow to take his own head in turn.

Angel stood up, Simeon holding him under his arm. Batiste leaned down, and picked up the vampire heart from the dust. He stood slowly, and spoke to Cian. "How long ago did you slay my child?"

Cian lifted his head, confused, but responded easily enough. "Less than an hour. His body is through there, Constantine." Cian pointed with his chin at the doorway in the roots. "And so are your remaining children. They live, all of them, but for the unfortunate soul from which I took the heart."

Batiste stilled, and even Angel could tell the Master was surprised. Angel was too, and Simeon tensed beside him. Batiste gestured, and Simeon pulled away from Angel, Bridgerton blurring as well. They went through the root doorway, and Angel turned back to Cian.

He walked over to the kneeling fae lord, and crouched beside him. Cian met his eyes, unashamed and peaceful. There was regret there, but Angel had a feeling it wasn't for killing innocent people. Nor was it for getting caught. He frowned, and asked, "You said you were away. Where were you?"

Cian was surprised, perhaps expecting Angel to shout or yell at him, but he answered. "I was searching for a priest of our people. I've been searching since Ruairí fell in battle and he was placed in stasis. My search was for naught—I gave up a few months ago, and attempted the restoration spell known only to our priests on my own. That is why I collected the hearts."

"But you didn't know the ritual, the specifics, so it kept failing," Angel said, and Cian nodded.

"I saw it performed once, millennia ago as a child, but could not duplicate it," Cian said, a wry smile twisting his lips. "For my failure, Ruairí nearly died, and I stole lives from worthy souls in a fruitless quest."

"You knew I was a necromancer. Why didn't you come to me directly?" Angel asked, utterly at a loss. Cian reared back on his heels, and the absolute shock on the fae's face left him surprised.

"I have never known a necromancer to offer their skills for nothing," Cian said, eyes wide and startled. "The ones I have known in the past were not trustworthy, or would have refused. Powerful sorcerers all, but evil men with rotted souls who would enslave Ruairí as soon as heal him. I thought to perhaps bribe you, or maybe take your brother as hostage, but the last fool to touch your brother you burnt alive. Then I learned you were bonded, mated, and the dishonor in harming a pair is unparalleled. So I sought to keep you out of my affairs, and strove to heal Ruairí on my own."

Angel gaped at Cian. He knew the reputation of necromancers. He wasn't a fool, or blind. He fought against that prejudice every day, no matter how well-deserved of a reputation it may be. His kindred across the globe weren't known for their acts of kindness nor charity. If Cian had been here when Angel was growing up, he may have known better, learned Angel would have helped simply because it was the right thing to do.

Ifs and buts were pointless, though, and Angel shook his head, standing.

"Ruairí is innocent of all his brother's transgressions," Angel said to Batiste, the Master glowering at him, but he nodded. "Do as you will to Cian. Stone is dead, his life for the human of yours he killed. Turn Cian over to the humans, or take his life, I don't care. I'm done."

Angel walked away, not looking back. His hellfire light still burned above them all, lighting the room. Angel skirted Stone's headless corpse, and walked to the tunnel.

A slight weight landed on his shoulder, and Angel reached up for Eroch, pulling his familiar into his arms and hugging him to his chest. "Thank you, wee beastie." Eroch chirred, snuggling, warming Angel as regrets that weren't even his own clouded his thoughts.

Eventually Simeon found him at the tunnel's entrance, his mate covered in blood, but uninjured. Simeon held his face between his palms and kissed Angel, a nearly chaste kiss full of comfort and love. Simeon tugged on his arm, and Angel held his mate's hand as they walked up the tunnel.

Simeon all but had to pull him to the top when the angle grew too extreme, but Angel didn't mind. He was tired, dirty, and wanted a shower. Angel didn't speak until Simeon returned them to the alleyway, jumping them up through the hidden door. He asked, "The vampire, the one Cian killed for his heart. Is he dead for good?"

Simeon led Angel to the end of the alley, where a limo idled, waiting for them. Vampires milled about, politely ignoring them both as they parted for their passage. Simeon opened the limo door, and said, "My Master was able to restore the soldier. It was close, though. His body had started to decay. Batiste's blood is powerful; he will survive."

"Gross. And good. But still gross," Angel muttered, climbing in the limo.

Simeon laughed, getting in behind him and shutting the door.

18

REDEMPTION

A crash made Angel jump, and he fell from bed, hitting the floor. He groaned, rolling on his side and clutching his knee. "What the fuck!"

Crashing and shouting came from the bathroom, and the bedroom door opened with a bang, Simeon blurring through the bedroom. Angel sat up, grumbling, and used the bed to get to his feet. Glass broke, and Angel heard Eroch screeching.

"Wee beastie, if you've brought the Pigeon Wars into the house I'm gonna be pissed!" he shouted, heading for the bathroom door. He made it just in time to see Simeon punch a bleeding Ballacree in the face, breaking his nose again. Eroch flew around the screaming man's face, tearing skin and belching out bursts of flame.

"Oh, what the hell," Angel breathed out. There was an unfamiliar dagger on the floor, some noxious chemical spilling from a vial, and to top off the insult, an ashwood stake. "You dumb fuck, you really thought you could sneak in here? Stake my boyfriend and do nasty things to me while I slept, drugged out my ass? Eroch, eat his face off. I'm calling the police."

Simeon yanked Ballacree all the way through the window that led to the fire escape, the man apparently having made it halfway through the space they kept open for Eroch to come and go. Ballacree was screaming, and Angel spun back just as surge of magic came from the wizard. A spell, orange and black and stinking of sulfur came from the wizard struggling in Simeon's arms, and Angel tried to shout a warning. He blocked the spell, sending it into the mirror over the sink, the glass shattering and the wall smoking as flames devoured the plaster. He was about to cast his own spell, but Simeon lifted Ballacree upright, and struck. His fangs sank into the wizard's neck, and Simeon ravaged his throat.

Angel shook off his surprise, feeling the soul bond cycle the harmful magic in Ballacree's blood into Angel, allowing Simeon to drink without dying from poisoning. It was odd, having another's magic come along the soul bond, but Angel stayed quiet. Ballacree came with the intent to murder Simeon, and just tried to kill Angel when he was stopped from carrying out his plan. Killing in self-defense was perfectly acceptable to them both.

Simeon drained Ballacree in moments, the wizard dying quietly. Angel stayed, witnessing, unwilling to give Simeon any doubts that Angel accepted this part of his nature. His mate was a vampire. He drank human blood. And sometimes, he killed that way.

THE CLEANING SERVICE eyed Simeon with some fear and a lot of respect. Angel smirked, holding the door for the humans as they carried their equipment and left the apartment. Daniel and Isaac were huddled together on the couch, snickering. Simeon crossed his arms and leveled a stern glance on the young men, who merely broke out in loud chuckles. Milly shook her head, sipping her tea and passing O'Malley a fresh scone. Angel closed the door with a bang, and rounded on the room.

"Evil bad guys need to stop interrupting my sleep," he said, cranky and owning it. "Do you forgive me?" Angel asked O'Malley, who glared at him as he chewed on a mouthful of cranberry scone.

O'Malley swallowed and said, "No, but I'm not gonna pretend I don't know you were acting in my best interest or that of my department. Officers would have died going down there into the temple."

"I am sorry," Angel said, heading for Simeon who opened his arms and gathered him close.

"No, you're not."

"Yeah, I'm not."

"I'll forgive you for another scone."

"Done."

"If only forgiveness were always so easy," Simeon said with a chuckle.

Everyone laughed but Isaac, his brother freezing. Angel watched as he got up from the couch, and headed for his bedroom.

Simeon spoke to O'Malley, discussing Cian, the fae having been turned over to the human authorities since the vampires he captured all made it, and Stone was dead. No fae had been tried for murder in Massachusetts, ever, so the state and the city were arguing about how to handle it. There was no death penalty in the state, and life imprisonment took on a new twist when the sentence could last eternity. Ruairí had disappeared when Batiste took Cian to the police, and Angel was worried for the fae lord. He'd been asleep the last two hundred years. The world was vastly different from what he once knew.

Simeon did explain one thing, that Cian and Ruairí were known to Batiste. The Master was over a thousand years old, and had met the twins centuries ago in the Old World, long before the Revolution.

Angel kissed Simeon, then followed after Isaac. He paused in the hall outside his brother's door, but he knocked. He waited, and entered after a long pause when no answer came.

Isaac sat on his bed, and Angel shut the door behind him at the tears running down Isaac's face. He knelt on the floor, and took his brother's hands in his, rubbing them. "Tell me what's wrong."

"I...I did something horrible, and you'll hate me," Isaac sobbed quietly, clutching at Angel's hands. "I can't tell you. I love you too much to tell you."

"What happened? I love you. Please believe me. I won't hate you.

You are the only person in this entire world that I can never hate. And that includes Simeon. Tell me, Isaac."

"The night they came for our family," Isaac whispered, meaning the vampire army that decimated their family and Angel eventually stopped almost accidentally, "The reason the wards didn't come up correctly that night wasn't because everyone tried to do it themselves and they fought over control...it was because that morning I was trying to control them. I did something to the runes by accident, and warped a few of them. I was trying to use the lessons Dad and August taught me earlier that week, and I wanted to impress everyone. But I fucked up."

Angel fell on his ass. His heart stopped, and his memories of the last decade blurred and twisted. Isaac gulped, and gripped his hands so tightly his bones creaked. "I killed our family."

CONTINUE READING to enjoy a bonus short story set in the BHS world. (The next book in the series after the short story is *The Necromancer's Reckoning*, Book Three of The Beacon Hill Sorcerer.)

BONUS SHORT STORY
THE NECROMANCER'S BIRTHDAY SURPRISE

Written for Crystal's Many Reviewers Blog Birthday Celebration, March 2016.

This short story takes place after Book #2 and before Book #3. Enjoy!

NECROMANCER'S BIRTHDAY SURPRISE

BY SHEENA JOLIE

A ngel huffed out a breath, watching as it fogged up before dissipating into the cold spring night air. The cemetery was quiet, and his breathing and the scuffing of his boots on the stone mausoleum's roof traveled farther than was wiser considering his errand that night. It was also way too bright, the moon full overhead, not a cloud in the sky, the stars almost as bright as the moon, illuminating the whole of the graveyard. So Angel decided he would be in plain sight, but hidden—and as long as he waited until his quarry was in range and in the act before leaving his perch, he would remain invisible behind his spells.

For the last two weeks, cemeteries around the greater Boston areas and surrounding burbs had been visited by grave robbers, digging up the recently deceased and taking everything from jewelry, clothing, and even organs. The last part was what made BPD finally call Angel, Detective O'Malley briefing him with a look of disgust on his face and confusion in his eyes.

"We've got 20 bodies desecrated, Angel, and no leads," O'Malley had grumbled to him yesterday morning when he stopped by Angel's studio, file an inch thick in his hands. The detective looked frumpier than usual, his red hair lightened by strands of gray and the lines on his face seeming to be deeper, etched by exhaustion instead of age. "I'm at a loss about what to do—and I finally figured if we couldn't track the stolen goods, we'd follow the stolen organs. But that was a bust as well, and now I need you."

It wasn't a bad idea, considering. Most grave robbers went after what the dead were buried with—as Angel was a sorcerer, and his people cremated their deceased, he was still floored by normal humans burying their dead with valuables and mementos. Since the cops couldn't track the sale of the stolen goods, that either meant the thieves weren't selling them yet, or the goods weren't taken for monetary gain. Along with the stolen organs, Angel had a theory—ghost calling.

It was a cruel, harsh, and complicated process, but boiled down to its essential pieces it meant pulling a departed soul back from the Other Side. Then it was anchored to an item that soul had a connection to as a mortal—like a favored watch or wedding ring—and then using the summoned spirit for some task. Historically, that meant revenge hauntings, guards for territory or homes where a ghostly warden would scare intruders off, even as spies.

In the modern era, it involved stolen identities and password theft. In the days and early weeks after death, unless the deceased had a definite plan for closing and freezing financial accounts after death, rarely did anyone handling the affairs of the departed think to change passwords or financial access codes. Angel's theory was that the organs were used in the spells to call up the ghosts, the items to anchor them on this plane, and then the information forced from the returned souls was used to rob the dead and their families.

Angel sighed, wishing he had thought ahead and brought something to sit on, but his desire to get out of the apartment for a night alone had overwhelmed his better sense. Angel came prepared for almost anything, and his traps were set around the two most recent graves in the cemetery, ready to go with a thought. This cemetery was one of the first to be hit, so the police had discounted it, but a car accident several days prior that killed an elderly and wealthy married couple had to be too much temptation for the thieves. At least in Angel's opinion. The police were on a stakeout at a few other cemeteries, but Angel was sure tonight, this cemetery, and these graves were too prime of a target for the culprits to pass up.

And Angel wanted, no needed, to get out of the apartment. Isaac was skulking about like a wraith, though his little brother was hardly dead, just not quite alive. He was still grieving for his boyfriend, killed five months before by a rogue vampire. Not to mention the revelation Isaac dropped on him about what really happened the night their family died. He had no idea what to do with that bomb of information. And Daniel, his apprentice, was the type to hover around Angel as if afraid Angel would disappear if Daniel let him out of his sight for longer than a minute.

And Simeon, his lover, the vampire Elder, was busy at the Tower, handling clan matters for The Master. And while Angel loved Simeon more than he had ever loved anyone or anything before, he needed to be alone. Especially tonight.

It was his birthday tomorrow, and he would be thirty years old. And he felt ancient. He hadn't had a happy birthday in over a decade and didn't know how to handle having one now.

A sharp chirp came from above, and the familiar flapping of wings warned him he had company. Eroch came winging in from above, slipping through Angel's illusion of a bare roof to the mausoleum, and landed on his shoulder. Angel held still while Eroch pulled his wings in, the tiny dragon chattering up a storm, poking at Angel's cheek with his snout, sniffing in his face. Eroch sounded annoyed and affectionate at the same time, probably scolding him for leaving the apartment without him when he left for the cemetery.

"Shhh, I'm trying to catch bad guys," Angel whispered, scratching under the dragon's chin, Eroch purring like a cat. The little dragon was the size of a housecat, with mannerisms to match, but he was sentient and as smart a human. More intelligent, some days. "Think we'll catch them?"

Eroch chirped, and Angel chuckled. "I think so, too, my wee beastie. Won't the cops be happy I got the bad guys first?" Eroch tipped his head, yellow eyes flashing, and Angel grinned. "No, I didn't think so either. At least, O'Malley won't mind all that much."

Angel shifted, his ass numb, glad the dragon took it upon himself to find Angel. The dragon was his familiar though Angel had yet to use the wee beastie in that manner. It smacked too much of ownership, and he wasn't comfortable making Eroch serve that purpose, no matter that the dragon apparently decided he would be doing so on his own. The tiny dragon gave off a surprising amount of heat, warming Angel even through his weather-proof sweater. Eroch draped himself over Angel's shoulders, head on one shoulder, tail hanging down Angel's opposite arm like a living shawl. He had to deal with a wing messing with the hair on the back of his head, but he was used to it by now. Eroch hung on him all the time unless the wee beastie was begging for scraps from someone's plate.

The wind picked up, whistling through the cemetery, the headstones almost glowing from the silver light from the moon, and Angel felt cold. Colder than he should be wearing a dragon and a magicked weather-proof sweater, but it wasn't the wind that chilled him to his bones.

A sound that wasn't the wind moaned long and low, seeming to echo off the stones upon which Angel sat. Careful not to move too much and disturb his illusion of an unoccupied roof, Angel peered through the distant shadows, checking the periphery of the cemetery. Eroch growled from his perch, and Angel agreed with him. Off to the east, near the direction of the groundskeepers' gates, came a shift in the black, a flicker of light. The moaning rose to a thin wail, the wind carrying it across the full field of graves, and the hairs all along Angel's body rose in one sweeping realization.

Zombies.

Angel reached for his bag where it was braced behind a statue of an avenging angel, out of reach of the wind, and pulled his athame from its depths, eyes locked on the gravel road that wound its way through the headstones and plots. Figures appeared from the blackness, two walking with an easy gait and carrying what seemed to be shovels, flashlights in hand. The other figures moved with a disjointed pace and pattern that was more a struggling shuffle, bodies bent and twisted as the spells that animated their corpses.

Two men, probably sorcerers and the likely grave robbers, and six zombies.

"Shit, I picked the wrong night to be the Lone Ranger," Angel muttered to himself, tucking his athame under his belt, and reaching for his bag. The sorcerers and their minions were getting closer, heading for the graves Angel had marked as the likely targets. And once they hit his spell traps, they would know they weren't alone.

Angel had underestimated his quarry. Expecting it to be a pair or small team of low-ranked practitioners, he had come alone and with minimal supplies. He had expected to catch them in his trap, call the police, and then release them once the cops were on site. He might get lucky and take out some of the zombies, and with enough time he could wrest control of them from the sorcerers, but he was unlikely to get that time. Neither man was a necromancer; he would be able to sense their affinity for death, but they were still sorcerers, and creating zombies was within their reach, especially if they pooled resources, and that made them dangerous.

A buzz and a sharp vibration on his hip made Angel gasp and jump, and he grabbed his cell before it could go off again and give away his position. The group was heading for the fresh graves, and Angel would have only a few minutes before his traps were set off. He glanced at the screen, and answered it, keeping his voice low.

"Simeon."

"Good evening, *a ghra*," Simeon purred in his ear, sexy as hell and the best thing Angel had heard all night. "Are you ready to celebrate your birthday?"

"Where are you?" Angel whispered, eyeing the group as the sorcerers directed their undead troops, making them shuffle out among the headstones. He ignored the mention of his birthday, as the company he had in the cemetery was more pressing. Two zombies headed in his general direction, and would be able to smell him once they got close enough. His illusion did nothing to prevent his scent from escaping. "Tell me you're near Heaven's Gate Cemetery."

"Angel, did you take that case?" Simeon asked, and Angel could hear the frustration in his lover's voice.

"I took that case. Yes, I went off on my own. Yes, I am an idiot, and I need to make better life choices. And now instead of a ragtag crew of B-list wizards, I am looking at two sorcerers and half a dozen zombies. And they are going to know I'm here in less than a minute."

"I am on my way, *Leannán*. Stay in one piece until I get there. Ten minutes."

"You better make it in five," Angel whispered, clicking off his cell as the two zombies came within a few yards of the mausoleum. Eroch growled from his shoulder, and Angel tucked his cell away in his pocket just as the two undead below him began to snuffle, their decomposing heads twitching left and right as they detected the presence of living flesh. They wouldn't attack their masters, not unless the bonds were broken holding them in thrall, and Angel reached out for the cloud of death magic hovering around the zombies.

Shovels digging into cold earth came to his ears, but Angel pushed aside distractions. He had seconds before his traps were set off. The zombies below him finally zeroed in on his location, growling and moaning as they shuffled forward, and Angel threw off caution and reached for the veil, opening a direct line to the maelstrom of infinite energy past the dimensional wall, and sent his will out.

The two sorcerers sensed him at the same time he opened the veil, shouts and deep growls from the other zombies coming just at the moment a shovel triggered his trap. A boom reverberated through the cemetery, the ground rolling and lifting in a wave as the earth beneath one of the sorcerers opened up, and the man fell into a gaping void beneath him. The other sorcerer pointed and yelled something, and the zombies all lost their disjointed pondering walk and raced over the distance between them and Angel's perch.

Angel gained control of the two zombies closest just as the others came scrambling over, and Angel sent them after the sorcerer who hadn't fallen into his trap. Eroch launched himself from his perch, screeching, and Angel tried to grab the tiny dragon before his familiar dive-bombed the nearest undead.

Angel dropped the illusion, and stood, throwing up a shield between himself and the other sorcerer, just in time to catch a red fireball flung his way. It splattered and hissed when it hit his shields, tails of fire whipping through the air as its remnants fell to the ground. Fingers, crooked into claws tried to find something to grab as the zombies clustered around the base of the stone mausoleum, and Angel cursed his lack of foresight in not taking a higher perch. He'd wanted something he could jump down from, but any minute now that would be his undoing once the zombies figured out how to get up there with him. He could keep them out with a shield, but even with the veil powering him he couldn't maintain it forever and deal with his opponents.

A roar and a wave of flame arched up from the ground, and Angel stumbled back on the roof, hands up, holding his shields in place as another roar and burst of flame cascaded up and over the gutter. The zombies that had been trying to crawl up the mausoleum disappeared in the fire, and Angel gaped, confused. He heard a shout, and Angel looked up to see the two zombies he'd sent after their former master chasing the sorcerer across the cemetery, the fool screaming, and tossing fireballs at the zombies, but they kept after him.

Angel crept to the edge of the roof, and looked down, but the beast that stood up...and up....and up made him jump and swear. Eroch huffed, a puff of smoke escaping his nostrils, and he tilted his head to the side, staring at Angel from one melon-sized eye. Eroch was huge, no longer his wee beastie, but a dangerous and devastatingly beautiful dragon of ancient lore. Crunching came from beneath Eroch, and Angel looked down to the ground, to see his familiar standing on the crushed and charred remains of a handful of zombies.

"You're sneaky, little beastie," Angel murmured with a smile, and he chuckled when Eroch grumbled and shoved his massive head into

Angel's chest, demanding scratches. "You have any more secrets I should be knowing?"

Eroch just sighed and let Angel scratch his scales; the dark emerald green lit up by the moon. And the red and blue of police car lights.

The cops screamed into the cemetery, and Eroch pulled away, hunkering down, and Angel laughed in delight as his familiar shrank rapidly, becoming once again his wee beastie dragon. Eroch chirped and flew up to Angel, who caught him in his arms and hugged him tightly. "I won't be leaving you behind again, my friend."

"Angel!"

Simeon ran into the cemetery, blurring as he came, following Angel's scent. Angel had a second to prepare himself before he was whisked off his feet and swept into Simeon's arms. Simeon jumped, carrying Angel and Eroch to the ground and away, past the cop cars and out to the street. Simeon put them down, hands running over Angel, looking for injuries.

"I'm fine! Simeon, I swear I'm fine," Angel said, trying to reassure his lover. "No one touched me, and the zombies never got to me."

"I had faith you could handle yourself *a ghra*, but I worried none-theless," Simeon said, cupping his face and kissing him deeply, as if he would only believe Angel was unharmed if he examined every minute inch of him, including his tonsils.

Finally, Simeon let him go and hugged him again. Angel snuggled back, watching as the cops swarmed the cemetery. "You got here quickly."

"I called Detective O'Malley immediately and told him what was going on," Simeon said, voice rumbling under Angel's ear. "I wasn't that far away."

"Heaven's Gate Cemetery isn't on the way home from the Tower," Angel said, thinking. "What were you doing out this way?"

"Stopping at the 24-hour bakery nearby," Simeon said, and Angel looked up at him, confused.

"A bakery? But you don't eat."

"No, I do not, but you do," Simeon said with a wicked grin, making Angel peer at him in suspicion.

"What did you do?"

Simeon backed up and blurred away. Angel grumbled, but Simeon returned in less than 15 seconds, a small box in his hands. Angel groaned, and rubbed his face, flushing in embarrassment. "No, please tell me you didn't..."

"Of course, I did. Turning thirty is a grand occasion, and should be celebrated," Simeon said with a grin, peeling back the cardboard box's lid to reveal a giant cupcake. It was a chocolate monstrosity that was covered with a mountain of frosting, sprinkles, and a single unlit candle.

"Says the undead man who's over 400 years old." Angel rolled his eyes. "That's not a cupcake. That's death by chocolate."

Eroch chirped in agreement, eyeing the giant cupcake hungrily.

Simeon looked at his watch, and walked over to Angel, kissing him on his cheek. "It's after midnight. Happy birthday, my love."

Simeon pulled out a lighter and lit the candle, holding the box up toward Angel. He tried to glare, but the love and joy on Simeon's face were impossible to resist. Angel bent down and blew out the candle, making a wish.

"Now I am a little bit lax on human custom. I should not ask you what you wished for, correct?"

"Well," Angel said, dipping a finger in the decadent frosting and sucking it off his finger, Simeon's eyes heating with lust as they tracked his movements. "You can, but you already know what I wished for."

"I do?" Simeon's voice was husky and deep, and made Angel shiver.

"It's something I already have," Angel teased, going for another lick of frosting.

"What's that, *a ghra*?"

"You."

Simeon blinked, and bit his lip. The old vampire was usually smooth and sophisticated, always in control, but Angel saw beneath that hard veneer to the real man.

"I love you, Simeon, and you in my life is the best present I could ever ask for," Angel said, and leaned in, kissing his lover.

Simeon broke the kiss after a moment, and said, "I love you, too."

"I want another cupcake, though," Angel said, frowning.

"Why? What's wrong with...Eroch!"

Angel laughed as the tiny dragon chirped from the box, covered in frosting, his belly fat from eating half the cupcake.

AFTERWORD

Thank you! I hope you enjoyed the book. Please consider leaving a review on Amazon, Bookbub, or Goodreads. Reviews help other readers decide to take a chance on self-published books. Reviews help indie authors like me continue to write and bring new books into the world.

—Sheena

Want more ways to support my writing? Join me on Patreon!

ALSO BY SHEENA JOLIE
AN INFINITE ARCANA SERIES*

THE WOLFKIN SAGA
Wolves of Black Pine
Wolf of the Northern Star

BEACON HILL SORCERER SERIES*
The Necromancer's Dance
The Necromancer's Dilemma
The Necromancer's Reckoning
A History of Trouble (Collection)
Mastering The Flames
Love Springs Eternal
Blood Omen
The Necromancer's War
The Edge of Fate

WEREWOLVES OF BOSTON*
Wolfsbane

REALMS OF LOVE
The Solstice Prince

The River Prince

SCALES OF HONOR
Knight's Fire

STANDALONE TITLE
Saving Silas
Treasured

Find my titles on Audible here!

ABOUT THE AUTHOR

My name is Sheena (they/them) and I write as SJ Himes (soon to be retired pen name), Revella Hawthorne, and now, as Sheena Jolie.

My companions are my furbabies: Wolf and Silfur, two cats who love me but hate each other, and together we reside in MidCoast Maine on the ocean. The sea breeze is always refreshing, and the seagulls are always annoying.

I write romances with an emphasis on plot and character development, and almost all my characters are LGBTQ+ and that's on purpose.
To keep current on what I'm working on and where to find me on social media, go to my Linktree:

https://linktr.ee/sheenajolie

Made in the USA
Columbia, SC
23 March 2025

55534948R00126